OF BLOOD AND SHADOWS

BOOK 1 IN THE DONATI CHRONICLES

CAROL KERRY-GREEN

Kelly + Kia

Carol Kerry-Green

Enjoy!

Of Blood And Shadows

This is a work of fiction. Names, characters, places and incidents are either the products of author imagination or used fictitiously. Any resemblance to actual persons, living or dead, business establishments, events or locales is entirely coincidental.

Editing by Penning and Planning.

Proofreading by Steve Kerry.

CONTENTS

PART III

My sister Linda (1950-2018) and my brother Steve (1957-2020) – always remembered in love, never forgotten.

Rossini Family Tree

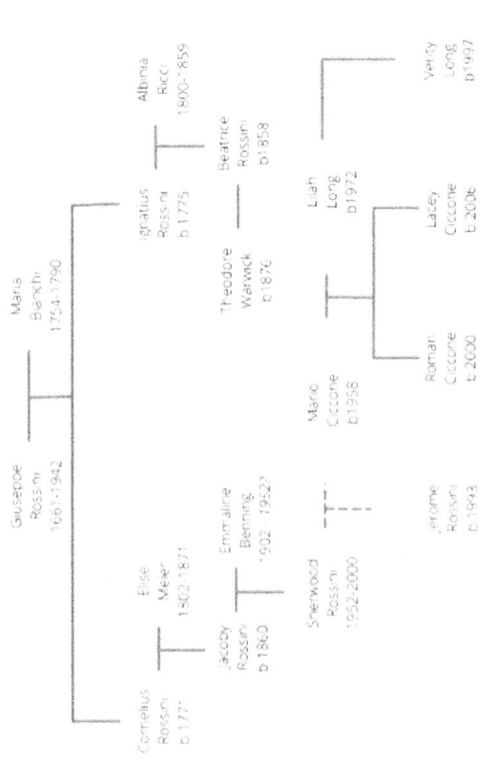

PART I

I

September 2010

Consciousness came slowly through the pain. Jerome Ciccone tried not to struggle as he realised his hands had been tied above him and he was suspended by ropes from the ceiling of the warehouse. His toes were barely touching the floor. He was freezing, dressed only in his underwear. He was finding it hard to keep his weight balanced on his toes, in his weakened state.

How and why he had ended up here in this moment still eluded him. He tried to chase the memory down, but he couldn't grasp it. A noise to his left made him jump. Pain radiated from his arms and feet as he tried to regain his precarious balance. Were his tormentors back? Part of him hoped they were, and that this nightmare would be finished. All he wanted to do was go home. To his family. There was a spark in the darkness and the memory came rushing back to him…

He'd been daydreaming in his economics class, listening to his teacher drone on about commercialism and the state of the World Bank. He'd gained his driver's license only a few days earlier, and he was looking forward to helping his father and Lilah, his step-mother out by taking on some of the running around for his younger siblings, Roman and Lacey.

The sound of the school intercom disturbed the class.

"Will Jerome Ciccone come to the principal's office?"

Everyone turned and looked at him, some of his friends giving him sympathetic grimaces, but he couldn't think of anything he'd done that would cause a visit to the principal's office. He looked up at the teacher who nodded his head to show he was excused. Gathering his belongings as it was nearing the end of the period, he headed down the deserted corridors of the school to Miss Beeching's office and entered the room.

"Pa…" he began, floored to see his father, Mario

Ciccone, standing there. Jerome looked at his father to see if he could work out why he was there, but he was looking at him with such an unusual look of sternness that he closed his mouth again.

"I understand it is your choice, Mr Ciccone," Miss Beeching was speaking to his father. "However, I would recommend against removing Jerome from this school. He is coming up to final exams and his future education could be in question."

"Thank you for your opinion, Miss Beeching. My mind is made up. Jerome, with me."

His father strode out of the office with Jerome struggling to catch up with him. He followed the older man to his car and got himself strapped in his seat, before turning to speak to him. They were already leaving the school parking lot, pulling out on to the main road.

"I don't understand. Pa? What's happening?"

"Don't call me that," Ciccone hissed through clenched teeth.

"But I've always called you Pa," Jerome began, even more confused now.

"Not anymore, you don't. You're no son of mine! That worthless bitch lied to me!"

"What…" Jerome shut up at the look of pure hatred Ciccone threw his way. Did he mean his mother? Sherwood Rossini had died in a car crash six years ago, when he was eleven. Mario Ciccone had taken him in, claiming him as his own son, bringing him up with his other children.

After a while, Jerome gave up on trying to talk to his father. When Mario Ciccone was in a mood like this, it was better to avoid antagonising him further. He watched the scenery go by. Unfamiliar with this part of town, he wasn't sure where they were going, never mind why.

After about an hour's drive, they pulled up to a warehouse. Jerome tried to see if there was anyone around, but he was hustled out of the car and dragged by his arm to a small doorway. Ciccone pushed him through the door and threw him onto the concrete floor, his schoolbooks and backpack, which he had unthinkingly brought with him, spilling out onto the icy floor.

"Stay there," Ciccone spat at him

Jerome sat up but stayed where he was. He didn't know what was happening. It was as if he'd never known the older man at all.

"Is that him?" He looked up to see a stranger walking towards them. The man had long stringy, greasy hair and looked very pale under the electric strip lighting.

"That's the bastard." Ciccone laughed. He walked over to Jerome and nudged him with his foot.

"And you're sure he's Donati?"

"His bitch of a mother was, so it stands to reason he is, doesn't it?"

The stranger nodded and approached Jerome. "Sit up properly," he ordered. Jerome did as he was told, spinning round to sit crossed-legged, his back to the door.

"He'll do." The stranger grinned at him, revealing dark stained teeth.

"Here." He thrust a package towards Ciccone. "That takes care of the debt."

"Huh?" His father opened the package and Jerome saw that there were bundles of cash in there. His father smiled for the first time since he'd picked him up from school.

"Nice doing business with you, Striga." He turned and walked out the door.

"Pa!" Jerome shouted, scrambling to his feet. The stranger backhanded him and he fell to the floor, knocking his head on the concrete as he landed. What was happening?

"Follow me," the man said, making his way to the back of the warehouse.

Jerome scrambled to his feet, his head ringing. It was only then that he noticed the other two men. They circled around behind him and pushed him in the direction where the Striga —whatever that meant — had gone.

There followed several weeks of hell for Jerome.

Nearly every day the stringy-haired man, whose name he had learned was Fenton, ordered for Jerome to be beaten. Sometimes just a little, sometimes a lot. He lost track of the number of times. His body was full of bruises and he was sure they'd broken his ribs. He didn't understand why they beat him. Their silence was unnerving.

They rationed his water and food intake. He felt weak and dizzy most of the time. The worst agony came weeks into his captivity. He had long lost track of what day or date it was, but he was sure he'd been there a long time. Fenton was absent, leaving only his underlings in charge of Jerome. That day's beating was one of the worst he'd yet endured, and they hadn't stopped there this time, brutalising his body in other ways. Ways his mind skittered away from.

His body shook again in the darkness as he hung from the rafters by ropes, the spark of memory receding away from him.

Fenton, when he was there, would poke and pry at him, asking him questions to which he had no answers. Jerome hated the sound of his voice almost as much as the physical damage the others did to him.

He heard a noise from the door. He froze. Not

again… not yet. He hadn't had time to recover from the last beating.

"Jerome." A whisper in the darkness. A woman's voice. They were using a woman now?

"Shh." A soft hand brushed his hair back from his face. He flinched, but the caress continued.

"It's okay. We're here to rescue you. My name is Beatrice."

"Please, please, no more," he croaked. He had had no water in a while and his throat was sore and parched.

"Here." Another voice; a man's. "Drink this, but only a little." A bottle of water was held to his lips and refreshing, cold liquid entered his mouth. He swallowed, the cold shocking him, but he still tried to drink more.

"Enough for now," the second voice said. "Beatrice, we need to get him out of here before the Striga come back."

"God what have they done to him?" she whispered with a sob.

Jerome didn't recognise either voice. "Who… who are you?" he finally managed.

The woman touched his cheek. "I'm Beatrice and this is Theodore, my husband. It's okay, Jerome, we're family."

He shivered. Family? He wasn't sure he wanted anything to do with family ever again, but her hand felt warm and the caress was the first touch he had received that wasn't a blow since… well, just since.

Jerome was gently lowered to the floor by Theodore, who covered him with a blanket, he tried to sit up but couldn't.

"Can you stand?" Theo asked.

Jerome shook his head. "I, I don't know." He tried to push himself up off the floor and keened in pain. His entire body ached. It felt like they had gutted him and left him to bleed out on the floor.

"It's okay," Beatrice calmed him, her voice soothing. "Theo will carry you. We're taking you to a hospital."

Theo reached out to him slowly. Jerome could just see his face now, in the low light that Beatrice was holding; kind brown eyes looking at him.

"It's okay, Jerome. I'm going to pick you up now. I'm not going to lie to you, this is going to hurt."

Jerome nodded. Together, he and Theo counted to three before Theo stood up with him in his arms. Jerome screamed. He couldn't help it. The pain was just too much. He collapsed back into darkness.

He awoke slowly. He was lying on a comfortable bed. For the first time in as long as he could remember, he was not in pain. He could hear a *swish whoosh* noise and the beep of machinery nearby. Soft blankets covered him, and pillows supported his head. He closed his eyes against the glare of the overhead lights. Surely this was a dream. A noise to his right caused him to open his eyes again. He moved his head slightly and could see a young woman, with olive skin and long black her. Her brown twinkling eyes were smiling back at him.

"Do you remember me?" she asked.

He nodded his head. "Beatrice," he breathed.

"That's right." She smiled at him "You're safe now. It's time for you to concentrate on getting better."

He closed his eyes again. Safe? He wasn't sure he'd ever be safe again.

II

Present day

Lying on his back in a deserted, dirty alley in New York, wasn't where Jerome Milton thought he would end up. His life of late had spiralled out of control. He lay there looking up at what he could see of the night sky through the rain. He was getting soaked, but he didn't move. In some ways, it was liberating not to care about what happened to him. If he stayed here and faded away, no-one would miss him. Well, maybe Chrissy, Hal's sister... His mind shied away from memories of Hal.

Looking around the alley, he could only see one streetlight high on the wall, but it hardly did anything to light up the area. Not that he needed the light to see what was around him. He had been there since early morning when there'd been plenty of daylight to see the squalidness of the place he found himself in.

Jerome was feeling light-headed, and his stomach was empty from lack of food. He'd had nothing to eat since the burger his friend Chrissy had pressed into his hands the day before yesterday. At least he thought it was the day before yesterday. His sense of time was slipping. Just as it had…

"No," he muttered to himself. He didn't want to go there. His memories of that time were still fuzzy, the betrayal he had felt when his father, Mario Ciccone, had thrown him away.

The aftermath and recovery that followed had been hard. He'd changed his name and slipped away to join the army without anyone knowing. But now the army didn't want him either. Bloody Improvised Explosive Devise! His best friend Hal had been killed instantly and Jerome had been medically discharged because of his injury.

His thoughts shied away from Hal. He couldn't think about him now.

Chrissy had half-adopted him, though he hadn't made it easy for her. He'd spent many nights on the sofa in her small apartment. She'd harangued him about his life and what he was doing. He really couldn't bring himself to care, which is why he found himself lying there passively in the alley.

"Well," a voice said from the darkness, "what do we have here?"

Jerome looked up through the rain, wiping it from his eyes, to see a tall man hovering over him. His eyes were a piercing amber and his red hair flowed around his shoulders. He was wearing a black trench coat, cinched in at the waist.

He was being sheltered under an umbrella held by a blond-haired, blue-eyed man who hung over his left shoulder, as if he belonged there.

Jerome scrambled backwards until his back was against the wall. He didn't have the energy to get up. He flopped back. Who was he kidding? If they meant him harm there was nothing he could do.

The man in the trench coat leaned down and examined Jerome.

He squinted back at the red-haired man, waiting for a blow that didn't come.

"Whaddya want?" he slurred, his head spinning from when he had pushed himself into a sitting position.

Blondie joined his friend in squatting before him and stared into his eyes. It felt weird, as though he was looking into his soul.

"Jerome," he breathed his name. Jerome jumped and the red-haired man said something which sounded like 'finally'.

"How to you know my name?" he asked, scrabbling round now to escape the two men.

"We've been looking for you a long time, Jerome." Red Hair smiled at him, his amber eyes shining, as his entire face lit up.

"What…?"

"Beatrice sends her regards," Red Hair said, and Jerome jumped, almost struggling to his feet, before slithering down the wall again.

"I don't know who you're talking about." He refused to look at them. Memories of a comforting presence and a beautiful smile accompanied the name Beatrice. She had been his saviour.

"Oh, I think you do." The red-haired man knelt before him and smiled. "My name is Cornelius Rossini, and it is so, so good to finally meet you."

Jerome shook his head, then wished he hadn't as the light-headedness returned. He keeled over to one side.

"It's okay, Jerome," Cornelius said, helping him to sit back up. "I know this will be hard for you to believe, but we really have been searching for you since you disappeared from the hospital."

"I don't understand," he admitted. "How… how did you find me here?"

"Your friend, Chrissy."

"What…"

"We finally traced you to the army, only to find

out you'd been discharged. Chrissy's address is in your file as being a contact address for you. She's very worried about you."

"I don't understand," he repeated. "What do you want with me?"

"Why don't we go somewhere where it's dry and more comfortable than this alley?" Blondie asked.

"Who're you? If he's Cornelius, what's your name?"

"Dastan," he offered.

Jerome sighed. Knowing the other man's name didn't really help him. He tried to sit up again, finally managing it with Cornelius's help. Obviously, his idea of lying in this alley until he faded away was not going to happen.

"Well?" Dastan asked.

"How do I know I can trust you?"

"You don't, not really," Cornelius replied. "I can offer you answers, though. Answers about Mario Ciccone… and your family."

"Ciccone's nothing to me," Jerome spat out. "He… he…."

"We know, Jerome, we know," Dastan said, as he helped Jerome to his feet. With Cornelius's help he managed to get his arm under Jerome's left shoulder.

"Let's get you somewhere more comfortable," Cornelius said.

Jerome tried to struggle away from them, but he

was too weak. His strength had been eroded over the last few weeks as he'd spiralled further into a dark depression. He'd stopped eating and his injured leg had gotten worse. He felt himself helpless in their hands. Giving up, he allowed them to take him where they would.

Dastan and Cornelius helped him walk towards the end of the alley where, for the first time, Jerome noticed that a large white SUV, its engine running, was waiting.

Fuck, he thought. I hope I'm not going to regret this.

III

Cornelius entered the bedroom where Jerome slept. It was 10 am the day after they had found him in the alley. He looked down on the young man and could just make out the boy he had been. He hadn't seen his great grandson since he was about five, when he had last visited his granddaughter, Sherwood.

He smiled as he remembered the bright, intelligent boy who had wanted to know everything he could tell him about the Donati. His mother had neglected to tell him anything about his heritage, only saying it had caused her more trouble than it was worth.

The young man stirred in the bed and Cornelius sat down in a chair near the balcony doors, which were open to let the fresh spring air into the room. It wasn't long before Jerome opened his eyes and tried to sit up. He winced in pain, but Cornelius was there to help him get settled and pull the pillows behind his back.

"How are you feeling today?" he asked.

"Confused." The young man shook his head, then grimaced. "Note to self, don't shake your head."

Cornelius smiled at him. "What do you remember from yesterday?"

"Not much. The alley, rain coming down, you."

"Do you know who I am?"

Jerome went to shake his head again, before changing his mind. "You said your name was Cornelius."

"Yes. Do you remember seeing me before yesterday? Perhaps when you were a child?"

"I don't know. You seem familiar but… it's all a blur." He swallowed. "I remember you mentioned Beatrice yesterday. Is she here?

His tone was hopeful and Cornelius was pleased. His niece was still in Italy but he was sure when he called her, she would come rushing to help Jerome.

"No," he replied. "I wanted to make sure you were in a state to meet her before letting her know you were here."

"Whaddya mean?" The young man bristled.

"Yesterday you were lying in an alley. To all intents and purposes, it looked like you would be quite happy to stay there until the end. Your friend Chrissy said she had been getting more and more worried about you. She said that she thought you'd given up on life. How you had stopped going to the VA hospital for treatment and physiotherapy for your leg. How you had stopped eating, washing, sleeping. She was very happy to see me and tell us where she thought you had gone."

"Some friend," Jerome growled

"Yes, she is," Cornelius replied, sternly. "When you're feeling better, you will have to contact her so she doesn't worry too much."

There was a knock on the door and Cornelius shouted for them to enter. An older man with craggy features and grey hair entered the room. He was carrying a tray with a glass of orange juice and a covered plate from which enticing smells wafted.

"Thanks, Shea," Cornelius said as he indicated that the other man put the tray down on the dresser nearest to Jerome.

"Jerome, I'd like you to meet my steward, Shea. He runs the house, our security, and generally makes our lives easier." Cornelius smiled at the older man.

"Er, hi," Jerome muttered quietly.

"Jerome," Shea replied, smiling. "It's good to meet you at last. Do you need anything else?" he asked Cornelius before turning to leave the room.

"No, I'm good."

Shea nodded once, then left, closing the door

behind him. Cornelius moved and helped Jerome sit up properly in bed, fluffing up the pillows behind his back, so he could sit back comfortably. Only when he was satisfied did he pick up the tray and place it over Jerome's knee, before lifting the cover from the plate. It revealed a light fluffy omelette with chopped ham and tomatoes.

Cornelius could hear Jerome's stomach groaning.

"Eat up." He gestured at the plate and Jerome glanced warily at him.

"It's okay, you need to build your reserves up."

"No coffee?" the young man muttered.

"Later, when you're up to it. Now eat up, then you can catch up on more sleep. I've arranged for my personal doctor to come in and see you later."

"Don't need no doctor..." The words were muffled as Jerome began tearing into the omelette. Cornelius smiled to himself. He reminded him very much of his own son Jacoby when he was ill or hurt – grumpy and reluctant to be helped.

"Where's the other dude?" Jerome asked him as he finished his food and drank his juice.

"Dastan? Downstairs answering his emails, I should imagine."

"Hmpf, thought he was your shadow."

Cornelius laughed. "Something like that. Now, do you need help to use the bathroom before you sleep again?"

Grumbling some more, Jerome attempted to get out of bed on his own. He realised he did need help so, reluctantly, the young man allowed Cornelius to help him to the bathroom before closing the door in his face. Several moments passed before he opened the door again, his face white.

"Okay," he said. "Guess I'm more out of it than I thought."

Cornelius only nodded and helped his young guest back to bed.

"Get some more sleep. Dr Browning isn't due until this afternoon. I'll be back up later with some lunch. If you need me press that button there. Shea will answer the intercom and let me know." He pointed to a small white button attached to the bedside cabinet, before helping Jerome get comfortable once more.

He watched for a while as sleep overcame the young man, then tray in hand he left the room to go in search of his lover.

He found Dastan in the library where he was just finishing checking his emails. Cornelius walked over and gave him a kiss before sitting down in one of the plush chairs across from him.

"How did it go?" Dastan asked.

"Okay. He's still pretty out of it, but grumpy with it, like Jacoby used to get."

"He remembered yesterday?"

"Yes." Cornelius stared off into space, and Dastan got up and joined him on the comfortable chair. Just enough room for two if they snuggled.

Pulling Cornelius into his arms, he said. "We got to him in time, Neely. Remember that."

"I know," he sighed. "I just worry for him. There's so much to tell him, so much he doesn't know. I only scraped the surface when he was a child, I thought we'd have all the time in the world."

Cornelius took comfort from his lover, as Dastan pulled him in and held him. He had done his best, but when Sherwood had died in an accident, his own son, Jerome's grandfather, had shown no interest in the boy. When Mario Ciccone had claimed him as his own, Cornelius had tried to oppose it, but Jacoby had accepted it and there was nothing he could do at the time.

He and Dastan had been in Rome, finishing up a task for the Donati Council, when Jerome had been removed from school by Ciccone. It was only his own misgivings that had had him ask Shea to keep an eye on the boy from time to time. Shea had reported that Jerome was missing, and Cornelius could only look on from afar as he sent Beatrice and Theo to find him.

They'd rescued him, only to have the boy

24

disappear a few weeks later. Thank goodness for the computer skills of Shea's son Donal in finding him.

"Shh," Dastan said. "I can feel your mind skittering all over the place."

He reached up and touched Cornelius's temples, gently massaging them. Slowly, Cornelius's mind stopped spinning and he smiled at his lover, forever thankful that he had found him. They sat like that for several minutes, communing silently with each other. The door opened and Shea entered with a tray of coffee. He raised his eyebrows at the couple and chuckled.

"Is it safe to come in?" he asked.

"Of course," Cornelius answered, taking the coffee Shea offered him. His steward had been with him a long time, over one hundred and fifty years now, since just before his wife, Elise had been murdered. He was part of the family and he didn't know what he would do without him, or his son Donal, if they decided to leave his service.

They settled down to their morning coffee. The conversation was kept light. There was nothing they could do until the doctor had been and they knew where they stood with Jerome's injuries from when he was in the army.

IV

Jerome woke slowly, stretching luxuriously. It had been several months since he'd had the pleasure of sleeping in a real bed, in a real bedroom. Most days he slept on Chrissy's sofa, but her new boyfriend didn't like him coming round. He hadn't been there in weeks, only managing to catch her for short periods of time, usually when she pushed food into his hands and sighed at him.

He had been out of it when they arrived at Cornelius's house last night, having fallen asleep in the SUV, a sure sign that despite his qualms he did trust the pair. He didn't remember the walk through the house last night, just his arrival in this room, collapsing into bed and falling asleep.

He looked around himself now, noting the balcony door was open as the drapes blew slightly in the breeze. The room was decorated in pale greens with gold highlights. Jerome liked it, he found it soothing.

He vaguely remembered Cornelius that morning, and the breakfast the other man, Shea, had brought him. He was still feeling weak, but he managed to pull himself into a sitting position.

As he did so, he became aware of Dastan standing at the open balcony doors looking in at him.

"The doctor has arrived. She's having coffee with Cornelius just now. Do you need the facilities before she comes upstairs?"

Jerome grimaced and nodded, allowing the other man to help him out of bed and to the bathroom. He noticed the toothbrush in its cellophane wrapper this time and made use of it. There was shaving gear as well, but he didn't think he could cope with that at the moment. It would have to wait until later.

When he re-entered the room, Cornelius and a woman were waiting for him. The woman had a doctor's bag with her and was smiling at him.

"Hi Jerome, I'm Doctor Jenna Browning," she held her hand out to Jerome, who took it and shook it. He nodded at her then sat on the bed.

"I understand, from what Cornelius has told me, that you were injured in Afghanistan when an IED exploded. He tells me you were injured in your right leg. Am I okay to examine it?" she asked as she approached him.

"Knock yourself out," he growled. He'd had enough of doctors in the VA hospital when he had been repatriated back to New York.

Dr Browning carefully moved Jerome's leg onto the bed so she could see it better. He was wearing sleep shorts, so she was able to examine the wounds on his leg, without removing further clothing. She looked at the skin grafts that had been done in the hospital in Germany, and examined the area where he had lost muscle.

"Thank you." She smiled at him as she pulled off her latex gloves. "Now I'd like to examine you, see your general health."

Jerome allowed himself to be pushed and prodded, breathing in when told to do so and answering her questions. She frowned a couple of times, obviously not liking his answers, but he wasn't sure he cared.

When she had finished, she helped him back into bed. He was glad to sit back against the pillows again. He wouldn't admit it, but the exam had been difficult for him.

"Your leg has healed nicely, but you could do with more physiotherapy." She turned to Cornelius. "I have someone I can recommend, who can come in here a couple of times a week to help build the stamina back up in that leg. A lot of the muscle was lost in the explosion, but there's enough that physio will help give it more strength."

Jerome sat and listened. This wasn't new to him, the doctors at the VA hospital had said the same, but he hadn't taken much notice.

"You're seriously undernourished." She continued. "Though that will be helped by good and regular meals. After a couple of days, I suggest walking as a good exercise, and swimming. Added with the physiotherapy, it will help you build up your stamina and return you to health."

"He'll be okay?" Cornelius asked.

"He'll be fine," Dr Browning answered, smiling at them all.

"Thank you, Dr Browning." Cornelius smiled back at her and reached past Jerome to press the little button attached to the bedside cabinet. "Shea will show you out."

"You're welcome," she replied. "If you need me again, you know where to get hold of me. It was good meeting you, Jerome." She shook his hand once more. "I don't think you'll have any difficulty recovering, and I know you'll be well looked after here."

A couple of days later, Jerome was beginning to feel a whole lot better. He had resented the intrusion of Cornelius and Dastan to begin with, but he had to admit they had only his well-being in mind. Though he had tried hard, he couldn't recall having met Cornelius before. Cornelius had just shrugged and said he'd explain another time.

He got out of bed and entered the bathroom, which was modern and bright white. A large shower cubicle boasted a rain shower head, along with several other detachable heads. It was just what he needed to make him feel better and being able to shave and brush his teeth was wonderful. He was still getting used to having a bathroom so readily available to him. Before Cornelius and Dastan had brought him here, it had been several weeks since he'd been anywhere near a real bathroom. Having strip washes in public restrooms was not the same.

With a towel around his waist, he returned to the bedroom to find that someone, probably Shea, had laid out some clothes for him. Boxers, jeans and a tee shirt, with crew socks for his feet. Getting dressed in clean, new clothes was a novelty for Jerome: it had been more than a few months since he'd had anything newer than Goodwill rejects.

As he pulled on his socks, he heard voices coming from the balcony. When he was ready, he followed the sound outside where he found Cornelius and Dastan having breakfast at a small table in the shade. Coffee, juice, fruit, cereal, and bacon and eggs were laid out on the table in various containers.

"Good morning." Cornelius smiled and motioned for Jerome to join them at the table. "Would you like some breakfast?"

Jerome's stomach took that moment to gurgle loudly. He grimaced.

"I would love some, thank you."

"You're looking better," Cornelius said. "The physio has helped?"

"Yes." Jerome agreed that the physio was helping. It had only been his own blockheadedness that had stopped him before. Being able to swim in Cornelius's outdoor swimming pool had helped as well. He had been on the swim team in school, and he hadn't realised how much he'd missed it. He was still limping a bit and the physio had suggested using a cane for a few weeks. He'd not been happy with that but had reluctantly agreed.

Jerome looked at the view in front of him. Lawn gave way to trees and from there open fields. He couldn't remember how long they had travelled for when they had arrived the other day. They had to be in upstate New York, a long way from the city.

"Are you going to tell me why you brought me here?" Jerome looked at Cornelius. Now that he was beginning to feel better, he was becoming more curious as to why Cornelius and Dastan had brought him to their home. Okay, he got that they were probably some kind of relative and that Cornelius had known his mother, but…

"Not yet. Dastan and I need to be somewhere this morning and we'd like you to accompany us, but only if you can keep your questions to yourself until we return this afternoon. If not, we will leave you here and you will be well looked after. Shea will provide for you, he is an excellent cook and will arrange lunch for you. If you come with us, however, you may learn some things that will help you with the road ahead."

Jerome frowned. It seemed he had come to a fork in his road – did he continue following the pair and find out more about who they were and what they wanted from him? He was still unsure of their motives, but up to now they had treated him well, getting a doctor for him and looking after his well-being. He was confused as to what was going on, but the only way to find out more was by going with them.

Shrugging his shoulders, he nodded his head at the men.

"I'm in."

V

———

Returning to his room after breakfast, Jerome found a Tom Ford single breasted suit hung up for him on the armoire in the corner of his room. He looked at it in consternation, he really couldn't remember the last time he'd worn a suit. He'd never graduated from High School, so hadn't had the opportunity to wear one then. In the army he'd been in uniform for several years.

Laid out on the bed were socks, a business shirt and a belt, and on the floor a pair of dress shoes. Next to them was a black ebony cane. Jerome shook his head. Someone, probably Shea, had thought of everything. He began getting changed.

There was a slight knock at the door, and a soft cough drew his attention. Turning, he found Shea standing in the doorway.

"Good morning, Jerome. Cornelius requested I provide a suit for you for this morning's outing. I believe this one should fit you, it's one of Dastan's. You look to be about the same size, though I should imagine you will bulk out more now that you've begun eating properly again."

"Thank you," he answered. "Do you know where we're going?"

Shea just smiled. "I do. It must be very confusing for you, and I can only imagine it's going to get worse in the next few hours. Once you're dressed, Cornelius will meet you in the foyer."

Shea turned and left before Jerome could even utter a thank you. Wherever Cornelius and Dastan were taking him they needed him to be dressed in business clothes. It didn't help him work anything out, but he got dressed. Leaving his bedroom, he found the stairs and descended, with the help of the cane, to the first floor to find Cornelius waiting for him.

Cornelius was dressed in a high-end bespoke suit. Jerome thought it was Armani, not that he had ever been up on fashion, but it spoke volumes regarding the amount of money he had access to. Jerome held his arms out, as though for inspection, and lifted his left eyebrow quizzically at Cornelius.

"Thank you for indulging me in this, Jerome. We are visiting a man who is a high-powered attorney in

New York, and I want us to make a certain impression."

Jerome shrugged, and Cornelius gestured him towards the doorway. They left the house together to find Dastan already seated in the white SUV from the other day. Cornelius slipped into the passenger seat and Jerome got in the back seat, meeting Dastan's eyes in the rear-view mirror.

"Thank you for loaning me your clothes."

"You're welcome. I'm glad the suit fits."

———

Jerome discovered that Cornelius and Dastan's residence was on the outskirts of Schenectady in upper New York state. It took them a couple of hours to reach the city. Before long, they arrived at one of New York's tall skyscraper office buildings. Ironically, it was not that far from where Jerome had been lying in his alley.

Dastan parked the SUV in visitor parking in the building's underground parking lot and they entered the elevator. Cornelius pressed the button for the 21st floor and Jerome perused the directory to see who was situated on that floor. He read the name Ciccone from the directory and his blood ran cold.

"What the hell!" He turned to Cornelius and Dastan, the colour having drained from his face, his bright blue eyes standing out starkly against his pale skin. He couldn't help himself; he was shaking. Shaking with fear and with rage. How dare they! His hand reached out to push the emergency stop button, but Dastan was faster than he was and pulled his hand back.

"Let this play out, Jerome," he said quietly, staring into his eyes. Jerome felt as though he was being judged. He felt power swirling around them though he couldn't say what it was. Slowly he calmed and nodded his head at them. He could do this. He could face his nemesis.

"Okay," he whispered as the elevator arrived at its destination.

The three men stepped off the elevator and walked to the reception desk. A slight young man was sitting behind the desk. He gave them a distracted smile as he talked quietly into the telephone headset. There was something about the young man that tickled Jerome's memory, but he couldn't quite grasp it. He sighed, so much was lost.

Jerome, Cornelius and Dastan waited for the receptionist to finish his call. Jerome took the time to look around the reception area. He had never been in an office area like this; the walls were painted a pale green and the artwork was chosen to fit in with them and the dark green carpet on which he stood. The wood on the reception desk was a pale colour and

Jerome could see that it was well polished and well kept; the man who owned these offices liked to show off his wealth. Jerome shuddered, though tried to hide it.

"I'm sorry for keeping you waiting," the man behind the desk said.

"That's okay," Cornelius replied. "Mr Rossini and associates to see Mr Ciccone, he's expecting us."

The young man in front of them consulted his computer and smiled up at them. "He's waiting for you in Conference Room One. If you'll follow me, I'll take you to him and his team."

They followed the man down a corridor and to the left of the building. A large area opened up where several desks were occupied by workers, who appeared to be glued to their computer screens. Not one of them looked up at them as they passed, which struck Jerome as strange.

They were ushered into a conference room where several people were either sitting at the large conference table or standing around the room drinking coffee and eating pastries.

"Mr Rossini and his associates," the young man announced.

A large florid man with a coffee in his hand turned to greet them and dropped his cup in surprise at seeing Jerome. He gaped for a moment before moving towards them. The receptionist tried to go to pick up the cup, but Ciccone brushed him off and sent him back to his desk.

"What is the meaning of this?" he roared, pointing at Jerome. Everyone else in the room turned to look at him. Men in their suits and women in their heels all looked at Jerome and his companions in shocked silence.

"Mr Ciccone," Cornelius began.

"So, son…" Ciccone turned to Jerome. "You run from me for years, yet here you are with these… these…"

Jerome looked in confusion at Cornelius and Dastan, and pointed to Mario Ciccone, his estranged father, the man he still had nightmares about, the man he hated so much he'd rather be anywhere else than in his company. The man he'd tried to forget.

Cornelius gestured with his arms. Jerome squinted at him, wondering if he had gone mad, but no, he stood there with a slight smile on his face. Jerome looked around him and gaped. All the people in the room, apart from the three of them, had stopped what they were doing and were… frozen, yes frozen, in place. One woman stood in the corner with her phone to her ear and another had a pastry half in and half out of her mouth. A man sitting at the table who had been tapping his pen on his legal pad was frozen as well.

Jerome turned to Cornelius and, as he did,

noticed that all the people out in the large work area were also frozen. "What?" he asked, gesturing to the frozen people around him.

"Time," Cornelius said. "Time is frozen. Look at the clock."

Jerome did as he had been told and looked at the large clock on the far wall. It had stopped at 10.47am. He watched for a moment or two, but it didn't change. Time really had stopped.

"I don't understand."

"I know, but trust us a bit longer." Cornelius said.

Jerome nodded as Dastan approached Ciccone, touched his head and grimaced. He stayed there for a while, his eyes flickering back and forth as though he were watching a film or reading a book.

"He's reading his memories, looking for information that only Ciccone knows. Trying to find anything that he knows about you, about his son, the one that got away, the one he can't control."

Jerome felt as though he was in some kind of sci-fi film. This only happened in bad fiction, right? He watched as Dastan gasped, then flung himself away from Ciccone. He turned to look at Jerome, and the sympathy and horror in his eyes were almost more than Jerome could take. He wrenched his eyes away from Dastan and returned to looking at the other people in the room, frozen in time.

"We should go," Dastan said. "I need to have

quiet and space to work through all the memories I've picked up from this vile man."

Cornelius nodded and leant over to touch Ciccone's chest, right where his heart was. Jerome thought he was going to kill the man, but all he did was touch him for a moment.

Cornelius gestured again and the room around them came back to life, no-one there aware that they had been frozen in time.

"I'm sorry, Mr Ciccone," Cornelius said. "This was obviously a mistake, I had hoped we could sit down and discuss business matters, but…"

Ciccone looked at him as though he had grown horns and pointed at the conference door. "I think it's best if you go. You can leave Jerome here though, he and I have some catching up to do."

Before Jerome could stop him, Ciccone had grabbed hold of his bicep and was squeezing his arm tightly, pulling him further into the room.

Cornelius reached out towards Ciccone again and the man's hand fell from Jerome's arm as he sagged, clutching at his heart. At the place where only moments before Cornelius had touched him.

"Quickly," Cornelius said to one of the stunned people in the room, "your boss is ill, you'd best send for the paramedics. We'll see ourselves out."

People jumped into action with several going for their phones. Ciccone gasped for air as he leant on the desk before one of the women helped him to sit on the floor. Though his face was creased in pain, Jerome could still see the man's hatred aimed at him.

The door was flung open, and the young man from the reception desk ran in. "Father," he said, reaching down to touch Ciccone. "What happened—"

Ciccone threw the young man's hand off him in irritation.

The door of the conference room closed behind them as Cornelius led Jerome and Dastan back out the way they had come in. This time the people in the large office stared at the commotion in the conference room as well as at the three men heading for the elevator.

Jerome looked back into the conference room. There *was* something about the young man, something familiar he couldn't quite grasp.

As the elevator car began descending, Jerome looked at Dastan and Cornelius. "What the hell? And who the hell was the young guy?"

"That was your half-brother, Roman. His mother was Ciccone's third wife. Roman takes after his mother and is not his father's favourite person."

Jerome shook his head as they got back in the SUV. Nothing made sense, none of this, none of what had happened. He put his head in his hands and Dastan drove them away. Perhaps he should have stayed in his alley and faded to nothing after all.

VI

Jerome sat at the table out on the balcony where they'd had breakfast yesterday morning. He was still reeling from having seen his father. He couldn't even begin to get his mind around the fact that Cornelius could stop time and Dastan could seemingly read memories. The shock of seeing his father was all he could feel. Obviously, he wanted him for something… His mind was spinning.

"Jerome." His musings were interrupted by Shea who was standing at the balcony door inside his room.

He looked up at Shea, who smiled at him. "I thought I'd find you here. There's been a development. Cornelius and Dastan would like it if you'd join them in the library."

Jerome sighed. Whatever this development was obviously involved him. He grabbed his cane and followed Shea through his bedroom and down the stairs. He felt as though his whole life had been turned around since the night he'd lain in the alley, and he still wasn't sure if it was for the better.

"It has to do with your family," Shea said, looking sympathetically at him as he left him outside the library.

Jerome entered the room and nodded to Cornelius and Dastan who were both sitting in comfortable chairs in a nook, surrounded by books, papers and laptops. The modern accoutrements seemed quite incongruous given the old-fashioned nature of the library itself, with its floor to ceiling shelves and dark wood desks and chairs.

"Shea said there'd been a development?"

"Yes, your half-brother Roman and his older sister Verity are at the front desk in the building we have in New York asking for you." Cornelius turned the laptop around so Jerome could see what looked like security footage showing the young man, Roman, whom they had met yesterday, and a slightly older looking woman whose blonde hair was pulled back in an elegant chignon style. Jerome stared at them. He felt he knew not just Roman but the woman as well. Verity, Cornelius had called her.

"The question is…" Dastan sat up in his chair. "Do you wish to see them?"

Jerome shook his head, not because he didn't want

to see them, but because he couldn't understand why they would wish to see him.

"Honestly, I don't know. What did they say?"

"Just that Ciccone is in the hospital. His heart is fine, but they are keeping him in for tests. He refuses to talk to them about you, refuses to answer their questions. They're hoping you can fill in the gaps."

"Fuck! I don't know anything myself!"

"Neely," Dastan addressed Cornelius, "I think it's time; an explanation for Jerome is long overdue, and for these two as well."

Cornelius nodded and pressed a button on his laptop. A security guard's face appeared in the window.

"Yes, Mr Rossini?" the man answered.

"I'm sending transport for Mr Ciccone and Miss Long. It should be there in just over a couple of hours. Please offer them refreshments and advise them of the timetable. Let them know that Jerome will be here to meet them, when they arrive."

"Yes, sir." The laptop went dark and Cornelius moved it off the arm of his chair where it had been resting.

Dastan got up and moved to the door of the library. "I'll go pick them up. Be back as soon as I can."

———

It was, if not an uneasy silence, a difficult silence between Cornelius and Jerome as they waited for Dastan to return with their guests. Shea served them coffee and handed Jerome the local paper. He thanked the man and settled down to wait. Not his best activity.

He broke the silence at last. "What's going on, Cornelius? I've spent the last fifteen years trying to stay off that man's radar and out of his reach. Yet once again he knows where to find me."

"I'm sorry, Jerome." Cornelius reached out and patted his shoulder.

Jerome sighed. There was nothing he could do about it now. The next few hours passed quietly, with both men trying to read, and failing.

Shortly after 5pm, the door of the library opening caused both men to start. Dastan entered followed slowly by Roman Ciccone and Verity Long; Jerome's half-brother and step-sister.

"Jerome," Roman gasped out, "it is you. I wasn't sure yesterday, and then all hell broke loose and you were gone." The young, slight man looked at him as though Jerome was the answer to his prayers. "Don't you know me? Jer?"

"I'm sorry–" he began before he was interrupted by Verity.

"I told you he might not remember, Ro," she said sadly looking at Jerome.

"But why…" Roman's words came out as a whine and Jerome looked up at him. There was something in that intonation, something in his voice – and hers – that he sort of, kind of, remembered.

"Shea is bringing refreshments," Dastan said as he re-entered the library. Jerome hadn't even noticed that he'd left after bringing his siblings in a moment ago. His head hurt. They were his siblings, weren't they?

"Lacey?" he asked, suddenly. "Where's Lacey?"

Roman's whole face lit up. "You do remember! She's at school. Mom decided it would be better if Lacey went to boarding school."

Jerome touched his temples, his head was throbbing. He turned to Roman and looked at him, really looked.

"I'm sorry, Roman, I remember bits and pieces. I know you – we – have a younger sister called Lacey, that Verity is your mother's daughter from a previous marriage… but it's like I'm seeing this through some kind of fog."

"That will be the memory block," Cornelius spoke up for the first time since the siblings had arrived.

"I'm sorry?" Jerome asked, looking pale.

"When you were young, after your mother died in the car accident," Cornelius began, "you lived with your father, step-mother and siblings. When you were in your teens, Ciccone began his mind games with you, taking you out of school–"

"But," Roman interrupted, "Father told us Jerome had run away!"

"I did," Jerome replied. "Eventually. I remember the pain, then Beatrice… She helped me escape, I think." He screwed his eyes up as he tried to remember. "I left. It's beginning to come back now." Roman smiled at him. "I… I can remember playing with you both, and Lacey, a baby, a toddler, then not much else, until one night…" He shuddered. "After that I joined the army and hoped I'd never see my father again."

"Jer…" Before Jerome knew it, he had an armful of siblings, as Verity and Roman tried to squash him between them.

Jerome turned to Cornelius and Dastan, "You I definitely don't know. How do you fit into the picture?" His head still hurt and though he remembered his siblings now, his memories were fuzzy and when he tried to concentrate on them, he skittered off them somehow. Cornelius had mentioned something about a memory block?

Cornelius said nothing to begin with, moving around the table to join everyone in the comfy nook, where they had been seated before. Shea had been and gone, bringing refreshments with him. He poured himself a cup of tea and stood in front of the bookshelves, his eyes looking into the distance.

"You don't remember me," Cornelius said. "Not

surprising really, you were so young. We only met a couple of times when you were a baby and a young boy. The last time we met, you were about five, six? Your mother, Sherwood, was my granddaughter. Jerome, you are my great grandson."

Jerome gaped at him. "Your grandson? No, wait, your great grandson? Just how old are you anyway?"

"Two hundred and fifty-four," Cornelius stated, looking him in the eye.

Jerome gasped, the number of the years of Cornelius's life floating between them.

VII

"Walk with me." Cornelius smiled at Jerome and gestured to the garden.

Shea had returned shortly after Cornelius had told them how old he was. He had ushered Verity and Roman from the library, saying he'd get them settled in connecting rooms. They'd meet again in a couple of hours for dinner.

Jerome had been surprised to find out that each sibling had brought an overnight case with them, as though they'd known they wouldn't be going home for a while.

Cornelius and Jerome walked silently for a couple of minutes enjoying the sunshine on their faces. The estate was covered in mature trees. Cornelius enjoyed spending time amongst them, and he unerringly led his great grandson down his favourite path.

"I still don't understand," Jerome spoke up, breaking the silence.

"About who you are, who I am?"

"All of it. It's like a different world here, a world where time can stand still and memories can be read. It's like some kind of psychic bullshit you see on those made for TV movies!"

Cornelius laughed. "You're right, it does feel like that sometimes, but believe me Jerome, it is very real."

"How?"

"I'm not sure I can answer how," Cornelius said, squinting into the sun, "but I will do my best to try and explain some things to you."

"You come from a long line of what we call the Donati, the gifted ones. Each Donati has a special gift. As you've already seen I can stop time for a while and restart it. I can control smaller things such as when I made Ciccone's heart beat out of sequence for a time. Dastan can read someone's memories and hold them in his own mind, Beatrice works with memories to help people, like a counsellor. Your gift will be different again. We are a long-lived people. As I said, I am two hundred and fifty-four, Dastan is one hundred and seventy-five and Shea is over three hundred years old."

"What the fuck!" Jerome stopped short on the path, and Cornelius had to turn to see where he had gone. "That's just..."

"Yeah, there are no words for it sometimes."

Jerome appeared to be thinking about what Cornelius had told him and when they came to a garden bench along the path, he sank down on to it. Cornelius watched his great grandson with care. He still wasn't sure how Jerome was going to take everything. He sat down beside him.

"I was born in Verona, Italy in the year 1771. My father Giuseppe was a mind-worker, similar, but different to both Dastan and Beatrice. He could help people change memories and create new ones. He always said it was something he only ever did when there were no alternatives, that it was a heavy burden to take on someone's memories and then to help them create new ones. I wish he was here now to speak to you, but though we Donati are a long-lived race, we can be killed. He was caught in London in the Blitz and didn't make it out. I still miss him, every day. My mother, bless her, was human, and died a long time ago.

"I married your great grandmother when I was in my forties and we had one child, a son. Jacoby was born in 1861 in Paris, where we were living at the time. By then I was working for the Donati Council, an organisation created hundreds of years ago to regulate the Donati and work with human governments when needed. Jacoby works for them now. We stayed in Paris until the Franco-Prussian war broke out and..." He stopped and stared into the trees.

"Anyway, your great grandmother Elise was killed during the Paris Commune. The rest of us – myself, my brother Ignatius, Jacoby, and Ignatius's daughter Beatrice – removed ourselves to London, where I continued to work for the council. I met Dastan, in Europe, during another war in 1914, and we've been together ever since. He helped me heal from the death of your great grandmother and followed me to New York when I moved here after the war. Jacoby stayed in London, where he met your grandmother, Emmeline, or Emmie as she was known. They both worked for the Council and consulted with the British Government during the Second World War. Eventually, Jacoby fell out with the Council and they too moved here. Your mother, Sherwood, was born in the early 1950s in New York. After Emmie died, Jacoby moved back to Washington, DC and began work with the Donati Council once more."

Cornelius stared off into the distance as though looking back through time. "We've been looking for you since you disappeared when you joined the army. It was sheer luck on our part that Shea's son Donal was visiting with us recently and he used his computer skills to track you down. We knew little about what had befallen you with Ciccone. When I tried to speak to you Ciccone told me you had ran away from home at seventeen and he'd heard no more from you. He was very unpleasant and seemed to have changed from the last time I spoke to him when you first went to live with his family when you were twelve. Theo and Beatrice were able to find you by backtracking his movements, and they took you from the warehouse you were being kept in to the hospital."

They sat on the bench for a long time until Shea called them in for dinner. Cornelius spoke about his long life, and some of what he had done. He spoke more about the gifts each Donati received, and their longevity. Jerome listened to him, gazing off into the distance.

───────

Cornelius stood at the balcony door to Jerome's room, watching as his great grandson slept. Dastan, as always, stood at his left shoulder. He remembered standing like this watching Jerome sleep as a young child. He and Sherwood hadn't always seen eye to eye, but she had encouraged him to visit with her son. She believed he needed a male role model in his life, and Jerome's father wanted no more to do with her or her child. How times had changed.

Dastan squeezed his shoulder. "Come to bed, Neely. He'll be okay."

Cornelius allowed Dastan to lead him to their

bedroom, where he undressed and got ready for bed still in a daze. He had not expected Jerome's siblings to turn up when they did, determined to find out what had happened to the older brother they remembered from childhood. He expected that would bring repercussions when Mario Ciccone realised where his wayward children had gone.

"Come here." Dastan opened his arms and Cornelius sank gratefully into his embrace, as he had been doing every night since they found each other over a hundred years earlier. His relationship with Dastan had seen him through difficult times in his life. He had already lost his wife, Elise, mother of Jerome's grandfather, Jacoby. He had loved Elise and still found her senseless death during the Paris Commune hard to deal with. He hadn't gone into details with Jerome but knew at some point he was going to have to explain about the Striga and other species who populated their world.

They lay together, taking comfort in their closeness and sharing with each other the doings of the day, and their thoughts and feelings. A habit they'd got into decades ago.

"It has to be soon, Neely," Dastan said, referring to the memories he had picked out of Ciccone's mind the day before. "I can hold them for a few days, but not much longer. I think it's important that Jerome sees what has been going on whilst he was held by

Ciccone and since he moved on. That man's memories are rank. I've been having trouble holding them closed."

Cornelius turned and studied his lover. "Are you okay?"

"Yes, nothing I can't cope with, but if we are going to expect Jerome to help us against his father in any way, we need to do it soon. He is confused and feeling betrayed, even if he doesn't say that much."

"Tomorrow," Cornelius agreed. "Let's get some sleep…"

———

Breakfast the next day was a subdued affair. The siblings Roman and Verity were expecting to be called to task by their father at any moment. Determined to remain and help Jerome, Roman decided to bite the bullet and phone his father before he could contact them. Cornelius asked him to put the phone on speaker so they could listen in, and he complied.

The phone rang a few times before Ciccone picked up.

"Roman, that better be you telling me you're not where I think you are!" His father's voice came through the speaker loud, clear and annoyed.

"And where might that be, Father?"

"You know very well where!" his father blustered.

"You and that good for nothing sister of yours get yourselves back here straightaway."

"I don't think so," Roman replied, grimacing at them. "If you'd have asked nicely, I might have come in to work today."

Cornelius could hear the tremor in Roman's voice. He knew the young man was not in the habit of going against his father. He had been brought up to follow the man's every order and he was struggling to go against his upbringing.

"This is your doing, Jerome," Ciccone shouted through the phone's speaker. "I know you're there and listening. Don't think you'll get away with—"

"Honestly, Mario, listen to yourself," Verity spoke for the first time, interrupting Ciccone's rant. "Roman and I will be visiting with Jerome for a few days. We'll be in touch."

She reached over towards the phone that Roman was still holding, took it out of his hands and switched it off.

"It's as though I don't really know him anymore," Verity said. "When he first married my mother and Jerome and Roman were boys, he was almost the perfect father. I worshipped him at one point as little girls often do their fathers. I just don't know what happened to him…"

"I'm afraid I do," Dastan spoke up for the first time. "When we visited his office the other day, I managed to obtain access to his memories and well, I guess you'd say 'downloaded' them into my mind. I can take on board another person's memories like this for a short time, but I need to look at them properly soon otherwise I'll lose them."

"That's…" Jerome spoke up for the first time, "that's some weird shit."

Dastan laughed. "You're right, Jerome, it certainly is."

Cornelius looked at Jerome's siblings to see if they'd picked up on Dastan's comments, but they were huddled together still talking about Ciccone.

VIII

Beatrice Warwick sat looking out of the balcony window of her Florentine home. She nursed an espresso in her hands as she contemplated the view in front of her.

Her husband Theo was still asleep, the coffee she had brought for him going cold on his bedside table. She sipped at the espresso, pleased with the new coffee machine that had been a birthday present from her father, Ignatius. Being able to make coffee by putting a small pod in a machine and have it do all the work was still a novelty.

She remembered her Aunt Elise in the house in Paris making coffee by boiling it on the stove, she'd have loved present day conveniences. Beatrice sighed. She still missed her aunt, even after over a century since the older woman's death.

Just as she was contemplating getting dressed, her cell phone rang. She looked at the screen and saw it was her father:

"Ciao, Papa," she answered the phone.

"Ciao, Beatrice. How's my favourite daughter?"

"I'm fine, Papa. Theo and I have been having a few days off."

"I'm glad to hear it," Ignatius answered. Beatrice and Theo ran an art studio in their home city of Florence. It was well known in art circles throughout the world, and they both worked hard to keep their reputation.

Beatrice listened in silence as her father told her that her uncles Cornelius and Dastan had found Jerome. She felt tears falling down her cheeks and wiped her eyes. She had been looking for the boy – well, man now she guessed – since he'd disappeared from the hospital. She knew the Striga hadn't recaptured him, but he had disappeared from sight. She took a deep breath to centre herself.

"Theo and I'll be on the next flight I can book to New York. How is he? Has he said anything about where he's been?"

"Slow down, bella. He's fine but very confused. Neely and Dastan need you to help remove the memory block you put on him after his captivity. His Ciccone half-siblings are with him. Even though he doesn't remember much about them, he knows they are his kin and…" He hesitated. "Dastan has Mario Ciccone's memories on ice, he's going to go through them today and see if we can start getting some answers."

Beatrice gasped. What Dastan had done was fraught with problems. "I'll phone him. It will be easier for him if I'm there to help."

"I thought you'd say that," Ignatius answered.

"I'll wake Theo, then Papa, and get going. Are you in New York?" Beatrice quickly worked out the time difference, it was 2am where Ignatius was.

"I just landed an hour ago and am on my way to them. I'll be there when you get here."

She put the phone down. Sniffing, she walked to her closet to get dressed. It was only as she turned away from its doors with the dress and leggings she wanted to wear that she realised Theo was awake.

"Tesoro." He sat up. "Why are you crying?"

Leaning down, Beatrice hugged her husband. "That was Papa on the phone, Zio Cornelius and Zio Dastan have found Jerome. He is at home with them now."

Theo grinned, his blue eyes shining in the reflected sun coming through the window. "That's wonderful news, bella. Are we going?"

"As soon as I can arrange a flight."

Theo jumped out of bed and headed for the bathroom for his shower. Beatrice found a flight that left Florence Airport in five hours. She dragged her luggage out of the closet and began packing for a few nights stay, anything more and she could buy new things in New York. She was looking forward to seeing Jerome again. Not just because of the relief that he was alive and okay, but also because she had become attached to the young man whilst he had been recovering from his ordeal in the hospital.

October 2010

Beatrice pushed open the hospital room door and smiled at her cousin. Jerome was now sitting up in the chair next to the bed. It wouldn't be long now before he could go home, and she was looking forward to helping him decide where and what he would do next. But before that, there was the painful decision to make about what to do with his memories of his ordeal. She knew that they kept him awake at night; horrible nightmares about the beatings and his father's betrayal. She was hoping he would let her give him some measure of peace.

"Bea," Jerome caught sight of her and smiled, his eyes lighting up as she entered the room. "Where's Theo today?"

"He had an errand to run for my father so won't make it until later this evening, but I'm here until then. Have you given any thought to what you'd like to do about your memories?"

Beatrice had given him some details of their Donati heritage, letting him know about her ability to alter and hide memories.

Jerome's face fell. "I'm… I… Damn it, Bea, I just don't know."

"I can understand that, Jerome. You went through a horrible ordeal and it would be great if you could forget about it. Yet, at the same time, you need to work with a counsellor and come to terms with what's happened, else it will affect you for the rest of your life."

Beatrice sat on the edge of Jerome's bed and took hold of the boy's hand. His face was still bruised, but the horrible swelling had gone down and his ribs were healing. It would be a while yet before the plaster cast on his left wrist could come off, but he was making progress physically.

"You can make me forget?" his voice trembled as he squeezed her hand tight.

"Yes."

"I never want to think of Mario Ciccone again. I'm changing my name as soon as I reach eighteen next week. One of the nurse's brothers is a lawyer, and he's going to help me."

Beatrice took the change in subject in her stride. They had discussed this as well.

"What are you going to change it to?"

"I'm not sure yet. I did think about Jerome K. Jerome." He grinned at her. "*Three Men in a Boat* was one of my mother's favourite novels. She read it to me when I was younger, but somehow it doesn't feel right."

Beatrice smiled. "I'm sure whatever you choose she would be proud of you."

Jerome ducked his head and smiled shyly at her. He looked up and caught her gaze. "Do it," he said. "Bea, I want you to help me forget."

She nodded. "When Theo gets here tonight."

"Okay."

The exchange had taken a lot out of Jerome and he fell asleep in his chair. Beatrice kissed his forehead before heading out to contact Theo to ask him to help her that evening.

———

Now, fifteen years later, Beatrice would meet Jerome again in only a few brief hours. The nine hour flight from Florence was nearly over. They'd be landing in New York shortly.

Beatrice checked her watch. 9.30pm. They'd get a room and travel tomorrow. Though she was keen to seeing Jerome, there was no point in exhausting them all.

She wondered if he would be happy to see them, maybe explain why he'd disappeared a week after his eighteenth birthday, just as she and Theo were prepared to bring him home to Florence with them, to finish with his recovery. They'd turned up at the hospital to take him to their hotel for a few days, only to hear from the confused and upset nursing staff that he had signed himself out against doctor's orders. There had been nothing they could do. He was an adult and able to make his own decisions. She had been upset and worried for him though – he was a young boy, eighteen or not, alone in the world where he had already experienced some of the worst things that could happen to him.

Theo held her hand as the plane landed at JFK airport and helped her gather her things. They made their way into the airport to collect their luggage and as they went through customs and entered the airport concourse, Beatrice saw her father waiting for them.

"Papa!" She smiled as she reached him. He smiled back and enveloped her in a bear hug.

"I didn't expect you to be here!" she exclaimed.

"Since I got in early this morning, I decided to stay and travel with you tomorrow," he replied, taking her overnight bag out of her hand. "I've booked us rooms at the hotel here, I have a hire car in short-term parking."

"Theo, good to see you, mio figlio," Ignatius said as Theo arrived with their larger cases. He pulled Theo into a hug as well.

Beatrice nodded, and taking a deep breath, she followed her father and husband out of the airport.

IX

"There's rather a houseful, I'm afraid," Shea said as he greeted Beatrice, Theo and Ignatius at the door, late the next morning.

Beatrice smiled at him. He had been with her uncles for almost as long as she could remember. At least since London anyway.

"It's great to see you again, Shea," she smiled, giving the man a hug. He was almost as much family as the rest of them.

"I've given you and Theo your usual room at the back of the house and Ignatius, you are next door to Cornelius and Dastan on the other side of Jerome."

He bit his lip and Beatrice could tell he had something he wanted to say to them. She smiled at him. "The young man has had rather a time of it... it's been hard on him." He sighed.

Taking her bag, he began leading the way upstairs.

"I'm hoping I can help," Beatrice replied. "I hope that unblocking his memories will help, though I worry it could have the opposite effect."

Theo, who was following behind Beatrice and Shea, squeezed his wife's shoulder. "You did what you thought you had to Bea; you have to remember he agreed to it."

"I know," she replied, "but Papa said he was in the army, then living on the streets. I'm worried about the effects the unblocking will have."

Shea remained quiet as he opened their room's door and ushered them in. He opened the drapes to let the late morning sunshine in, and as she always was when she visited her uncle's estate, Bea found herself drawn to the view of the lake with the sun shining off the water.

"Where is Jerome now?" She turned to Shea after putting her backpack down by the bed.

"He went for a walk. He's a rather difficult young man to read."

Beatrice nodded and headed back for the door. "I think I'll just see if I can find him. I hope he is happy to see me."

"Zio Neely!" Beatrice threw herself into her uncle's embrace as she found Cornelius in the foyer, having just come in from outside. He drew her close and pressed a kiss to her forehead.

"Beatrice." He sighed. "Lovely as always, my dear."

She stepped back out of his embrace, so she could see into his eyes. He wasn't a small man – few inches taller than she was – but for a woman she herself was quite tall. She placed her hand on his cheek as she had been doing since she was a child and smiled at him. "It's good to see you. It's been too long."

Cornelius drew her arm through his and they headed for the back of the house and the deck that looked out over the lake and the dock. "He's out there now, sitting on the dock. I think he'd like to see a familiar face."

"Does he know I'm coming?"

"No, I wasn't sure when you would be able to get here, and I didn't want to raise his expectations, so I haven't told him you were coming. He knows how you are related. I told him about Elise and how I met your Zio Dastan, and a little about being Donati, but he may relate better to you. I see in his eyes sometimes how confused he is. He's had a hard time. He was discharged from the army after being injured in the line of duty. The doctor says he'll recover, but he still needs physio and probably therapy."

Beatrice shook her head. "How did he end up on the streets?"

"When he returned, he shared an apartment with two other vets, but they were not paying their portion of the rent and their landlord evicted them. Then he lost his job and everything spiralled from there. I'm just so glad we found him when we did!"

She held up her hand to shield her eyes from the sun and saw the figure of Jerome sitting on the dock.

"I feel so guilty that I didn't do enough to find him when he went missing."

Cornelius hugged her to him. "Don't. You did what you could. Perhaps he will talk to you and tell you what happened, and why he left the hospital early. Will you unblock his memories?"

"Yes, if he asks me. Though I'll try to muddy the waters a bit on some of them – what happened to him, Zio… even now I can still remember what he told me he had gone through. I'm not sure he'll want to remember; he was only seventeen."

"Shh, it's okay. He's a strong young man, despite his recent difficulties. He's not that scared young boy anymore. He's been to war and seen things that eclipse some of those memories in many ways. We have to remember he's in his thirties now and able to deal with what happened then and what must come next."

"You're right. All this time I've been remembering

him as he was in his late teens. I have to remember to treat him as an adult now and not the child he was back then."

Beatrice leaned up and kissed her uncle on the cheek before making her way down to the water's edge, where her cousin sat.

As Beatrice approached the dock, Jerome turned and his eyes opened wide in shock.

"Bea? Beatrice… is that you? My god, you don't look any older!"

She grinned wide. "Yes, it's me. I'm not the only one that doesn't look too much older! Though you've lost that gangliness you had."

"Hah," he shouted, grinning back at her. "I can't believe you're here."

"Yes, well, as soon as Zio Neely called my father, he called me and well… here we are."

"Theo is here?" Jerome asked as he stood up.

She nodded. "Your uncle Ignatius is here as well. They're back at the house. I thought I'd come and see you first."

Beatrice pulled Jerome into a fierce embrace.

"I am so pleased to see you, Jerome." She smiled at him through her tears. "I've looked for you for years. What happened? I went to the hospital one day, and you were gone. All the staff said was that you had signed yourself out, and there was nothing they could do as you were an adult."

Beatrice's words tumbled out as she tried to convey to Jerome how much she had missed him and how it had hurt to find he had gone and not told her.

"I had to go." Jerome held her hand and led her to one of the Adirondack chairs on the dock, sitting back down in his own.

"Will you tell me?"

"I'd like nothing better. I wanted to get in touch with you back then, and for years afterwards I thought of contacting you. But then I came out of the army and was back in a hospital again, it was just too much." He squinted, looking at her. "I... I wasn't in a good place when I left the army and made some questionable decisions. I'm still not sure all this is real."

He swept the surrounding area with his hand and Beatrice smiled at him. "It's real. I told you back then we were related, just not quite how. I was going to, but by the time I felt you were ready... well, that's past now."

"Yes, I'm sorry, Bea. Grandfather has explained a lot to me, and Dastan has been a great help. I'm afraid I wasn't too open with them at the beginning. Now, though, Roman and Verity are relying on me. It feels strange. I remember them, but don't... As though they're characters I've read about in a book? It just doesn't make sense to me. I know they're my siblings, though. I feel it's time to move on and embrace who and what I am."

"That's brilliant, Jerome." She smiled at him. "I'm glad you're calling Cornelius Grandfather already – though you might want to try the Italian version – Nonno?"

"Nonno," Jerome repeated. "I can do that." He grinned at her.

"Maybe we can all move on from this, I've–" Beatrice gasped as Jerome pulled her down off her chair to lie flat on the dock. "What–" she started to say, but he put his finger to his lips, then she heard it. The thwack thwack thwack of a helicopter. She lay shielded by Jerome's body and watched as the helicopter landed not too far away from them on the lawn. Several men dressed all in black and carrying sub-machine guns jumped to the ground and began running for the house.

"Stay low," Jerome whispered and began a running zig-zag pattern in a low position towards the helicopter and the house. Beatrice followed him, worry for her family gnawing at her.

Gunfire was heard from the house, then it was cut off suddenly. Jerome rose up as he felt the world stop. Cornelius had stopped time again.

He and Beatrice rushed into the house to see

Theo disarming the would-be assassins as they stayed frozen in place. With Shea's help Theo set about tying them up.

Jerome ran to his great grandfather. "Are you okay, Nonno?" He asked, assessing the room quickly, looking for other threats.

"I'm fine, Jerome." His great grandfather's hand came to rest on his shoulder. "I managed to stop time before they hit anyone, just things."

"But who are they?"

"The question," Dastan said, appearing with Ignatius from the library, "is not just who are they, but how did they find us? This place is guarded by a glamour, and is not registered in any of our names. No-one should be able to just find it."

Cornelius nodded, looking at the men in front of them. "Theo, Shea, get everyone ready to move out. We leave in ten minutes."

Both men nodded and left the room at a rush.

"Where are we going?" Jerome asked, confused.

"Back to New York. We have a safe house there that only Dastan and I know about, and we'll be taking these men with us."

He gestured with his left hand and time began again, the tick of the hall clock loud and clear. Gasps came from Roman and Verity as they tried to catch up with what was happening. The four men in front of them gaped as they realised that not only had they lost their weapons, but that they were tied up as well. It would have been funny if it wasn't so serious.

Jerome turned to his siblings. "Come on, we're leaving. Help me get ready."

Slowly, still in shock, they nodded and began moving as Jerome chivvied them along. Explanations, it seemed, would have to wait until later.

X

They took two large Hummers as they left Cornelius's estate behind them, Dastan driving the first and Ignatius the second. Cornelius phoned Beatrice, who was in the second vehicle and had her put her phone on speaker, so they could all hear what was being discussed.

"How are our guests?" Cornelius asked.

"Confused," Theo answered, a smile in his voice. "Not sure what they were expecting but losing their weapons and being tied up and gagged wasn't it."

"The question," Cornelius answered, "is how did they find us? I know Ciccone sent them as a scare tactic. He doesn't have all the details on us, and he'd love to know more."

The cars went quiet as everyone was thinking on the conundrum of how Ciccone had tracked them down. The estate was in the name of an alias with nothing to link it to Cornelius, or his family.

"Okay," Ignatius's voice came over the open line. "There's a turn-out coming up. We need to pull over and check a couple of things before we get any closer to New York."

Cornelius agreed with his brother and had Dastan pull the Hummer to a halt in the turn-out. They all got out. Theo even pulled the four aggressors out with him.

Meanwhile, Dastan was rooting around in the back of one of the Hummers.

"Jerome," he called.

Jerome joined him and saw that Dastan was pulling out what looked like one of the latest security wands used for checking for electronic bugs. He had used something similar during his time in the army.

"Want me to check over our guests?"

"Yes, do them first. I'll check out the cars. Then we need to check everyone else."

Everyone waited in silence as Jerome and Dastan ran their wands over the four captured men, under the watchful eye of Theo. Nothing. Dastan ran them over the cars and even got down on his back on the ground to check underneath them. Jerome started checking everyone else.

He'd checked Cornelius, Shea and Theo before motioning Roman over to him. Nothing on his front, but when Jerome ran it over his neck, a red light lit up on the wand and a slight beeping noise followed. Jerome touched his brother and motioned for him to stand still whilst he repeated the exercise. It had the same result.

"But…" Roman began.

"It's okay, Rome." Jerome squeezed his shoulder. "We'll get back to you in a minute. Here, stand with Shea."

Roman moved over to stand next to the older man, who put his arm around his shoulders to comfort him, as Jerome and Dastan quickly completed the exercise.

"Just Roman then," Dastan said as he joined Shea, Jerome, and the young man in question.

"It's not in his clothes," Jerome said as he finished checking his brother over once more. "It's in his neck, I think."

Roman blanched and turning, he vomited into the bushes near him. Jerome could see that he was shaking as shock took hold of the younger man.

"Rome, hold on to me," Jerome said as he wrapped him up in his arms. He looked at Cornelius over his brother's shoulder. "Ciccone chipped his own son! He fucking chipped his own son!"

Roman was shaking in Jerome's arms. "I didn't know." His voice quavered. "I didn't know…"

"It's okay." Cornelius approached. "We believe you."

Jerome closed his eyes. Who would chip their own child like an animal?

"Dastan? Is there a first aid kit in one of these monster cars?"

"I'll get it," Shea spoke up for the first time since they had stopped and moved away to the back of one of the Hummers.

"I'm sorry, Rome, but we're going to have to remove it. You know that, right?"

His younger brother looked up at him, trusting Jerome to do what was right. His face was still a pale sickly colour, and he was still shaking as he stood in the circle of Jerome's arms.

"Okay," Cornelius spoke up. "Jerome, hold Roman so his head and neck aren't moving. I'm going to spray his neck with antiseptic gel, but there's no anaesthetic, so it will sting at the very least."

Jerome nodded and held Roman in place. Cornelius took out a pair of gloves from the first aid kit and put them on, spraying the gel as he'd said he would. Afterwards, he removed a fresh scalpel from its packet and eyed up the young man's neck. With precision, he slit the skin and with a flick of his wrist removed a tiny chip.

Roman flinched but kept still in Jerome's arms, his eyes closed and his breathing heavy. Jerome watched as his great grandfather quickly stemmed the bleeding and applied a butterfly bandage to the wound. Dastan came over with the wand again and checked Roman over one more time. This time there were no beeps or lights; there had only been the one chip.

"Fuck." Jerome staggered a little as Roman passed out.

"Here, give him to me." Theo appeared at his side with Beatrice and took Roman out of his arms. They laid him gently in the back seat of their hummer with Verity to watch over him.

Cornelius and Dastan examined the bug they had removed from Roman's neck. It was tiny and blinking red, on off, on off.

"That's it," Cornelius said. "Though what I don't understand is why it took them so long to act on the information it was sending them. Roman has been with us for a few days now. Why wait until today to attack?"

"Think about it, Neely," Ignatius said. "Bea, Theo and I arrived today. Maybe he was trying to take as many of us out as he could. He may know we're Donati, he may know we have memory skills, but your ability to stop time is a closely guarded secret."

Jerome considered what his great uncle had said and had to agree with his assessment. It horrified him that anyone could treat their own son that way, and he was more horrified that it was his little brother, who

85

had been chipped like an animal. He could feel himself getting angrier the more he thought about it. He knew he had to control that. His family needed him; both the one he was beginning to remember and the one he'd only just met.

"What are we going to do with it?" Jerome motioned to the bug in his great grandfather's hand. "We could crush it, but then he would know we'd found it."

"Give it to me," Theo said. "When we get into New York, I'll plant it in a taxi. It will take Ciccone a while to figure out it's not his son driving around the city. It will give us a chance to get to the safe house and get settled in, before we decide what to do next."

No-one could think of anything better than what Theo suggested, so they all piled back into the cars. Jerome made sure he got into the one with Roman and hugged the young man tight.

"You okay?" he asked.

"I think so. It was just the shock. How could he do that, Jerome? I mean, I've heard of parents having an app on their kids' phones so they can track them, but to put a chip inside me…"

"I know." Jerome was quiet for a moment. "When we get settled in the safe house, I'm going to ask Bea to work with me on the memories she blocked when I was seventeen. Maybe there'll be a clue there."

He shivered. He didn't want to remember, but

knew he had to. He had to keep his family safe. He felt a small hand squeeze his and smiled at Beatrice, who was sitting in front of him.

When they arrived on the outskirts of the city, they dropped Theo off and watched him get into a yellow cab, then they drove off to the agreed meet-up point. The four attackers sat in the back of the Hummer, and Jerome could feel the confusion and fear rolling off them. Their day had not gone as planned. He hoped there would be no more surprises today.

XI

Jerome sat in the Hummer driven by Dastan as they entered an industrial area, with several large warehouses side by side. Some had activity outside them, but others were quiet.

He shivered as he remembered another, different, time when he had been in a vehicle driving into an industrial area such as this.

"You okay?" Bea asked him as she squeezed his hand.

"Yeah, just remembering that other place. Though this is nothing like that area, it still gives me a scary feeling."

She smiled at him in reply.

He turned his face to the window to see where they were going. Cornelius must have used an electronic control as up ahead, the other Hummer was driving through a large door into a dark, empty warehouse.

Only a few seconds passed before overhead lights flickered on, due to a hidden switch being activated.

"We're here," Dastan announced, as he drove through the doors and into a wide-open space.

It was mostly empty with a few old pieces of equipment scattered around. An office space was off in one corner, and a wonky ladder led up to another storey. It didn't look like a safe house to Jerome.

They all tumbled out of the Hummers with Theo dragging the four assailants out, none too gently. Their eyes were hard and blank behind the duct tape covering their mouths.

Theo and Shea shoved them forwards and made them sit on four chairs that Dastan had pulled over from the old office space.

Verity put her hand in Jerome's and looked up at him. "What's happening?"

"I'm not sure, but I think they're going to question them, to see what they know."

She turned her head into his shoulder. "I don't want to watch them being tortured."

He smiled and put an arm around her shoulders. "I don't think that will happen. For some reason that doesn't strike me as Cornelius or Dastan's way."

"No," she agreed. "Though I'm not sure about Theo."

"No torture," Bea said as she approached the siblings. "Though they might deserve it. They didn't seem to care if anyone got in their way back at the estate."

"I know." Verity pushed her blonde hair off her face and smiled at Bea. The younger girl appeared to have developed a bit of a crush on Jerome's older, dark-haired Italian cousin. "I'm just a wimp, I guess."

Beatrice squeezed her arm and smiled at Jerome. "Are you holding up okay?"

"I'm fine, Bea. This is nothing like that other place, and I must admit I am curious to see what happens next."

"Watch," she said, motioning them to look at the four assailants. They were now tied to the chairs in the middle of the warehouse.

Theo and Shea were circling the attackers looking at them from all angles. It was like watching large predators circling their prey. They were silent as they assessed their attackers.

"I don't know, Shea," Theo spoke conversationally. "Maybe…" He wiggled his hand back and forth. They had been arranged on the chairs by height, so the tallest, dark-skinned man sat nearest to Shea, and the smaller, pale man sat on the end. There was no reason Jerome could think of why they had been seated that way, but he assumed Theo and Shea knew what they were doing.

Shea moved round to the front of the men at the same time that Theo came from the other direction. They held their hands out in front of them and in unison hit all four in the forehead at the same time. They murmured, "Sleep."

Immediately, all four of their would-be attackers heads slumped onto their chests, as if they had been hypnotised by the pair.

Verity squeezed his hand, and Jerome pulled his arm from her shoulder. She seemed fascinated by what Shea and Theo were doing and moved to stand closer to them.

Dastan pulled her to him. "Not too close, bella," he said. She nodded and leaned into him to watch the two men in front of her work.

Theo tapped the second man on the shoulder, and he lifted his head. His long, dirty, blond hair was pulled back into a queue, which hung limply down his back. His eyes were open, but Jerome wasn't sure how aware he was of what was going on around him.

"Who are you?" Theo asked, his voice soft, so that the man really had to strain to hear him.

"Jim Bowen."

"Who do you work for?"

"Mario Ciccone."

"Why did you attack us today?"

"Ciccone sent us." He went quiet for a moment.

"He called us in to see him, and that other guy, the pale dead-eyed one was there. He called him Fenton."

Jerome felt himself freeze and stare at the four men. He could no longer see anyone else in the warehouse. He felt sick on hearing the name Fenton. He'd not thought of it for years, but now he was reacting to the name and description. His body was shaking and all he could see was black around the edges of his vision.

"Breathe, Jerome."

Cornelius stood in front of him. He realised his great grandfather had moved him away to a different part of the warehouse, away from the others. "That's it, come on, breathe with me."

Cornelius began an easy breathe in, breathe out movement, with Jerome's hand over his chest so he could feel its rise and fall. After a moment, Jerome fell into the same pattern of breathing as his great grandfather.

"That's it," he said. "Feel better?"

Jerome nodded and smiled shakily at his Cornelius. "I'm fine Nonno, really. It was just a shock hearing that name after all this time. I remember that Fenton was the worst of them."

"We'll talk about that later. Come on, let's see if Theo has found anything else out."

Jerome walked with Cornelius across the warehouse floor to where Theo was still questioning the four assailants. He was talking to the first guy now, the dark-skinned, short-haired, African American man who was as least 6ft 5in. He was talking to Theo about their preparations for the raid.

"Did Ciccone tell you he'd placed a chip on his son Roman?"

"Yes, the tracking program on his laptop showed where y'all were hiding. He pulled up Google Earth and zoomed in until he found your house on the lake. I don't know all that computer shit, but he managed to show us the layout of your estate. Where it was and the best place to land and enter the house."

Dastan looked at Cornelius and whispered, "I doubt very much he was using Google Earth, the estate doesn't appear on there. He must have had help to see through the protection on the house. That worries me more than the attack itself."

"What were your orders?" Theo continued to question the African American man who was called Manny.

"To cause as much chaos as possible. Grab the boy and Ciccone's wayward children and take them to Ciccone and Fenton."

"Why? Why does he want Jerome?"

Jerome perked up again at this. It was a question he wanted – no, needed – answered.

Ever since the man he had looked up to and called 'Pa' had dragged him out of his classroom and delivered him to Fenton and his goons, all he had wanted to know was why?

"He didn't say." Manny answered in the monotone voice he had been using throughout Theo's questioning of him. "But I know he blamed Fenton for letting him get away in the first place. He was the one that was supposed to play hero, not anyone else."

"Explain." Theo leaned closer to Manny. "What do you mean by that?"

"I've worked for Ciccone a long time, since before the boy was taken to Fenton. It was supposed to be a scare tactic, supposed to cement his loyalties to Ciccone."

"Funny way to go about it," Jerome muttered to himself.

"It was a ploy," Manny continued. "He and Fenton came up with it together. Ciccone would pretend that the boy wasn't his, that he had been cuckolded by his mother. He'd deliver him to Fenton, who would rough him up a bit and threaten him. Ciccone would arrive like a white knight on his charger to rescue the boy a few days later. He would be crying and wailing, claiming Fenton had threatened his younger children with all sorts of dire things unless he went along with the kidnapping and roughing up. The boy would be so grateful to see him, to get his father back, that he would do anything for him, use those weird powers of his to help his father and Fenton in their fight against the rest of his kind."

He continued. "But Fenton's people went too far. Much further than they were supposed to. By the time Ciccone got there, the boy had been rescued. They tracked him down to a local hospital. They arranged to get in to see him, but by then he'd checked himself out and disappeared."

The man's voice ran down as he ran out of information. Jerome just stood there, numb. He felt like all the blood had drained from his face. Ciccone was his father. He could have his family back, but even as he thought that he knew he would never call the man 'Pa' again. He had engineered his own son's kidnapping and torture, without a care for how he would suffer. Just so he could reap the benefit of Jerome's Donati powers. Which, quite frankly, he still didn't know himself.

"Come with me, Jerome," Bea was talking to him. "Let's get settled."

"What about them?" He pointed to the four assailants who were once again 'sleeping' on their chairs.

"Don't worry about them. Theo and Shea will alter their memories and dump them outside Ciccone's office. They'll remember setting off on their raid, but nothing else after that."

Jerome allowed Beatrice to lead him away. They

followed Cornelius and Dastan, and entering a doorway he hadn't seen earlier, he was surprised to see an elevator tucked away into one corner.

"Come." Cornelius herded them into the elevator car. "Let's go somewhere more comfortable."

XII

Cornelius inserted a key into the pad on the elevator and pressed a button. The car began to descend rapidly. Caught by surprise, Jerome grabbed the chrome bar and held on. A short while later they came to a smooth halt, and the doors opened. Stepping out, Jerome gasped. He'd expected a concrete bunker of some sort, but what he got was a marble covered floor in a foyer which wouldn't have looked out of place in some upmarket, high rise penthouse. The door in front of them was also pretty amazing. It looked like something out of a steam-punk drawing. His eye was caught by the swirls and depictions of girders and metal work, with billowing airship sails behind. It was all carved out of wood.

"It's pretty swanky, isn't it?" Beatrice asked, noticing Jerome's amazement. "Zio Dastan made it.

Woodworking is one of his hobbies, when he gets some downtime."

The man himself turned round from unlocking the door and grinned at Jerome. "Took me a good six months to get this to how I wanted it. When Neely and I first bought this place, it had a 'serviceable' iron door. I couldn't wait to get my hands on a new one for the entrance."

Jerome smiled at his great grandfather's partner's enthusiasm for his work on the door. He had a sneaking suspicion that he hadn't seen the last of the wonders this place had to offer.

Once the door was open, he followed Beatrice and Dastan into the open space and down the staircase, which flowed towards a large open area below. He gaped; he had never seen anything like it. The open area was like a large warehouse penthouse conversion, except it was underground in what had once, he presumed, been a bunker of some kind.

"It's… it's amazing!" were the only words he could come up with to describe what he saw in front of him. "Is that a swimming pool?"

Dastan laughed at his reaction. "You should have seen the place when we first bought it. As you probably guessed, it was built as a bunker during the cold war, but the guy who had it before us had turned it into a pleasure palace! It had a swimming pool and a stream running through it, 'open air' barbecue areas, party corners, dance floors and space to sleep up to twenty. His guests used to park upstairs in the warehouse and party down here until the wee hours."

Cornelius smiled at his lover and continued the explanation. "We visited a few times in the early 2000s for parties, even though it's not really our thing. But Dastan is right, it was a sight to behold. When the guy who owned it died, his widow wanted nothing to do with it. It had never been her favourite place. It seems he'd been partying with several 'playgirls' when he died down here. She couldn't wait to get rid of it."

All Jerome could do was gape as he wandered around the place. He noticed the same attention to detail he'd found at his grandfather's estate. All the artwork complemented the furniture, and he was captivated by a portrait of a young woman in a crinoline that hung on one wall.

Beatrice slipped her hand into his and squeezed. "Aunt Elise, your great grandmother." Jerome nodded. He had wondered...

"She was beautiful," he found himself whispering.

"She was. I was only a child when she died, but I still remember her well." She tugged on his hand.

"What?"

"Now would be a good time to sort out that memory block, whilst the others get settled in here. I know Shea has his routines, and I know that Zio

Dastan will enjoy showing your siblings around. The pool is always a great attraction."

Jerome swallowed. It wasn't that he had forgotten about sorting out the memory block, just that he had put it out of his mind in the hope of not worrying about it too much. He felt his breathing beginning to speed up, and he felt as though he couldn't get enough air as he began to sweat. Black dots appeared before his eyes and he felt himself begin to sway. He recognised the symptoms of a panic attack. He'd suffered from them a lot shortly after he let the army.

"Jerome, breathe with me." Beatrice put her palm on his chest and breathed with him. "In, out, hold; in, out, hold." She repeated this until Jerome was breathing normally again.

"I'm sorry."

"There's nothing to be sorry for." She smiled at him. "I'm not a stranger to panic attacks myself. I still occasionally get them from remembering the events around when Aunt Elise died. I've learnt to manage them and they're rare now, but they still occur every now and again when I least expect them."

Jerome squeezed her hand and smiled at her. "Thank you."

"You're welcome."

Beatrice led him to a small room off the main area. It was comfortably furnished with sofas and matching soft furnishings. A coffee table sat in the middle with a few books and magazines scattered around. The only thing missing was windows, though the artwork on the walls and the judicial use of drapery and soft lighting helped to alleviate that.

"This room is shielded for memory work." Beatrice smiled at him as she got two bottles of water out of a small fridge in the corner. "I've used it several times before. I hope it's okay?"

He gave her a nervous smile and nodded his head.

"I'm not going to go in and just release the hold I put on your memories. I will examine each of them with you, and help you deal with them. Some will need more attention than others, depending on how you react to them. In all honesty, I'm hoping that you will remember something that will help us with what Ciccone and Fenton are up to, and why your father felt the need to go through the charade of giving you to Fenton. Even with Manny's explanation, it still feels far-fetched that they would torture a seventeen-year-old boy that way."

Jerome shivered. Even though he didn't remember all of it. he did remember the feelings of helplessness as he was hit and kicked by Fenton's men in that cold warehouse.

The following couple of hours were difficult ones.

They examined his memories of the day that Ciccone took him out of school and left him in the warehouse. They looked at his memories one by one of the following few days, as he was tortured and assaulted by Fenton's men. Beatrice helped him work through each and every one until they were examined, dissected and filed away. It was only when they came to his last day that Jerome balked and called a halt.

"How are you doing?" Beatrice handed him another bottle of water and watched him whilst he took a few sips.

He scrunched up his nose. "Not sure really. It's hard, yet easier than I thought it was going to be. If that make sense?"

She nodded her head. "Everyone deals with it differently, Jerome."

He sighed. "Yeah. It's just that I know this last day was a doozy and yet, at the same time, one of the best things that happened to me was when you and Theo turned up to rescue me."

"Do you want to continue? We could take a break, join the others for dinner and resume later?"

"No!" he almost shouted. "Sorry, let's get it finished. We know that Dastan wants to feed back on the memories he took from Ciccone that day at his office. The sooner we get this done, the sooner we can get on to that. Not that I'm going to admit I'm scared."

"It's okay to be scared, Jerome," Beatrice answered, "I think I'd be more worried if you weren't scared."

He nodded and squeezed her hand before once again leaning back into the sofa and opening up to Beatrice. It was like being enclosed in comfort and it mostly protected him from the horrors of that day.

October 2010

The day started as they all did since he'd been taken to the warehouse. He was kicked awake from where he lay on the floor, covered only by a thin blanket. He had been allowed to use the bathroom, and he'd pissed blood again. He would be worried about the state of his kidneys if he could be bothered, and if he thought there was any chance of him ever escaping from this warehouse.

He was chivvied back to the main room and his hands were cuffed again before he was thrown back onto the floor. He shivered as he realised that Fenton, the guy his Pa – no not his Pa... Ciccone – had given him to was here. He hated that man with a vengeance. He looked pale and had stringy hair that hung down almost to his collar.

His smile was almost inhuman as he approached Jerome with a swagger.

"Your old man wants you back, boy." He grinned, showing off rotting, uneven teeth behind his thin lips. "I think you're nearly ready, what do you say?"

Jerome looked at him in confusion. "What old man?" he asked through split lips.

Fenton laughed. "You'll find out soon enough. He thinks he's in charge, but he'll soon learn otherwise. All he wants are your Donati skills. He thinks you'll be thankful. Thinks you'll be so grateful when he rides in here on his white charger, that you'll do anything he asks…"

Jerome hardly understood what Fenton was going on about. Though the Jerome who was buffered by Beatrice in the present now understood that the 'old man' Fenton referred to was his father, he also understood that there was some kind of power struggle between Ciccone and Fenton.

Fenton grinned at Jerome once more and Jerome was sure he saw fangs peeping out of his mouth as he did so.

"I'll be back later. Your friends here are looking forward to spending some time with you…"

Jerome shivered and looked at the two other men who were his main torturers. They leered back at him and he did his best to scrabble away as Fenton left the room, laughing.

Present day

With the help of Beatrice, Jerome relived that awful last day until the point where he was rescued by his cousin and her husband and taken to the hospital. They quickly went through the rest of his memories until the time at the hospital when he had awoken with a feeling that something wasn't quite right. He'd slipped from the bed and into the corridor outside his room. It was here that he caught sight of Fenton talking to a nurse.

He shivered, Beatrice had blocked many of his memories, but he still remembered some of what had happened, and Fenton. It wasn't until they moved that he noticed that Fenton wasn't alone.

Talking to the nurse also was his father, Mario Ciccone.

He managed to slip closer without being seen and listened as Ciccone told the nurse that he was looking for his teenage son. He explained to her that he'd been missing for several weeks. He showed photos. From his position behind the doctor's office door, Jerome saw the nurse look towards his room. Ciccone also saw the movement and smiled at the nurse.

Ciccone and Fenton headed towards his room,

and Jerome slipped further into the doctor's office, out of their line of sight. He changed into some scrubs he found in there, before peeping out once more, thankful that the doctor was on his break. Jerome liked Dr Sharman and didn't want to get the man into trouble.

Keeping an eye on the door to his erstwhile room, he'd headed for the stairs where he went up one floor before heading to the elevators, getting lost in the throng of people waiting there. He merged in with the crowd of nurses and doctors, also dressed in scrubs, and members of the public. He left at the first floor and melted into the press of people in the lobby.

———

Jerome looked up at Beatrice and managed a watery smile for her.

"Fenton was not beyond taunting you about the way Ciccone still wanted to control you. And they both turned up at the hospital, looking for you." She closed her eyes a moment, her hand squeezing her cousin's tightly.

Jerome tilted his head to one side and looked her. "I remember Fenton showing up at the hospital, but not my father – Ciccone."

"What happened next? When Theo and I got

there that night, all they would say is that you had left against doctor's orders."

"When I got to the first floor of the hospital, I didn't think about what would happen next. I was dithering round the entrance when Dr Sharman, whose scrubs I was wearing, recognised me." He smiled for the first time since they had entered the room.

"He asked me what I thought I was doing, but I really couldn't give him a coherent answer except there was no way I was going back to my room. After some argument, he agreed to take me home with him for a few days. He was great. He made me aware that it was against all medical advice, and he could get fired for doing it. But without him... he helped me get my ID sorted out. He knew someone who knew someone." Jerome grinned at Beatrice. "I'd already got the paperwork emailed to me for changing my name, thanks by the way." He grinned at Bea. "So we went through with that, just changed it to Milton instead. When I was better, he went with me to the bus station, where I got a bus to Chicago. Once there, I went to the nearest army recruitment centre and joined up."

"It was good of him to help you. He could have gotten into a lot of trouble."

"I know. When I was discharged from the army and came home to New York, I sought him out at the hospital." He grimaced and sighed. "He'd been killed in a road traffic accident only a couple of days after I left."

"Ciccone." Beatrice sighed.

"I think so. Somehow he found out what Dr Sharman had done for me and arranged for him to be killed. The crash was a hit and run – witnesses said an SUV drove deliberately at the doctor's small Smart car. No way was he walking away from that. They never caught the driver of the SUV."

Beatrice put her hand on her cousin's shoulder and offered him a fresh tissue and another bottle of water.

"Ready to join the others for dinner?" she asked as Jerome drank from the water bottle. He nodded his head, slowly.

"Thank you, Beatrice, for everything. For rescuing me, for helping with the blocks back then, and for today. I can see were the blocks where and where you have removed them. I… I think it's going to be okay, though there's a lot to take in."

She smiled at him. "I think you'll be okay, Jerome. There's still a lot for you to learn, but hopefully it won't be as painful as today was."

He stood up and offered her his hand to pull her up. "Dinner?"

"Dinner," she agreed.

XIII

Dinner that night had been a quiet affair, everyone seemed to have a lot on their minds and not much to say. Cornelius and Dastan were lost in thought, as though they were plotting something only the two of them knew about. Dastan looked tired, but he had just finished reporting back on Ciccone's memories, which Jerome had found upsetting. He was still thinking through what Dastan had told them. He was jerked from his inner contemplation by Verity nudging him.

"What's your gift, then?" Verity asked.

"I don't know," Jerome replied. "I never gave it much thought."

"But you do have one?" she persisted.

Jerome turned to Cornelius who had leant forward upon hearing Verity's question.

"She's right, you will have one, Jerome." He thought for a moment before asking, "Have you ever used a skill that could be construed as 'different'?"

"Not that I know of..." Jerome shook his head, thinking.

"Though..." He raised his head. "My old army commander said I was very good at blending in with my surroundings, even without camouflage covering. He even said he'd missed seeing me in the rec room once, as he hadn't seen me in the corner. I just figured I was good at hiding!" He laughed.

"Hmm," Cornelius returned. "You probably don't know this, but Ignatius's gift is to be able to gather shadows around him, and use them to mask his presence in a darkened alley, room etc. Maybe you have something similar?"

Ignatius popped his head up from the corner where he was talking to Shea. "That could be interesting," he said.

Everyone looked at Jerome. He sat on the sofa next to Verity going red, whilst he tried to think of anything else that might be construed as his gift.

"Look, I don't know, okay!" he finally burst out.

"I'm sorry," Verity said. "I didn't mean to make you uncomfortable."

"I'd be happy to work with you on your gift," Beatrice spoke up. "Every Donati has a gift of some kind, as you know. Usually, they manifest in their teens but given what was happening to you in your teens, and early twenties, it's no wonder it hasn't appeared yet."

"How do you mean 'work on my gift'?" Jerome asked, curious now.

"Meditation exercises and yoga can help clear the mind. This in turn will allow you to be able to look inside yourself and discover what your gift may be."

Jerome sat in silence for a few moments. He hadn't given it much thought since he met Cornelius, Dastan and the others. He'd just taken their gifts at face value, without thinking that he might have one of his own.

He leaned over and squeezed Verity's hand. "Thanks, Verity," he said. "It's not something I'd thought about, so thank you for bringing it up."

Verity smiled at him and nodded, her blue eyes crinkling at the edges as she twirled her long bangs around her fingers.

"That's what big sisters are for."

Jerome laughed, breaking the tension in the room. He turned to Beatrice.

"Is it okay if I give this some thought?"

"Of course," she answered. "We went through a lot today, maybe take a bit of time to think about this. We can use the same room as today when you're ready."

"Thanks, Bea."

Cornelius and Dastan stood up. "Well, I don't know about you youngsters, but we're ready for bed." He grinned. "Don't stay up too late."

———

Later the next day, Jerome found himself lying on the sofa in the small room he and Beatrice had used for his memory work. He was trying to relax as Beatrice played some soothing music in the background.

"Have you done any meditation before?" she asked as she lit a vanilla candle on the low table in front of them.

"A little," he said. "One of our medics was keen on it. He led a couple of sessions."

"So, you know the basics?"

He nodded, then realised she had her back to him. "Yes."

Beatrice came round to sit in the chair next to his head. "Okay, we'll begin with some breathing exercises."

For the next fifteen minutes, Jerome practised various breathing exercises, until he was nice and relaxed. Next, they moved on to meditation and Jerome found himself enjoying the soothing sound of Beatrice's voice as she talked him through the experience.

"Okay," her voice came to him as if from a

distance, "I want you to find your centre and feel deep within yourself. Our gifts are within us, and sometimes, we need to reach deep inside ourselves to free them. Take a deep breath then let it go, slowly."

Jerome did as he was prompted, then followed her instructions for slow breathing until he felt that he was almost floating away. He felt as though Beatrice's voice was the only thing anchoring him to reality.

He reached deep within himself, noting the way his heart was beating slowly and steadily. He slowed his breathing even further and looked around his inner mind. He was really far out of his comfort zone, but it felt okay with Beatrice there to catch him if needed.

"Jerome," Beatrice said, "what do you see?"

"Blue," he answered slowly, his words slightly slurred. "All round me, blue."

"That's good," she encouraged. "Reach into the blue and think about what your gift might be."

Jerome followed her instructions and reached into the blue, sinking deeper within himself as he did so. Then he gasped, sitting bolt upright.

"What?" Beatrice was by his side straightaway. "Are you okay?"

"Beatrice…" Jerome smiled at her. "I found it!"

"I'm glad." She smiled back at him. "Now lie back down and see if you can find it again."

Jerome obeyed her, though he felt as giddy as a

schoolboy as he did so. His gift was there, he knew it now. Just as he knew himself. It took him a few precious minutes to return to the calm, blue place he had been before, but he did it.

Dreamily he began to talk. "I think I take after Zio Ignatius a bit," he said. "I can see myself, but no-one else can. It's as though I've flipped a switch and disappeared into the background."

"Chameleon." Beatrice said.

"Yes," he replied.

"Let's test it."

Jerome nodded slowly, and at Beatrice's prompting began to pull his gift towards him, until he slowly merged, visually, into the sofa he was lying on. When Beatrice gasped, he knew he'd succeeded. He let his gift go and opened his eyes, grinning at his cousin.

"That's brilliant, Jerome!" Beatrice grinned back at him. "Let's try again."

For the next couple of hours, Beatrice and Jerome worked on his chameleon gift. Slowly he found he could reach for the blue place and his gift without having to be lying on the sofa in a meditative state.

By the end of their session, he was exhausted but he could access his gift quicker and use it anywhere in the small room. Despite his exhaustion, he wanted to show the others straightaway. Beatrice laughed at his excitement.

"Slow down, okay," she said. "You need to rest for a while first, then you can show the others tomorrow."

He grumped for a while, but knew she was right. He had spent time in the morning doing his physiotherapy for his leg and it was aching now. Though he was excited to show everyone what he had learned, he didn't want to push things too far.

"How about tomorrow afternoon?" Beatrice asked. "You could spend some time meditating after your physio in the morning."

"Okay." He grinned. He couldn't wait to show the others, but he knew he had to be careful. He was still recovering from being undernourished, from when he'd been homeless, and knew he shouldn't overextend himself.

───────

After spending more time the following day practising meditation and his gift, Jerome was ready to share it with his family. He asked them all to gather in the living area at 3pm so he could show them what he'd learned. What he didn't tell them was that he was already there, standing by the portrait of his great grandmother, Elise.

He watched as they all came into the room from various parts of the Redoubt, as they had begun calling the underground safe house. They were laughing and chatting, trying to discover from Beatrice what his gift was. She was keeping quiet though, with a secret smile on her face. Bea was the only one who knew he was already there.

After a few moments, everyone settled down and began to relax.

"He's not got lost, has he?" Dastan joked, after a few moments of silence.

Everyone laughed, including Beatrice. She stood up and walked over to Elise's portrait. "Okay, Jerome, you can come out now."

Jerome let his chameleon cloak drop and stepped closer to Beatrice. There were a few gasps, then clapping.

"Hah," Dastan crowed. "I knew it! Pay up, Theo."

Theo growled, but reached inside his wallet and slapped a twenty dollar bill into Dastan's hand.

"You bet on my talent?" Jerome groaned.

"Yep." Dastan was unrepentant.

Cornelius laughed at his partner. "This deserves a celebration," he said, indicating Jerome. "Shea can cook a special meal as Jerome explores his gift further."

Everyone cheered up at that; it would be good to have something to celebrate.

XIV

Jerome was feeling restless and unable to settle to anything. It had been a good celebration the night before, giving them something good to think about. It had been difficult to hear from Dastan that Ciccone had been grooming him from the start. That he wanted to use his eventual Donati powers for his own gain.

Dastan had learned that Fenton had approached Ciccone, back when Jerome was only a toddler. Ciccone had just married Jerome's step-mother, Lilah, and Jerome's own mother, Sherwood, had still been alive. Somehow Fenton knew what and who he was. He had been instrumental in persuading Ciccone to take him in after Sherwood had died in the car crash.

Dastan had only shared some of the memories with Cornelius and himself, as they were personal to them as a family. These included several memories of his mother. He'd cried as he once again saw, heard and smelt his mother.

Jerome had seen Ciccone and Fenton discussing bringing him into the family after Sherwood was killed. Even from the beginning, Ciccone himself, hadn't wanted anything to do with him. Jerome watched from Ciccone's point of view some of his childhood activities. He was stunned by the different emotions coming from the man he had considered his father until he was seventeen. Hatred and speculation had been amongst them.

There were still many things left unanswered. Especially the question about who Fenton was. Neither Dastan nor Cornelius knew him, though they were sure they had seen him before.

Jerome's own memories, that Beatrice had helped him recover, hadn't been able to fill in too many gaps. He had a completely different view of his father than the one Ciccone had of him. He couldn't believe how he had been duped. But Dastan reminded him that he had been a child, and that Ciccone was a controlling bastard at the best of times. Jerome had only to think of how Ciccone had controlled Roman until recently to realise that he wasn't the only one duped by his father.

Thoughts like these had been going round and round in his head since the previous day. He'd tried to do more meditation earlier that day after his physio, but he hadn't been able to. Beatrice had suggested a complete break from all work with his gift for the moment. He needed time to rest. She suggested he join his siblings, but they had gone swimming and he was not in the mood. He sighed. Even Theo and Beatrice were somewhere else in the Redoubt, catching up on emails and dealing with a crisis at their Florence gallery. And he hadn't seen Cornelius and Dastan since the previous evening's celebration after the discovery of his gift. Once everyone had cleared up in the family room and retired for the night, Jerome had gone over and over his returned memories and those from his biological father. He hadn't got much sleep.

He was heading back towards the swimming pool with the idea that he might join Verity and Roman after all, when he found a corridor he hadn't been down before. A few feet in brought him to an open door, and as he looked inside, he found Shea watching several monitors at once. He recognised views of the estate and the grounds and the area around the Redoubt. He didn't know why the use of modern technology surprised him. After all, just because they'd been around for a few hundred years didn't mean Shea, and the others, hadn't embraced changing technologies. He'd seen it with his own eyes with the wands they'd used to find Roman's chip.

"Good morning," Shea smiled at him, looking up from the monitors.

"Hi Shea, keeping an eye on the assets?" Jerome smiled.

Shea laughed and pointed to various monitors, naming the areas for him. There was even one showing Ciccone's now empty law office, the outside of his apartment building, and inside and outside views of the estate.

"Nothing much happening at the moment, for which we can be grateful." Shea sighed and pointed to a hot plate with a pot of coffee on it, in the corner. "Help yourself."

Jerome picked up a mug and poured himself a coffee. He brought it, and one for Shea, back to the board of monitors.

"Have you seen Cornelius and Dastan this morning?" he asked.

"They left about a few hours ago." Shea grinned. "They were heading to a meeting in Washington with the Donati Council there."

Jerome blinked. "I didn't notice anyone going to the elevator."

Shea snorted. "They left by one of the 'secret' doors." He even air quoted secret.

"What does that mean?"

"There are several entrances and exits from this place. The guys who built it originally were paranoid, but it has proved useful for us. Dastan somehow thinks he can hide these places from me."

"And you know where they all are?"

"Yep, first thing I did when we moved everything in here was to check it all out. I believe they left by the east corridor. Good precaution to take, as we don't know if Ciccone or Fenton has found this place yet. Oh, not the Redoubt, but the warehouse. They might be able to work out it belongs to Cornelius, if they dig deep enough. Doubt they will though."

Jerome nodded and sank back into one of the chairs in front of the monitors, watching them with Shea. After a while he almost dozed off, and it was only Shea grabbing his hot coffee mug that stopped him from getting scalded.

"Whoa. Thanks, man." He grinned as he stretched. Just then something on one monitor caught his eye.

"Where's that?" he asked, pointing at a screen on the left.

"Industrial estate one over from here." Shea said, sitting up and taking a closer look. He quickly shared that screen to all of them to make one large monitor.

"Bloody hell!" Jerome shot up as he realised that a car chase was taking place not that far away from them, and that the two cars were getting closer to the warehouse.

"Call Theo," he shouted as he took a run for the elevator.

———————

He arrived at a small exit at the main entrance that they had entered through the previous day and opened it. There wasn't anything to see, at least not to begin with.

"Here." Theo appeared next to him and handed him an ear mic. He quickly put it in his ear so he could hear Shea and Beatrice in the control room.

"Thanks." Jerome also took the small handgun that Theo handed over. He tucked it into the small of his back, hoping he wouldn't need it.

"Jerome," Bea's voice came through his ear mic. "The first car has shaken its follower for now and is heading straight for us. I have an uneasy feeling that this is where they're heading. Are you okay to go investigate? I know you're only just feeling your way with your gift, but if anyone can blend in out there it's you."

"It's okay, Bea," he answered. He nodded to Theo to open the door and stepped out into the clearing around the warehouse. With a clang the door closed behind him. Theo would monitor him through the app on his phone, which was connected to the control room.

Jerome left the safety of the Redoubt for the first time in a few days. He felt exposed as he saw the small SUV come roaring round the last bend towards him. He knew they didn't have much time as the other SUV couldn't be that far behind. He'd only just discovered his chameleon gift but he took a deep breath to steady himself, then allowed it to take over.

The SUV careering towards him was being driven erratically, leading him to wonder if the driver was injured. As he watched, the vehicle came to a screeching halt in front of him, almost toppling over in its urgency. He could see there were two people in the front of the car – a man and a woman. He gasped as he recognised them both and dropping his chameleon shift, he rushed to the car and pulled open the passenger door.

"Mama Lilah!" he exclaimed. He reached in and pulled his shaking step-mother out of the car. She lunged at him and pulled him into a tight hug, hiding her face in his neck.

"Jerome, Jerome…" she chanted.

Holding his step-mother under one arm, he turned to the driver, Mario's brother Marc.

"Uncle Marc!"

"Get her out of here Jerome!" he growled

"But how…?"

"No time. Go, boy, go now!"

Acting on the urgency in his uncle's voice, he pulled Mama Lilah along with him. He headed towards the door of the warehouse, where Theo waited.

"Incoming!" Bea's voice in his ear warned him. Jerome just had time to stop, turn and cover both himself and his step-mother with his chameleon gift before the other vehicle pulled to a stop next to his uncle's car. He had to stop himself from gasping as Ciccone got out. He held a gun complete with silencer in his hands as he approached Marc.

Jerome tucked Mama Lilah's head into his neck, turning her so she couldn't see, though he could do nothing about her hearing.

"Marc." Mario had reached the car and was talking to his brother. "Where is she?"

"Who, dear brother?" Marc answered.

"My bitch of an ex-wife."

"I don't know what you're talking about," Marc tried to bluff, but even from this distance Jerome could see he was losing blood, and having a hard time breathing.

"Why here?" Ciccone asked looking around him at the industrial landscape.

"Why not?"

Ciccone sighed and aimed the gun at his brother's head. "Pity it's come to this, Marc. You could have taken your place at my side." He squeezed the trigger and Jerome saw his uncle's body shudder then slump forward.

He had his hand over his step-mother's mouth to stop her crying out, and held his own breath, as the man he'd called Pa looked through them both to the brick wall of the warehouse behind them. He shook his head once more, before getting back in his car and driving away. In the distance Jerome could hear the wailing of police sirens.

He let his step-mother go and took a couple of steps towards his uncle, before Bea's voice in his ear told him to get inside before the cops arrived. They didn't need them to start asking awkward questions. He nodded and led Lilah towards the door once more visible behind them. He tucked Lilah under his right arm and led her inside the warehouse.

"Oh god, oh god, oh god," Lilah was chanting as Jerome held her tight. "He's gone crazy, Jerome. My babies… god, where are my babies?"

Verity and Roman came running to reach their mother. "We're here, Mama," Verity soothed, taking her mother from Jerome's arms.

"Verity, Roman…" Lilah reached for them and pulled them tight then looked around her. "Where's Lacey? Where's your sister? Where's my baby?"

Verity blanched. "We thought she was at school in England."

Lilah shook her head, tears running down her face. "She's not there! I thought she was with you, they said she'd run away…"

Jerome looked at Theo and they both knew without any doubt that Mario Ciccone was holding his youngest daughter hostage somewhere. Jerome felt sick.

"Mama Lilah." He took her hand. "Come on, let's get you settled. We'll find her, I promise, we'll find her."

XV

Cornelius grinned at Dastan as they travelled along the East Corridor, away from the Redoubt. They both laughed at the same time. They were using segways, a nod to a scene in a Dr Who Christmas episode, where the Doctor, and Donna in her wedding dress, travelled on similar vehicles. They both loved the show, and watched it whenever they got a chance, laughing at some of the sillier episodes.

They had left the Redoubt at 5am for a trip to Washington DC, to visit with Cornelius's son Jacoby, who was the current Legate at the Donati Council there. For historical reasons, which Cornelius had never understood, there was no Donati Council presence in New York.

When they got to the end of the corridor, a steel door led up to a short flight of stairs to the garage of an unremarkable house, in a sub-division a couple of miles from the Redoubt. Cornelius paid the homeowner a small stipend for them to keep a jeep there, and make sure it was kept fuelled and ready to go, whenever it was needed.

Before getting into the jeep, Dastan used a security wand to go over the whole vehicle to check it for bugs and other devices. It paid to be extra careful, especially at the moment. Nothing showed up on a visual inspection, and the wand remained silent.

They left the garage, with Dastan in the driver's seat, and headed out of the residential area, towards the I-95 south to Washington. It was a 4-5 hour journey depending on traffic, and they intended to split the driving between them.

They'd stocked up on bottled water and protein bars before leaving New York and agreed to stop for breakfast in Baltimore at a diner they both enjoyed there. The Broadway Diner was just off the I-95 next door to a Home Depot, and their Crab Cake Benedict was superb.

———

Dastan wiped his mouth after finishing his breakfast and sat back to sip his coffee. He watched his partner enjoy the last few bites of his own breakfast. It was good to be out and about again. He worried about those they'd left behind in the Redoubt but was pretty sure Shea and Theo could handle any emergencies that cropped up. Ignatius had returned to Italy that morning. There was nothing he could do about it, except be extra careful. He'd called Cornelius from the airport saying he didn't think he'd been followed. He said he would call again when he was back in Florence. Ignatius had said he would also try and get back to them as soon as possible, to support his brother, and family.

"Better?" Cornelius asked Dastan, smiling at him fondly.

"Much better," he agreed.

Cornelius's phone rang with the ringtone he'd assigned to Shea, and they both stiffened as he answered the phone.

"What's up?" he asked.

There was a silence whilst Cornelius listened to Shea on the other end. "Is everyone okay?"

He listened again. "Do you need us to come back…? No, okay, keep us informed, we'll see you tomorrow as arranged."

He put his phone down and frowned. Dastan leaned forward. "What happened?"

Cornelius shoved his hand through his hair; a sure sign that he was agitated. "Jerome's Uncle Marc showed up being chased by Mario. He had Lilah Ciccone with him, Jerome's step-mother. Jerome managed to get her to safety, but Mario killed his own brother."

Dastan sucked in his breath and shook his head. It was well known that the brothers were often at loggerheads.

"Is the Redoubt compromised?"

"Shea says no and Theo agrees."

"What next?" Dastan asked.

"We continue with our plan." Cornelius called for the check and paid the cashier in cash as they headed out. He didn't know what resources Ciccone and Fenton had, but he didn't need them tracing him through credit card usage.

———

Once back at the jeep, Dastan repeated his earlier security checks before Cornelius got behind the wheel for the last part of their journey. Less than an hour later they were turning in to the underground parking lot at 15th Street North West. The Council rented a floor of the modern glass-fronted building. After parking the jeep in a designated Council visitor's parking spot, they took the elevator up to the fifth floor.

Exiting the elevator, Cornelius grinned as he found his son Jacoby waiting for him. Jacoby was slighter than he was, tall with dark hair and an olive complexion. Now that he looked with fresh eyes, he could see Jerome's resemblance to his son.

"Papa!" Jacoby greeted him with a hug, before going in to hug Dastan. "Dastan."

"Jacoby, it's great to see you my boy. I just wish it were under better circumstances."

"Me too." Jacoby turned and led the way to a small conference room, where another man rose from the chair he had been sitting on.

"Lord Dunstan!" Cornelius moved around the table and pulled his erstwhile colleague into a quick hug. "Damn, it's good to see you, Peter."

"Good to see you too, Cornelius, Dastan."

Cornelius nodded as he sat down next to Dastan at the conference table. On the screen in front of them were photos of Fenton and Ciccone, along with Ciccone's brother Marc.

"I take it Shea has updated you?" he asked his son.

"Yes, I had a FaceTime call with him about an hour ago. He said everyone is okay and Jerome, Roman and Verity are looking after Lilah Ciccone, who was in shock when she arrived. It seems Fenton and Ciccone have her youngest daughter Lacey, who is only fifteen, held somewhere."

"God, let's hope she's okay," Dastan voiced all their concerns. "Any idea where she's being held?"

"Nothing. Last anyone knew she was in England

at a boarding school near Oxford," Lord Dunstan chipped in.

"Any news on Fenton's whereabouts at the moment?" Cornelius studied the photo of the man, who they were pretty sure was a Striga. He inwardly promised retribution for what he'd done to Jerome when he was younger.

"Nothing concrete," Jacoby answered, breaking into Cornelius's thoughts. "Though we do have more information on the man himself."

He sighed as he moved away from the conference table a moment, to get himself a coffee from a pot near the window. He filled cups for everyone and distributed them around.

"His full name is Michael Fenton Bartok, and he is, or should I say was, a Donati."

Cornelius and Dastan stared at Jacoby. "You're sure?"

"Yes. I've accessed his records. He was born in 1900 in New York, son of Hungarian immigrants who arrived at Ellis Island the year before his birth. His parents were Taavi and Ebele Bartok from Gyula near the Hungarian-Romanian border. They settled in New York and took local manufacturing jobs. Ebele was Donati and her gift was being able to anticipate people's needs. Not a very powerful gift in some ways, but in the right hands it could be used to advantage."

"What happened?" Dastan asked.

"Ebele and Taavi were murdered in 1950 in their apartment but no-one was ever brought to account for it. Fenton was supposed to be at work but his gift is the power of persuasion. It could be that he 'persuaded' the police to believe him."

"Shit." Cornelius glanced at his son. "And we think what... that he persuaded a Striga to change him at some point?"

"Precisely," Dunstan added. "For whatever reason, he sought out a Striga and persuaded them to change him and see him through the change, and then he killed them. We're not sure of the sequence of events, but our intel states that this is what happened. Why? We're still not sure. What would make a Donati, any Donati, become a Striga?" He sighed. "We don't know. He must be strong to overcome the blood lust. Most Striga don't live that long, once they've been turned. But a Donati-Striga crossover, that's a new one to me."

"Do we know how long ago that was? He and Ciccone have been working together for over ten years now. Though his gift of persuasion may explain why Ciccone has joined with him." Cornelius looked round the room. "What now? Any suggestions?"

Jacoby looked uncomfortable to his father's eye. "What is it?"

"There are more Striga than ever before, and they're stronger than they've ever been. They're living longer before giving in to the blood lust. Some have been around for a few decades. Something has changed, but what we don't know. We can't get close enough to them to find anything out. Dunstan here suggests we reach out to Laertius."

Dastan grimaced. Laertius was a member of an older related species to Striga, that of vampires. Unofficially, he was seen as the Elder of the Vampires. There were rumours that he'd been around since the days of Pericles in Ancient Athens, though Cornelius had never been able to confirm that. Striga were a wilder, bastardised version of vampires, some even said older. Their downfall was their lust for blood; they didn't seem to be able to stop themselves from its call. Vampires were considered the older and steadier species. They consumed blood as it gave them life, but they weren't consumed by a blood lust, balancing it with food. Normally they weren't really interested in getting involved in Donati-Striga confrontations.

"Didn't you save Laertius's life once?" Dunstan leaned forward towards Cornelius.

"Yes." Cornelius remembered it well. He had stopped Laertius from losing his head in a fight with a blood crazed Striga in the early twentieth century. "He wasn't exactly grateful, claimed he had everything under control!"

Dastan laughed. "If that was under control…"

"Do we know where he is?"

"Being Laertius, where would you expect him to be?" Jacoby grinned at his father.

"The last place you'd expect a vampire to hang out."

"Exactly. Last I heard he was running a surf shop on Bondi Beach in Australia." Jacoby laughed at the look on his father's face.

"Fancy a trip?"

PART II

I

After one of the longest flights he'd ever been on, Jerome was pleased that they were on the final approach to Sydney airport. He, Cornelius and Dastan had undertaken the journey to visit with Laertius. He was glad his great grandfather had the wherewithal to pay for first class seats for them, making the journey more comfortable than it could have been.

He'd been surprised at first when Cornelius had asked him to accompany them to Australia to see the mysterious Laertius. The meeting the day after they returned from Washington had been rambunctious, with everyone having a view as to who should go and why. In the end, they had decided that Cornelius and Dastan would go, given their friendship with Laertius, and that Jerome would go with them.

Now, less than a week later, they were nearly there. Dastan stood up from his cubicle across the aisle, catching Jerome's eye as he stretched. Even with the spacious lay-flat seats, it had still been a long flight staying in much the same position. Cornelius had his seat already set back in day mode, and a flight attendant was sorting out the rest of the seats in the first class cabin.

"How are you?" Dastan asked Jerome as he leaned against the surround of his cubicle. "Did you manage to sleep at all?"

"I did actually," Jerome answered sounding surprised. "I wasn't sure I would, but I guess first class has its advantages."

Dastan laughed and replied, "Better than three weeks on a ship, which is how we did it last time."

Jerome gaped. He knew of course that both Dastan and Cornelius were several centuries old, but it still surprised him when faced with instances of their longevity. The idea that he might live for that length of time as well completely boggled his mind.

Cornelius joined them and slipped his arm around Dastan's shoulder. "Best three weeks of my life!"

Dastan grinned at him and Jerome forbore to ask them any further questions. He was happy that his great grandfather had such a close relationship with Dastan and looked to them both as father figures. He grimaced; they certainly did a lot better job of being his father figure that his own father ever had.

It had been a strange few weeks. He'd gone from being so depressed he'd nearly taken his own life, to having a loving family once more. Not only had he gained his great grandfather and Dastan, but Theo and the others as well. Getting his siblings back as well, had been amazing. He winced, remembering the fear in Mama Lilah's eyes when she had arrived at the Redoubt. He only hoped they could help find Lacey and that she was okay.

Which brought him back to today. They had left the Redoubt yesterday, in the early morning, and boarded a 10.15am flight at JFK Airport, for Sydney. Now, they were about to come into land.

Cutting into his thoughts, one of the flight attendants approached. "We'll be landing soon, gentlemen. If you could take your seats and fasten your seat belts."

"Thank you, Maisie," Jerome replied. He'd enjoyed being looked after on the flight by all the flight attendants and had tried to get to know their names and a little about them. He hoped they'd have at least some of the same ones on their return journey, whenever that would be.

He turned his attention to the window out of which he could now see the sea. They were fairly low already and he could feel the plane descending. The pilot tipped the wing to the right and he could see a beach coming into view.

"That's it," Dastan said. "Bondi Beach!"

"What the hell Laertius is doing here, I've no idea," Cornelius added.

Jerome watched as they came into land. The airport was busy, very busy. They were amongst the first to deplane and head towards luggage retrieval and customs. He hoped they wouldn't take too long to go through them. It was 9am local time and though he had slept on the plane, he still felt tired. He was glad that he didn't need his cane anymore to help with his walking, though Dastan had bought him a fold-up one that he could keep in his luggage, 'just in case'.

Cornelius and Dastan retrieved their luggage from the carousel, and Cornelius squeezed Jerome's shoulder as they prepared to go through customs. "Come on, let's get out of here and pick up a car."

They made it through customs with no problem. As they came out onto the concourse, a young indigenous man was waiting near the exit holding a placard with Cornelius's name on it. They stopped.

"Are you guys Cornelius, Dastan and Jerome?" he asked.

They nodded, and the young man grinned. "Great, I'm Jack, Lai sent me to pick you up." He reached for the bag Cornelius was carrying.

"Lai?" he asked.

Jack laughed. "He said you'd know him better as Laertius? Some of us call him to Lai to annoy him!"

"I see." Cornelius appeared perplexed. "I don't remember letting him know we were coming."

Jack laughed again. "Of course he knew! It's what he does."

"Would you mind if we confirmed this with Laertius?"

"He said you'd be wary. He said to remind you that – and I quote – 'I had everything under control, Corny'."

Cornelius sighed. Laertius was the only one who had ever called him Corny, and he'd insisted that he did have everything under control when Cornelius had stepped in and saved him from losing his head. Cornelius still begged to differ – a few minutes more and they would have been down one Vampire Elder. Still, the entitled git had insisted he'd have been okay.

Jerome and Dastan were grinning at him. Fuckers! He gestured with his hand for Jack to lead the way and they all followed the smiling man out of the terminal.

A black SUV was waiting for them in short-term parking and Jack helped them load the luggage into the back of the car.

"Lai's out of town tonight, but he said to take you to the guest quarters at his apartment and he'll catch up with you tomorrow. The place has been set up, so there should be food in the kitchen."

Cornelius nodded. "Thank you Jack, it's very... kind of him."

Jack laughed, his dark eyes twinkling.

As they were waiting to get out of the parking lot, Jerome switched his phone back on and immediately answered a call from Roman, on FaceTime.

"Hey," his younger brother said.

"Hey yourself," Jerome replied. "We just landed in Sydney. We're off to Bondi now. How are things at the Redoubt?"

"We're fine." Rome smiled. "Beatrice has been brilliant in helping my mother settle in here and soothing her fears over Lacey. Shea has been working on looking after everyone and security. Did you know he had a son – Donal?"

Roman continued before Jerome could reply. "Donal has been tracing where Ciccone and Fenton may have hidden Lacey. He's some kind of scary hacker from what I can work out."

Jerome smiled. He'd not met Donal yet, but had been amused at Shea's pride in his son's somewhat ambiguous abilities.

"Let us know if there's any movement there and pass my love on to Mama Lilah."

"Will do. I just wanted to touch base with you." Roman looked tired and Jerome wished he could have brought his younger brother with them. "I'll let you go now. Contact me later?"

"I'll do that, Rome. Try and get some sleep, eh?" He cut the call and smiled wearily at Cornelius. "Just Roman checking in."

Cornelius nodded. "Glad your step-mother is doing okay. Beatrice will make her welcome."

Jerome nodded and turned his head to look out the window. He watched the Sydney scenery go by as they headed away from the airport towards the beach. Jack told them it would only be about 10-15 minutes depending on traffic. Jerome was looking forward to collapsing into a comfy bed for a few hours when they got there. The lay-flat seat on the plane had been good, but his body clock was all over the place.

———

Jack pulled the SUV up behind a row of shops and businesses right on the main drag of Bondi, overlooking the beach. He jumped out and began unloading their luggage.

"The guest suite has its own entrance and parking space," he said as he gestured to a black door in front of them. "The car's yours as well for whilst you are here."

"Thank you," Cornelius replied as he helped the

younger man pile their luggage up in front of the door.

Jack pulled out an iPad from his messenger bag and passed it to Cornelius.

"If you'd just put your right palm on this," Jack said. Cornelius followed his instructions. "Now your left." He then turned to Dastan and Jerome and repeated the process.

"I've uploaded your palm prints to the security system," Jack informed them. "They control the entryway into the suite and enable you to set and turn off the security alarm. They'll also work on the safe upstairs if you have anything valuable to store whilst you're here."

Dastan smiled. "That's great – we're just revising our security systems back home. I'll have to mention this to a couple guys I know."

Cornelius laughed, he was sure Shea and Theo were already investigating new security systems, but there was no harm in making suggestions. He placed his palm on the plate next to the door and the door opened silently allowing access into a wide, cool foyer. He helped Jerome place the luggage inside.

"Are you coming in?" he asked Jack.

"Not at the moment, I have to get the shop open and catch up on stuff. Lai will be back in the morning and he said to invite you for breakfast. There's a door upstairs like this one that leads to the foyer outside his apartment. Your palm print will open the door on your side, but you'll have to wait for either him or one of his people to let you in. Until then, enjoy the scenery, maybe go surfing!" Jack laughed as he passed the keys for the SUV to Dastan and disappeared around the corner.

"Okay." Cornelius sighed, the jet lag catching up with him. "Let's go see our digs for the next couple of days and get settled."

"You're okay trusting this Jack?" Dastan asked.

"Despite appearances, I trust Laertius and if he trusts the young man to help us…"

"Yeah, okay."

Jerome went on ahead of them and used his palm print to call the elevator. They all piled in with the luggage and pressed the only button available with a big G on it.

The door opened directly into the guest apartment. As it did so, Dastan went on alert. It wasn't as if he was expecting trouble, but he'd found it really useful to be prepared wherever he was. He quickly glanced around the large open plan room but could see nothing to give him pause. He stepped into the room, allowing Cornelius and Jerome to follow him.

The room opened out revealing a communal lounge area, with a kitchen to one side. Moving further into the lounge area, Jerome could see that there were several open doors off a nearby corridor, which he could see were bedrooms.

"I'm going to crash. Let me know if you need me."

"Will do," Dastan replied. "You get some sleep, and we'll get together for dinner if you're not up before."

Jerome nodded. Picking up his messenger bag and rolling his suitcase behind him, he chose one of the doors at random and disappeared from view.

Dastan leaned in and kissed his lover's cheek. "How about you?" he asked Cornelius. "Do you want to get some rest?"

"Soon. Let's check out the kitchen and get some coffee going, then I want to touch base with Shea before getting some sleep."

"I'll just go put our luggage in one of the bedrooms then," Dastan said as Cornelius began exploring the kitchen.

Jerome managed a few hours' sleep before he woke up with a headache. He sighed and reached for his messenger bag, rummaging around in it before coming up with some aspirin. He'd been having these headaches for a few days now and they were starting to really bother him. At first, he'd thought they were to do with Bea opening his memories back up, but now he was beginning to think there was more to them. As he unpacked his luggage, memories of Hal, his army buddy, began pushing their way into his mind. He blinked and sat back on the bed, the tears coming quick and fast. Before he knew it he was sobbing uncontrollably. He curled up on the bed and tried to push the memories of Hal's sweet face away. He'd died in the same attack which had ended Jerome's army career, and Jerome could still see his twisted, mangled body as it lay on the roadside.

He reached over to the phone on the bedside table where he had put it to charge earlier and checked the time in New York before punching in Beatrice's number.

"Hey, Jerome. How's Sydney?" Her cheerful voice came over the line.

"Okay, I guess. Haven't seen much of it yet." His voice was creaky as he tried to clear his throat.

"You okay?"

"Not really. Sorry to bother you, Bea. Just… I just had a crying jag after I remembered what happened to Hal… sorry, Henry Greene. We went through basic training together and were deployed at the same time. He was Chrissy's brother. I just… just can't get what happened to him out of my mind. Weird, I've not really thought of him for a few weeks, then bam!"

"You've had a lot going on, Jerome." Beatrice's

comforting voice came over the line. "You've been recovering memories from years ago, and for a while there they may have pushed more recent memories to the back of your mind."

"Yeah."

"Is there anything in particular that might have set the memory off?"

"Maybe," Jerome replied, thinking of Jack, the young man who had picked them up at the airport. Now that he came to think of it, he'd had a look of Hal about him, or maybe it was just his infectious grin, he wasn't really sure.

"Sorry, Bea. I just wanted to… well, hear your voice, and know I'm not going mad."

"It's okay, Jerome. I understand. Your memories are all over the place at the moment and it could be that you'll have other flare ups like this. Feel free to contact me any time and talk it over if you need to. He obviously meant a lot to you. It's hard to lose a friend, especially in combat."

"You're right. He was a constant in my life, then suddenly he was gone."

"You'll get there. I'm not saying it's going to be easy, but your recovered memories will integrate with everything that's happened since."

"Thanks, Bea."

"You're welcome. Now, tell me… what's Laertius like?"

"Don't know yet, he's away tonight. Letting us stay in his guest suite and we're to meet him for breakfast in the morning. I'm going to go see if Nonno and Dastan are awake yet, see if they want a walk along Bondi beach before dinner."

Beatrice sighed. "Now you're making me jealous. Go on and enjoy your walk. I'll talk to you soon."

"Will do, and thanks again, Bea. I'm just not sure what I would have done without you."

11

The next morning, Jerome joined Cornelius and Dastan in the living area of the guest quarters. He felt quite rested and had been out for a morning run. Now that his leg was a lot better, his physio had suggested he take up running again. He found he really enjoyed it, so long as he didn't go too far.

Dastan stood up from the sofa and stretched.

"Have to find a gym soon if we're going to be here much longer," he said, smiling at Jerome and Cornelius.

"You could have joined me on my run this morning," Jerome replied.

"Maybe next time."

"Ready to join Laertius for breakfast?" Cornelius asked.

They both nodded and followed as Cornelius led

the way to the door that Jack had mentioned. Across the foyer from this door was another one, also with a palm print reader next to it.

Cornelius pressed his palm against it and then waited.

"Good morning," Jack's cheerful voice came over the intercom. "Just a moment and I'll open the door for you."

The black door opened as silently as all the others, and they entered the lobby of the other side of the building. Looking around, they could see that it opened out into a New York style loft. A mezzanine ran round the outside of the upper level. They could see several rooms leading off it, presumably bedrooms.

"I hope you slept well," Jack said, as he led them towards a row of large windows, through which the morning sunshine and Bondi beach could be seen.

"Yes, thank you," Cornelius replied, smiling.

As they approached the table, one of the men seated there got up. "Corny!" He laughed and pulled Cornelius into a bear hug.

This then was Laertius, Jerome thought. Laertius was a big man with long, black, curly hair, and his dark eyes were glinting with mirth as he pounded Cornelius on his back.

"It's good to see you again, old man." Cornelius grinned at him. "And Dastan."

Laertius moved around and gave Dastan a quick hug. "And who is this?"

"Laertius, let me introduce you to my great grandson Jerome, Jacoby's grandson. He is staying with Dastan and I in New York at the moment."

Laertius shook Jerome's hand then motioned to the table in front of him.

"Dastan and Cornelius, you know most of the people here. Jack, of course, Rupert Greene, Bill Coates, Cassius, and my PA Persephone Galanis. This young man is Jerome."

They all nodded or smiled at them. Jerome found himself taken with Persephone, her long, blonde hair swirled around her shoulders as she gave him a sweet smile.

"Please, join us." Laertius nodded towards the table and Jerome could see that it was filled with breakfast items: sausages, bacon, eggs, toast and many other things, as well as coffee.

Taking the offered seat, he said yes when Persephone asked if he would like some coffee pouring. Then, as everyone else around him did, he helped himself to breakfast. The only one it seemed not eating was the tall, well filled out Cassius.

Persephone laughed. "Cass prides himself on not eating 'human' food. He's a blood only vampire." He scowled at her amusement.

"Now you know that's not true, Perse." Jack

laughed. "We all know his weakness is cinnamon rolls."

The good-natured banter went on around Jerome as he ate. Occasionally, Cornelius and Dastan would join in, and Jerome realised they must have known the vampires – Laertius, Rupert and Cassius – for at least some time as they all appeared friendly. Though he caught a wary vibe from Dastan whenever Rupert spoke and occasionally saw Rupert give Dastan the stink eye, when he didn't think anyone was looking.

There was obviously a tale there.

"Well..." Jack swallowed the last of his orange juice and stood up from the table. "Bill and I have to open the shop up; some of us have to work."

Everyone laughed good naturedly as Jack and Bill said their goodbyes and left to open the surf shop in the parade of shops below them. At some point during breakfast Jerome had realised that Laertius's loft-style apartment and the guest accommodation they were staying in covered the whole area above the row of shops below. That was quite a bit of real estate on Bondi beach, and he wondered just how much Laertius was worth.

"More coffee?" Laertius asked. "I suggest we retire to the lounge area now that Jack and Bill have left us and discuss what brings you three to Bondi."

They all agreed and followed Cassius and

Persephone as they led the way over to a group of couches further down the apartment.

As they settled in, Jerome looked around himself and wondered at the vampires amongst them. None of them met his pre-conceived ideas of what vampires would look and act like.

"Thank you for receiving us, Laertius, and for letting us use the guest accommodation," Cornelius began. "Though I'm still not sure how you knew we were coming to Sydney."

Rupert laughed. "That's easy, old boy. We have contacts everywhere."

Jerome cringed at hearing Rupert call Cornelius 'old boy' in that tone; there was obviously history between them.

Cornelius nodded his head. "Okay, then you probably know what's been going on in New York?"

"Some." Laertius smiled. "We know you were attacked at your New York estate a couple of weeks ago and withdrew to one of your safe places, though we haven't worked out which one yet. We also know that the Striga are making a nuisance of themselves again in your part of the world. We've heard that a leader has begun organising them, a Donati-Striga cross, called Fenton."

"A fair summary. We only realised recently that Fenton was Donati and that it looks like he has been a Striga for several years now." Cornelius continued.

"He appears to still be in control of himself, having somehow managed to subvert the blood lust. He's also plotting with Mario Ciccone, a New York lawyer, who also happens to be Jerome's biological father."

All eyes turned to Jerome, and he squirmed under their scrutiny. Persephone smiled sympathetically at him and he returned her smile, grateful for the support.

"Ciccone was seen in Melbourne in the last few days," Rupert slipped into the conversation. Jerome went white and jumped up, swirling round to face the Englishman.

"Did he have a girl with him? A young girl about seventeen?"

"Not that we know of," Laertius replied. "Who is she?"

"My baby sister. Ciccone kidnapped her from her school a few weeks ago and no-one has seen her since." He deflated and sat down again with a bump.

Cornelius squeezed his shoulder in support.

"Have you any idea what he was doing in Melbourne?" Dastan asked.

"Not much, it was a fairly low key visit. He did meet with a couple of Striga in the area, but nothing appears to have come of it. He tried to meet with some of my fellow vampires, but few wanted anything to do with him. Fenton wasn't with him, but I imagine he was in close contact with him. Ciccone also met with some of your people Cornelius, though I don't believe the Donati council representatives here are aware of it."

"He's recruiting," Cassius said. "He must be looking for supporters in Australia. He hasn't been seen in Sydney yet, but—"

Cassius cut off what he was saying when the door into the apartment was flung open and Jack came stumbling in.

"Lai" he breathed out. "Attack... Bill's dead... Striga waiting for us..."

The young man collapsed on the hardwood floor and Laertius rushed to him. "Everyone stay back."

Persephone joined Jerome near where he had jumped up when Jack had made his entrance. They watched as Cassius joined Laertius as they tried to see what was wrong with the young man.

"He's bleeding too much," Cassius said as he worked desperately to stop the flow of blood.

"Should I call triple zero?" Persephone asked.

"No," Laertius said, sighing. "It's too late for that. He's too close to dying. They wouldn't get here in time."

Cassius stood up with Jack in his arms.

"You know what to do?" Laertius said.

Cassius nodded and swiftly took the stairs, two at a time, carrying Jack in his arms.

"You're just going..." Jerome began

"It's okay, Jerome," Persephone said. "Cassius knows what he's doing. Jack, like all humans who work for Laertius, have signed a living will. Some of us ask to be turned, others don't. Jack asked that it be Cassius who did the turning."

"To a vampire?" he asked. She nodded. Jerome didn't say anything, he wasn't sure he could. This was foreign to him. He was still getting used to the idea of Donati and Striga, never mind anything else.

Laertius turned away from the blood on his hardwood floors. "Rupert, Dastan, would you go downstairs and make sure the area is clear? Advise the other shops to close. Make sure there are no more Striga hanging about."

He closed his eyes as the two left the room, Rupert at almost a charge.

III

Dastan rushed down the stairs after Rupert, just catching up with him at the bottom. Putting his hand out on to his shoulder, he found himself being roughly thrown against the wall with Rupert's right arm across his neck.

"Rupert... stop... think..." he gasped. "They could... Striga."

Rupert loosened his hold on Dastan. "I'm not crazy."

"I know." Dastan leant down and put his hands on his knees, catching his breath. "Look, I know we haven't always got on, but still... I didn't want you rushing out into a trap."

Rupert sneered at Dastan and pulled out his iPad from his jacket pocket. He showed him the view from outside the back of the door. There was no-one around. Cautiously, they opened the back door and stepped out into the car park.

There was no movement anywhere.

"I've already sent the signal to the other shops to close up and retreat to their safe rooms," Rupert said as he showed Dastan a view from the front of the parade of shops. Metal shutters were already coming down on them all. "Listen…"

A mechanical voice came over the speaker. "Be aware. Be aware. This parade of shops is closed. This is due to a gas leak. The correct authorities have been informed and the leak is being dealt with. The shops will re-open as soon as they can."

Dastan watched as a few people who had been milling around the front of the stores shrugged and left the area. Rupert changed the view on the screen to the inside of the surf shop. They couldn't see if there were any Striga, but it didn't mean they weren't there. They could just make out Bill's body, lying on the floor near the till.

Reaching into the inside of his jacket once more, Rupert pulled out a sharpened wooden stake, and held it in his right hand. Dastan nodded at him, and reaching down to his ankle, pulled out the dagger that he kept in a sheath there.

He'd never been Rupert's biggest fan. He hated his 'old English gentleman' persona and was aware that he and Cornelius had once had an affair, back in the day. Which Cornelius assured him had been casual, at least on his side. Years later, he'd confessed to Dastan that he hadn't been aware that Rupert's heart had been involved. Dastan knew Rupert still carried a torch for Cornelius, even after all these years.

They waited at the door, trying to sense anything out of the ordinary. There was nothing to give them any clues as to what was happening inside. The place was completely silent. Rupert nodded and Dastan crouched down as the door opened. As if they had been doing this for years, they moved in unison through the door, Rupert going high and Dastan low, sweeping the inside of the shop for any movement.

Slowly, they made their way through the staff room at the rear of the shop. Rupert peeled off to check the storeroom, as Dastan continued to check out the shop itself. Suddenly, Dastan felt a weight land on his body and felt something scratching at his neck. Throwing his weight to one side, he was able to dislodge the Striga, which had obviously been waiting for them, and had dropped from the ceiling when Dastan walked by.

"Come into my parlour, said the spider to the fly…" the Striga said in a sing-song voice, as he came in close again for an attack. Dastan feinted right and managed to shrug the Striga off. It landed on its back amongst a rack of wet suits for hire. Before he could move further though, Rupert was there with the stake, and plunged it deep into the Striga's heart.

"Thanks," Dastan whispered. He touched his hand to his neck and his fingers came away bloody. It didn't feel too bad, but he'd check later for infection. A Striga's fingernails were never clean.

They nodded at each other and continued to search the shop, making sure they looked upwards at the rows of surf boards hanging from the ceiling, and the racks and racks of wet suits. Just as they reached the end of the shop, another Striga leapt out at them.

"A Donati and a vamp, how cute," he said, pulling a knife from behind his back. His grin showed off his blood encrusted teeth. Dastan tried not to think about it being Bill's blood.

Rupert attacked, his body whirling round and round the Striga. Dastan watched Rupert's back, prepared to step in if need be. It was over quickly as Rupert stabbed the second Striga through the heart with his stake.

They spent the next few minutes searching the shop top to bottom but the two Striga appeared to be the only ones there. When they were sure it was clear, Rupert sent the all clear signal to the other shops, and told the employees to go home for the rest of the day. He also contacted Laertius to update him and advised that though he was pretty sure there weren't any other Striga hanging about, a quick check of the other stores was probably in order, before they reopened the next day. Laertius agreed. He had called in several more vampires and humans from their coven, and they were waiting out the back for them.

Dastan knelt down by Bill's body. He had hardly said a word to him at breakfast, but he felt saddened by his death. He thought of Jack and hoped he'd survived his re-birth, knowing that not every change was successful.

"We'll arrange to burn his body, and that of the Striga," Rupert said, as he knelt down next to Dastan and sighed. "He was a good man, such a waste."

They opened the back door to the surf shop and several people from Laertius's coven were in the car park with a large van. They would load the bodies into it and dispose of them after dark. Most of those present were either human or older vamps like Rupert, who could survive in the sun's rays for several hours.

Dastan had just finished talking to Cornelius on his cell phone, as Rupert opened the door to Laertius's apartment and motioned Dastan through. He felt like a sort of truce had been called between them, as they ascended the stairs to report back to the others.

IV

Cornelius watched as his lover and Rupert dashed out of the door. He hoped there weren't too many surprises in store for them. A moment later, he heard the clang of the shutters going down on the shops below and in the apartment. All the windows were shuttered as well, and the lights came on. Laertius was taking no chances.

"Persephone." Laertius turned to his PA. "Please stay here whilst I take Jerome and Cornelius to check a few things out." She nodded and sat back down with her laptop and began checking emails. Jerome could just see the slight tremor in her hands, and it was his turn to give her comfort by smiling at her on his way by.

Laertius led them to the other end of the apartment where he put his palm against the plate next to a large black door. Once it opened, he ushered them inside and closed the door again.

"My control centre," he explained as he gestured with his right hand. Lights had come on automatically as they entered and Cornelius could see bank upon bank of computer screens, with several workstations scattered around the room.

"Only Rupert, Cassius and myself have access to this room," he explained as he powered up the nearest workstation. With a few flicks of his fingers he shared what was on his screen, to the larger screen in front of them. They watched as Dastan and Rupert entered the shop carefully and found Bill's body, before going further inside. Cornelius pulled in a deep breath as he saw Dastan get attacked, but the pair had it under control. They watched on the screens as Dastan and Rupert cleared the shop below them of Striga.

Laertius pulled up footage from before Dastan and Rupert entered the frame. They watched scenes from the various shops downstairs as they flew by one by one. Each shop was working normally until it came to the surf shop.

He slowed the images down and watched silently as Jack came into view from the back of the shop, laughing at something Bill was saying to him. A moment later, Bill turned round and gestured to someone behind him. Silently, the Striga that had entered the shop from the back after Bill, stalked through the shop heading for Jack. Laertius swore as they watched the attack on Jack unfold, whilst Bill stood back and watched. Jack's eyes had widened when he realised his friend wasn't going to help him, fear showing on his face.

Somehow Jack managed to get free of the Striga and pull a sharpened stake out from behind a display case. Whirling around, he struck the Striga in its side. Bleeding from his stomach, where he had been attacked, Jack headed for Bill, still with the stake in his hand. Bill began backing away as he realised that Jack was coming for him. Cornelius and the others watched as the fight between Jack, Bill and another Striga took place in the surf shop. Even though it was two against one, Jack was very well trained, and he eventually struck Bill in the chest, blood flowing freely from his wound.

Even though the Striga behind Bill and Jack had managed somehow to ignore the blood of his colleague lying dead, he appeared to go mad after Jack had stabbed Bill. They watched as the Striga's nostrils flared as he drew in a deep breath. He lunged forward and began to drink from Bill, his fangs striking his neck time and time again. Jack staggered back, still clutching the stake, then ran for the back door.

Laertius changed to the view from outside, which showed Jack stumbling out of the back of the surf shop and up to the entrance to Laertius's apartment. Jack managed to make his way through the door and close it behind him. The rest they knew.

———————

Cornelius could see that Laertius was dumbfounded and angry at Bill's treachery. He didn't know how long he had been in Laertius's confidence, nor how the Striga had recruited him, but he could see that Laertius was deeply affected by his actions.

"I'm sorry," he said, reaching out to Laertius.

Laertius lowered his head. "I… I just don't see it," he said. "Bill has been with me for years. He was loyal to the core…"

"Perhaps they threatened him, or his family," Jerome broke in.

Laertius was shaking his head. "We were his family."

Cornelius watched the screens below as Dastan and Rupert exited the surf shop and greeted other members of Laertius's coven, who had congregated in the car park to help with clear up. He drew out his phone and rang Dastan's number.

"Hey."

"Hey," came the reply. "I'm fine, we're fine," he amended.

"I know, we watched you on camera. Can you get

Rupert and bring him back upstairs? Laertius needs him. Bill was not an innocent victim in this." Cornelius heard Dastan draw in a breath.

"Understood, we'll be there in a moment."

"Tell Rupert we're in the control room."

———————

Less than five minutes later, the door to the control room opened as Rupert, followed by Dastan, arrived.

Cornelius pulled Dastan into his arms and checked his neck out. The bleeding had stopped, and the scratches weren't deep but…

"Here." Jerome approached them, as Rupert and Laertius huddled together whispering in a corner.

Cornelius turned and saw that Jerome had found a first aid kit. He raised his eyebrows and Jerome gestured towards a small bathroom set behind a bank of workstations.

"Let me see." He gently moved Cornelius away from Dastan and donned a pair of gloves, asking Dastan to lift his head so he could examine the wounds. As he did so, Dastan winced as Jerome applied pressure.

Carefully and methodically, Jerome cleaned the wounds, using an antiseptic to clear out any infection from the Striga's fingernails where they had scored his neck. Once he was satisfied it was clean, he applied antibiotic ointment to a small bandage and secured it with a sticking plaster.

Lifting his head, he met Dastan's gaze. "It'll be okay, your skin may feel tight for a while whenever you move your neck, but it should be okay."

Dastan nodded. "Thanks, Jerome." He kissed the younger man's cheek and Jerome smiled at him, before moving over towards where Rupert and Laertius were standing.

As he approached, they stopped talking and Jerome held up the first aid kit. "Are you injured anywhere?"

Rupert shook his head, then seemed to re-evaluate. "My right shoulder," he acknowledged.

Jerome had him sit down on one of the chairs and strip off his shirt. The shoulder looked raw and messy. The Striga who had attacked him had done a good job of messing it up.

Laertius moved forward. "Let me see." He peered down at Rupert's shoulder as Jerome set about cleaning it up.

"It looks nasty, but he should heal quickly." He spoke to Jerome. "Vampires have fast healing powers, but it still needs cleaning out. Infections can be nasty."

Jerome just nodded and got on with the task whilst the others, including Dastan and Rupert, watched the footage from before they entered the store.

Rupert's reaction to Bill's treachery was loud and

the air was blue from his swearing. His face grim, he winced as he watched the footage, and not just from Jerome's ministrations.

Jerome smiled inwardly. There were a lot of words there he'd never heard before, and here he'd thought Rupert was a gentleman!

Finally, he finished the bandaging and offered Rupert a pain killer which he turned down with disdain.

Jerome shrugged and went to check on Cornelius and Dastan.

"I'm fine," Dastan reassured him.

***

"Okay, listen up," Laertius said. "I'm calling a coven meeting for tonight. Bill was part of my inner circle, though he didn't know everything, thankfully. We just don't know how much, if anything, he shared with his Striga friends, and I suspect with Ciccone and Fenton too."

Cornelius nodded. "Agreed. Do you want us there?"

"Yes. We need to find out if there are any other traitors. I'm hoping Dastan will be willing to use his memory skills tonight and read those who turn up. I'm cursing myself now that I didn't ask him to do so at breakfast. We could have avoided this."

175

"You had no idea to suspect anyone at breakfast," Jerome broke in. "How could you have known?"

Laertius shook his head. "I should have suspected."

"Don't be too hard on yourself Lai," Rupert said, but Laertius was having none of it. Betrayal did not sit well with him.

He pressed an intercom and Persephone's voice came over the line. "Is everything okay?" were her first words.

"Damn. Sorry Persph, too much going on," Laertius replied. "Yes and no. We need to call a coven meeting tonight. Can you send out a message to everyone? 8pm at my club."

"The club? Not here?"

"Not this time."

"Okay. Leave it with me." Laertius switched the intercom off and sighed.

"If you gentlemen could spare me some time, I'd like you to go over the footage from the shop and car park for the last few days. I want to see if the Striga have been hanging around for a while. I never thought… Obviously they had some help, not many Striga can go out in the sun. Rupert and I are going to dig into Bill's friends and see if they knew anything or have any ideas. Jack obviously didn't."

Cornelius nodded. "We'd be happy to help, Laertius. We came to you for help with the Striga and what's happening at home. It seems it might all be tied together. All linked to Ciccone and Fenton in some way."

Laertius nodded and began logging them on the computers. It was going to be a long day.

V

Later that evening, Jerome stood in the large open space of Spiders, the nightclub that Laertius and his coven owned. It was closed, and with the lights up it was hard to imagine it as a place where people came to drink, dance and meet each other. He had never been a big fan of clubbing, though he had done his fair share during downtime whilst in the army. Looking around the large room, he could see that the whole place had a neo-classical look about it, and he wondered if that feel came from Laertius, or one of the others.

Laertius, Rupert and Cassius were standing near the bar, engaged in a private conversation. They had taken Bill's defection hard and were worried about how many others of their coven – humans or vampires – could have been tempted by Fenton and

Ciccone. As vampires congregated together in covens, they often faced a lot more scrutiny from their Coven Elders than Striga, who were loosely organised and largely free to pursue their own agendas. Rupert had explained that coven rules were often a bone of contention, particularly amongst younger vampires who often fought against them. But they were there for a reason: vampires had an uneasy truce with humans and often relied on the Donati to intervene on their behalf. Striga reasoned with no-one.

Jerome had learned from Dastan that there was a large coven in New York, and that he and Cornelius had approached them first about the situation with the Striga. They had been reluctant to get involved at the time and had agreed that Laertius was the best vampire to get in touch with. His long life had brought him into contact with the Striga more times than he liked to contemplate. He was also considered to be one of the Old Ones. These were a group of vampires who had been around since the time of the Pharaohs in Egypt. Laertius, having been born in a later period in Greece, did not consider himself a part of this group, though he was the oldest vampire known to be 'awake' at this point.

Jerome recalled the conversation he had had with Persephone whilst they had been driving to the nightclub.

"Many of the Old Ones sleep through centuries,

returning only when they feel the need," she had explained. "Laertius himself slept through much of the 16th and 17th centuries when there were plagues and wars around the world. He woke when he felt that times were changing, just in time for the Industrial Revolution. He has tried to keep up with technology ever since, claiming it is the best and the worst thing that humanity has ever done for the world."

"That could be dangerous," he'd replied. "What if their sleeping place is discovered and they are killed?"

"It happens," she agreed. "Laertius's own maker Anuk was killed by tomb raiders in Egypt. His sleep-watchers had abandoned him when the tomb raiders attacked. He was two thousand years old when he turned Laertius."

Jerome knew that Laertius was at least two thousand years old himself, but he couldn't imagine anyone being of such an age. Cornelius had explained to him that as a Donati, he should live to at least five hundred years. He would be as hale and hearty as he was now, until near the end, but the years the vampires lived were unthinkable to him.

Dastan's hand on his shoulder startled him out of his thoughts and he turned and gave his great grandfather's lover a smile. He would not have survived the events of the last few weeks without

Dastan and Beatrice by his side. He had come to love Cornelius as a father, but Dastan and Bea had been the ones to help him with his memories, and learning he was Donati and what that meant.

"Are you okay, Jerome? You look deep in thought."

"I'm fine," he replied. "Just thinking of something Persephone said in the car. She was explaining about the Old Ones amongst the vampire culture. I guess I just can't fathom living that long."

Dastan nodded. "That's why so many of them sleep the centuries away, hoping to awake rejuvenated and ready to live life again. Some never wake, dying in their 'sleep'. Others are killed, either deliberately or accidentally, and still others decide to take their own lives when they wake. There are still at least a dozen or so scattered around the world, sleeping the centuries away, at any one time."

"Can I have your attention, please?" Rupert said as he stepped into the middle of the floor, followed by Cassius and Laertius. The rest of them formed a loose circle around the trio.

"I'm sure you have all heard by now of the attack on the surf shop, the death of Bill, and Jack's injuries and subsequent turning." Everyone quietened down. Attacks on vampires by Striga were not unknown, but for them to attack Laertius on his home territory during daylight was a very unusual occurrence.

There were murmurs amongst the fifty-odd vampires and humans in attendance. Many had known both Jack and Bill and were outraged by the attack.

"This is what happens when you allow humans into your inner circle, Laertius. Don't say I didn't warn you," a woman with long black hair set off by two streaks of blonde through her bangs and piercing green eyes spoke up.

"Yes, thank you, Agatha," Laertius spoke. "You have made your case quite firmly before. However, my reasons still stand."

He looked at all members of his coven before continuing. "Somehow, Bill was seduced into working with the Striga. We haven't found out how yet, though I am hoping to get some answers tonight."

"How?" another voice cried out from the crowd.

Laertius didn't answer, instead he turned to Cornelius. "Ready?"

Cornelius nodded and with a sweep of his hand he stopped time. The room stilled, all except Cornelius, Jerome and Dastan frozen in their tracks. Cornelius quickly touched Rupert, Cassius and Laertius, leaving the rest of the humans and vampires frozen.

"Dastan," he said, indicating that Dastan should walk amongst the attendees and check their memories to see if anyone else was a traitor. All he needed to do was a quick touch of everyone, only skimming the surface of their memories, looking for any trace of them working with Striga, Fenton or Ciccone. Anything else would be a violation of their privacy, and he felt he was on dodgy enough ground even doing this.

As he moved through the vampires and humans, he indicated to Jerome and Cornelius those whose thoughts betrayed them. They moved those he indicated, with Cassius's and Rupert's help, to the middle of the dance floor, isolating them near to where Laertius now stood. By the time he had completed his work, Dastan's face was drawn with fatigue. Three vampires and two humans were isolated from the rest.

Laertius sighed and wiped his hands over his face. Cassius and Rupert moved to support him as they saw who was involved in the treachery. Remy, who had helped in the clean-up at the surf shop, Philip who was fairly new to Laertius's coven, and Bessie who had been with him for hundreds of years. The humans he knew less well – Carter and Daisy. They were servants and day watchers to the younger vampires who still felt the need to sleep during the day, both of whom served Philip.

"Thank you," he said. "Corny, can you leave these in stasis and return the others?"

Cornelius did as he asked. He touched each

vampire or human lightly on the arm in passing, and they became aware that several of their companions had been moved and now stood stock still in the middle of the floor.

"What…" Agatha, the vampire who had challenged Laertius earlier, began.

Laertius held his hand up asking for silence. "Apologies," he said. "I couldn't take any chances, we had to weed out those who were working with the Striga." He gestured to the three Donati. "Cornelius here is Donati. As some of you know, he can stop time and freeze people in place. Dastan here touched your surface memories slightly – no more than that – to check you weren't working with the Striga."

There was an outpouring of outrage from nearly everyone there. They felt betrayed and attacked, by their own leader no less.

"Enough!" Cassius roared. "You forget yourselves. Laertius is your coven leader for a reason, you all trust him. He only has the coven's best interests at heart. Would you rather we left them to seed dissension and treachery throughout the coven? We did it for you, for us."

The mutterings faded and some began to discuss those who were still frozen in time in the centre of the room.

"What will happen to them?" Jacques, another of

those who had help clear up at the surf shop that morning, asked.

"That we have yet to decide. First, we will see what we can find out from these five. Jacques will you help Rupert to restrain them before Corny frees them from stasis?"

Jacques and Rupert turned to do his bidding and once they were all restrained, Cornelius freed the five coven members from the stasis.

All of them were surprised to find themselves singled out and restrained, but it was Remy who spat at their feet and raged.

"You think you're better, but you're not really. Donati scum," he aimed this one at Jerome who was checking his bindings at the time.

"Be quiet," Laertius said. "We'll deal with you in a short while." To everyone else he said, "Thank you for coming. We will reconvene here tomorrow after closing. I will update everyone then."

A few of the vampires looked like they were going to argue and try and stay to see what happened next, but Rupert and Cassius herded them to the doors.

"You too, my friends," Laertius said to Cornelius, Dastan and Jerome. "Persephone will drive you back to the apartment. I will speak to you in the morning."

"Can we help?" Jerome asked.

"No, thank you. I… we… need to do this on our own."

Jerome nodded. Following Cornelius's direction, he joined Dastan and Persephone at the door.

"Don't," Cornelius said.

"What?"

"They have their own way of finding things out. They needed our help to narrow the field, if you like. The rest we leave to them."

Jerome nodded again as he followed them out into the sticky night air. He was glad he wouldn't be involved in what came next. He joined Persephone and the others at the car. She smiled wearily at him.

"It's been a long day. I'll take you all home so you can get some rest."

Jerome got in the front seat next to her while Dastan and Cornelius got in the back. Dastan was already beginning to droop – he had expended a lot of energy that night and needed time to recoup.

As they joined the main road heading back to Bondi, Jerome glanced out the side window and shouted, "Fuck, brace for impact!"

In the next moment, a large, black truck slammed into the passenger side door. Jerome screamed in agony as the airbags went off, and he lost consciousness.

VI

Impressions of screaming metal and the smell of fire followed Jerome as he struggled to regain consciousness. His left side felt crushed as he tried to breathe in. He coughed and it hurt. A lot. He came to, to find himself lying in the middle of the road whilst paramedics worked on him. He couldn't hear what they were saying properly, but it didn't sound good.

"Nonno," he groaned, asking for Cornelius.

"It's okay, we've…" the voice began before he faded out again.

The next time he became aware of what was happening around him, he was in a hospital bed with the sounds of machinery in the background. He pried his eyes open and rolled his head to the right where he could feel someone holding his hand.

Cornelius was slumped on an uncomfortable looking chair, one hand in Jerome's, the other in Dastan's.

Jerome moaned as a wave of pain hit him, and Cornelius jumped.

"Jerome," he croaked. He looked as though he hadn't slept in a few days, unshaven and unkempt in a way that Jerome had never seen before.

"Nonno? What happened, where am I? Hurts…"

Dastan was already up and out the door in search of a nurse or doctor to see to Jerome's pain. Cornelius leaned down and placed his forehead against his great grandson's.

"You worried us all, Jerome." He sighed. "What do you remember?"

"A truck?"

Cornelius nodded. "You just had a chance to shout, before the truck struck. I didn't even have enough time to act, stop it happening…"

Jerome squeezed his hand. "Shh, it's okay, you can't stop everything." He looked around the room. "Persephone?"

"She's fine. A broken arm and shaken up, but fine. Laertius showed up and took her home. I've never seen him looking so old."

Dastan arrived then with a doctor in tow, who proceeded to examine Jerome and hummed whenever he winced in pain.

"You're a very lucky young man," Doctor Greening finally said. "You gave us a right scare. I had to rush you straight into surgery when you got here. One of your lungs had collapsed and you've got several broken ribs. I had to set your left arm and leg as well, as you had compound fractures in them both. You were fortunate Dastan and Cornelius were there to help you, they were able to stop the bleeding and keep you alive until the paramedics could get to you."

Jerome looked questioningly at Cornelius.

"It's okay, Dr Greening is Donati and one of the best trauma surgeons in Sydney. Also..." He coughed. "Laertius gave you some of his blood. It will speed up your healing processes, but you will still be in a lot of pain until your ribs heal some more."

Dr Greening had called a nurse into the room and he was in the process of adding drugs to the IV bag attached to the stand near Jerome's bed.

"These are pain killers with an anti-biotic added in to fight any infections you may have received from the compound fractures. You should begin to feel the benefits in a few minutes."

Jerome nodded his head. He could already feel the drugs taking effect, and with them came drowsiness.

He wanted to know more about what had happened, but he couldn't stay awake.

———————

The next time he regained consciousness, it was to find Dastan sitting by his bed working on his iPad.

"Hey," he said. "What time is it?"

"Late, gone midnight. I sent Cornelius back to Laertius's place to get some rest. He hadn't moved from your side since the accident."

"How long?"

"Two days," Dastan replied.

Jerome tried to take that in... he had lost two days.

"Water?"

"Here." Dastan lifted a glass from the table by the side of the bed and helped Jerome to sit up and take a drink. "Just a little for now, you can have some more in a moment. How do you feel?"

"Better than before. Still hurts, but not as bad."

"Good. Dr Greening thinks you should be kept in another couple of days. After that you can go back to the guest quarters at Laertius's place. You'll need a good couple of weeks to recover, even with the help you've gotten from Laertius."

"Leg?" he asked.

"You were lucky there," Dastan answered. "The

compound fracture you received was in your left leg, not the one damaged in the IED explosion.

Jerome winced, and with Dastan's help he was able to sit up and feel a bit more awake and presentable.

He was still hooked up to the IV, but the drugs weren't as strong as before.

"Are you okay, Dastan?" he asked. "Nonno is okay?"

"We're fine, Persephone too. You seem to have taken the brunt of the collision. It could have been a lot worse."

"Do you know what happened yet? How did we get hit? What about the driver of the truck? Was he okay?"

"The driver deliberately rammed us then ran off before we even knew what was going on. The car was pushed halfway across the street. It took a while for us to work out that you were badly injured. We got the bleeding stabilised before the paramedics arrived. It was a mess. We're just thankful that you weren't more badly injured, and that apart from a few bruises and scrapes, the rest of us are okay."

"Do I remember you telling me that Laertius gave me some of his blood?" Jerome asked.

"Yes, not much. Just enough to help with healing. He was incensed that anyone would attack us in his city. He is beginning to realise that the Striga conspiracy is more widespread here than he thought. It has been a hard wake up call for him."

"Did he find out much from the vampires he was interrogating that night?"

"He hasn't shared much with us yet, though he says he's made progress. He... we wanted to wait until you were feeling better before going further. He has not been in a good mood. Some of those plotting against him he has known for a long time, centuries in some cases, and he just can't understand why they would do this."

Dastan sighed. "He's called a meeting with ourselves, Rupert and Cassius for the first evening after you're home. If you are up to it," he emphasised.

"I'll be ready."

Even after a couple of days and major surgery, Jerome was feeling better than he had when recovering from the wounds that led to him leaving the army. He was impressed that Laertius had given him some of his blood. Blood that was obviously helping him recover from the worst accident he had ever been in.

Dastan leaned over and kissed Jerome on the forehead. "Get some rest, I'm going back to the guest quarters to sleep and check on Cornelius. We'll be back in the morning. And you should phone Beatrice and Roman, they have been worried sick about you. Don't forget the time difference though."

With that Dastan left and Jerome reached for his cell phone which someone had kindly plugged into a charger near his bed. It was 2am in Sydney, it would be midday – the previous day – in New York. After he talked to Bea and Roman, he would need to sleep again if he was going to get out of here in a couple of days.

VII

Cornelius rolled over and winced. He felt his full two hundred and fifty-odd years and more. Though not badly hurt in the crash like Jerome, he and Dastan had been banged up a bit and the bruises were beginning to show.

He reached out to find the other side of the bed was empty. It was unusual for Dastan to be up before him. He must have really been out of it the previous night.

They were expecting Jerome to be discharged today, and he and Dastan had said they would go to the hospital to bring him back. When he remembered the aftermath of the crash, he could cry. His great grandson had become special to him, even more so perhaps than his son Jacoby… He let that thought go. He loved his son, but he'd been a difficult boy and even now, Cornelius didn't always understand his moods.

He and Dastan had taken the younger man under their wing, though Cornelius still felt guilty about forcing him to meet Ciccone that day. He still wasn't sure if it had been worth bringing Ciccone's attention to his son again. He grimaced. Time to get up and begin the day.

The door to the bedroom opened and Dastan entered bearing a tray with coffee and breakfast. He set it on the bedside cabinet and helped Cornelius rearrange the pillows behind him, so he could sit up more comfortably. He had lost count of the number of times either one of them had nursed and cosseted the other back to health.

"How are you feeling?" Dastan asked as he slid back into bed on his side and sat up drinking his coffee next to Cornelius.

"As though I've been hit by a truck." His slight smile let Dastan know he was recovering.

"What time is it?"

"Just gone 11am. I thought you deserved a lie in as Jerome is coming home later." Dastan grinned at him. It was rare for either of them to still be in bed much beyond 8am, so an 11am start was more than just a lie in.

"Thanks, love." Cornelius smiled as he buttered the croissant Dastan had brought him, still warm from the oven, then slathered it with strawberry jam. For a short while he ate and drank his coffee, enjoying the view of Bondi from their window facing the beach.

"Has Laertius returned?" he finally asked Dastan, turning from the view out of the window.

"Not yet. I spoke to Cassius this morning on the phone and he said they still intended to be back here by this evening. He wants to discuss a few things with us, and Jerome after he is back. I warned him that Jerome won't have much stamina."

"I still can't believe he gave some of his blood to Jerome…"

"I think he feels it's his fault that we got hit by the truck. He helped Persephone as well. She'll be there tonight; I spoke to her earlier." Dastan grinned. "I think she has a thing for our Jerome."

Cornelius laughed, then grunted as his bruised ribs protested. He had been sitting on the same side of the car as Jerome, in the back.

"Jerome certainly seems smitten. We'll see."

"Do you want to shower?" Dastan asked, going round to Cornelius's side of the bed to help him stand. They had kept the extent of Cornelius's injuries from Jerome. It wasn't really anything bad, just bruised ribs and a twisted ankle, but they hadn't wanted to worry the young man.

"I think I can manage," Cornelius said, standing

up and putting weight on his bandaged right ankle. "It's better than yesterday. Hopefully it'll be hardly a limp by the time we pick Jerome up this afternoon."

Dastan hummed and stood ready to help if Cornelius needed him. Cornelius smiled at his lover as he managed to make it to the bathroom on his own.

The soothing hot water of the shower helped loosen up his muscles, and by the time he was out and dressed he felt a lot better.

It was nearing midday when he joined Dastan in the living room of the guest quarters.

"What time did Dr Greening say we could pick Jerome up?" Cornelius asked Dastan as he joined him on the sofa, taking the glass of water he handed him as he sat down.

"Any time after 2pm, so long as he has his meds."

"Probably closer to 4pm then." Cornelius grinned. Getting prescriptions filled before being able to leave hospital always seemed to be the longest part of any discharge routine, no matter where in the world you were.

"I thought we could have lunch out, then head over to the hospital," Dastan said, as he set his mug down on the coffee table. "There are plenty of places between here and the hospital. A little time out for just the two of us, before this evening's meeting."

Cornelius nodded. It was a good idea. Who knew

when the next time they would get just for themselves would be?

They had to take it in little pieces, doled out one by one at the moment.

"Have you heard from the Redoubt today?" he asked.

"Yes, I spoke to Shea before. Everything is quiet there. They're starting to get bored, even with the facilities available. Roman is worried about Jerome and it was all Beatrice could do to stop him from booking a flight here to see his brother. For now, she's managed to persuade him that it's best he stays where he is but she's keeping an eye on him. He's a headstrong young man."

"He's just got his brother back; I can understand his worries." Cornelius grimaced. "How's his mother doing?"

"Bea has been working with Lilah, trying to help her with the fall out of her escape from Ciccone's clutches, and her worry over her daughter. There is still no sign of Lacey. All her school knows is that her father turned up one day with an affidavit 'signed' by Lilah to remove her from the school. The document appeared genuine and they didn't see there was any problem letting her go with her father."

Cornelius shook his head. Ciccone had obviously felt the need for the extra insurance of having Lacey in his possession.

"Oh, I've been meaning to ask Laertius, but with everything else going on… how is young Jack? Did he survive the turning?"

"I asked Cassius that this morning when I spoke to him. He said he is doing okay. They have taken him up country to a place they have there where he'll be able to learn how to act around humans now that he's a vampire. His base instinct will have changed, but Cassius seemed to think the young vamp could adjust quite easily."

"I'm glad. It all seems such a waste…"

***

Cornelius and Dastan arrived at the hospital to find Jerome up and dressed and ready to leave. His left arm and leg were still in plaster, but he seemed to have adjusted to using a crutch under his right arm to get around with.

He grinned at Cornelius as he entered the room. "Nonno!" Jerome accepted Cornelius's kiss on his cheek and returned it, then gave one to Dastan, before showing off how dexterous he had become with his crutch.

"I take it you're ready to go then?" Cornelius grinned, watching as the young man manoeuvred his way around the room.

"Can't wait," he said. "The pharmacist has just

dropped off my meds, and the nurse has my discharge papers. I'm all yours."

"Then let's go." Dastan pointed towards the door and they made their way down the corridor.

Cornelius stopped at the nurses' station to thank them once more for their care of Jerome. As he was opening the door to let Jerome out with Dastan, Cornelius felt like there were eyes boring into him from behind, as though someone was watching him. He turned slowly to check behind him but couldn't see anything. It was just a feeling.

He shook his head and followed his lover and great grandson out of the hospital, and down to their car in the underground car park. No matter how he tried though, he couldn't shake off the feeling that they were being watched.

VIII

The next two weeks as Jerome healed were quiet.

The promised meeting with Laertius didn't take place. He, Cassius and Rupert had gone 'up country', following up with other covens in the wider New South Wales area about the treachery Bill and the others had supported in the Sydney coven. Then he had been called away to see Jack, the young man who had been turned after the attack on the surf shop. He wasn't doing very well, despite an auspicious beginning, and Laertius had gone to help him cope. Cassius and Rupert had gone with him.

Now Cornelius reported that Laertius had gone 'walkabout', which didn't help the tension building in the guest quarters any.

The last couple of days Cornelius and Dastan had left an almost recovered Jerome in Sydney, whilst they had visited the Donati Council in Canberra. They were due back the next day. Jerome hadn't been left on his own though. Persephone, who had an apartment above the guest quarters, had been a frequent visitor, keeping Jerome as up to date as she could.

FaceTime on his phone jingled and Jerome smiled when he saw his brother was contacting him.

"Hey you," he answered. "How are things in New York?"

"Quiet," his brother's answer came back as he made a face into the camera. "Theo still won't let us go anywhere!"

"You know it's important that you stay there, right?" he asked, concerned.

"No, you're right, I do know, it just gets boring at times. Mama and Verity have been doing Zoom calls with their friends and Mama is even teaching that way. I don't know, I guess I'm just feeling antsy."

Jerome laughed. At twenty, his younger brother was typical of his age and missed his social life.

"It won't be for ever, Rome, you know that, right?"

"Yeah." His face brightened. "Hey, is Persph there?"

Persephone had been around for several of Roman's FaceTime calls and he had developed a crush on her. Jerome couldn't blame his brother; he wasn't any better. He laughed at Roman's hopeful look.

"No, she's gone to visit her father today, she'll be back tomorrow to take me to the hospital to have these casts off. She got hers off last week. I never thought I'd have a vampire blood infusion, nor how much it would help me. Damn, wish I'd have had this when I got injured in the army."

Roman fell silent. They had talked a bit about Jerome's time in the army over the last couple of weeks, catching up on the years they had missed out on.

"So," Roman began. "Shea's son, Donal, turned up a couple of days ago and Shea put him to work on teaching me some self-defence moves."

Jerome smiled. He had spoken to Shea himself in the last week, suggesting something similar, though he had wondered if Theo could do it. He hadn't realised Donal was there yet, though Shea had said he was on his way.

"How's that going?"

"S'cool…"

"Well, don't push yourself too much."

"I better be off," Roman said. "Mama suggested I audit a couple of on-line classes since I can't attend in person at the moment. There's still lots of courses offering on-line tutoring after the Covid pandemic, more than I thought."

"What are you auditing?"

"Physics and chemistry. I was doing a college degree in law, but that was Father's idea not mine, which is why I was interning at his office that day you and Cornelius came by. I always wanted to teach kids, so maybe I'll be doing that later."

"Good for you! Say hi to everyone and we'll have to set up a group call when Nonno and Dastan get back from Canberra. Hopefully things will start moving again soon."

"Yeah, be careful what you wish for, bro." Roman raised his hand in farewell. "Laters."

The hospital trip the next day went to plan, and Jerome was glad when one of the nurses in Dr Greening's clinic took the casts off his arm and leg. X-rays showed that the fractures were all healed.

Dr Greening warned about putting too much strain on them straightaway and gave him some physio to do. Jerome had sighed – more physio!

"Where to?" Persephone asked.

"Lunch?"

"Sounds good, we should be okay if we stick to the Bondi area. Hey, do you feel like fish and chips?"

"Could do. Not had it much, it's not really a thing in the States."

Persephone laughed. "It is here. Fish and chip shops and restaurants are a Greek thing and my family own a chain. There's one a few blocks away from the beach in Bondi."

"Okay, lead on." Jerome grinned; it was good to see Persephone smiling. The last two weeks she had been serious, and though always happy to sit with Jerome and watch movies and eat ice cream, there had been a lot going on that had concerned her.

They pulled up a short time later into the car park of a small restaurant advertising Galanis Fish and Chips. Inside, they were shown to a table by the window by a smiling waitress.

"Hi, Christa," Persephone greeted her. "Jerome, this is my cousin Christa. Her father Eric runs this branch of the business. Jerome has been staying in the guest quarters," Persephone told Christa.

"Good to meet you, Jerome. What do you guys want to drink?"

"Just water's fine for me," Jerome answered, and Persephone ordered a soda.

"I'll be back in a moment for your order," Christa answered before walking away to get their drinks.

"So," Persephone began, "great to get the casts off?"

"God, yes," Jerome answered, stretching his left arm out. There were still a few bruises, but apart from that there was nothing to show for the breaks he had suffered only a fortnight ago.

"What do you recommend?" he asked, looking at the menu.

"Just plain old fish and chips," Persephone said as Christa came back with their drinks.

"For two?" the waitress asked.

Jerome nodded his head, trusting Persephone's choice.

"So, Greeks and fish and chips?" he asked. "How did that happen?"

She laughed. "Not sure. Just did I reckon. My family followed Laertius out here in the 60s and it was already a thing back then, so when my grandfather retired as Laertius's seneschal, he opened up his first shop and with Laertius's help he made a go of it."

"Your grandfather worked for Laertius?"

"Yes, then my father and now me. It's kind of a family business as well."

"How did that happen?" Jerome asked, curious as to how her family had become mixed up in Laertius's world.

"We're all descendants of his human family. He's always employed us in various manners over the centuries. As day watchers, butlers, seneschals – as my father and grandfather were – or now as me, his personal assistant. Which I much prefer to seneschal!" She laughed.

"Wow, I had no idea. So, you what… grew up knowing about him?"

"To an extent, yes. I knew he was Daddy's employer and that we followed him around whenever he moved. Fortunately for me, by the time I was in school he'd pretty much settled here. Daddy said he went to several schools as Grandad followed him from Greece to Australia. When I was eighteen, they let me in on the secret. I was a big Twilight fan, so you can imagine my reaction!" They laughed together as their meals arrived. As they ate, Jerome found he enjoyed the food as much as the company. Eventually, he pushed his plate away and smiled at her.

"When did you take over from your father?"

"Five years ago. I made some changes in the way Laertius's affairs were run. Cassius and Rupert had already begun changing the way they carried out security. The technology required to set up the monitoring was an ongoing project then. That's why he brought Remy on board," she said, naming one of the vamps who had betrayed Laertius. "He had been in IT in his human life, and though he was only young in vampire years, less than ten I think, he had a lot of experience in his field. It's been a mess…"

She broke off and Jerome reached over and held her hand, offering comfort. He had begun to get the impression that they had been a tight knit community and that the treachery caused by Bill and Remy and the others had hit them all hard.

"Thank you," he said.

Persephone looked at him. "For?"

"Being here for me these last two weeks. I get the feeling that if you hadn't been injured yourself you would have gone with Laertius and the others."

She nodded. "Yes, but someone needed to stay behind as well, and run things from this end. There's been a lot going on in the background as you've probably guessed. Laertius was hit bad by this. It's not the first time he has faced treachery from members of his coven, but this is the worst for several centuries, involving Striga as well!"

Jerome nodded. He had worked out that Laertius, who had been around for several millennia, not just centuries, would have made many enemies over time. He seemed such a laid-back person, but Jerome was coming to realise that despite that he kept a tight rein on his coven members. For them to betray him like they had, must have rankled with him.

"Do you know when they'll be back?" he asked.

"Soon. A couple of days, I think. How about Cornelius and Dastan?"

"They return tomorrow, their flight gets in just after 2pm. I said I would pick them up at the airport now that I'm able to drive again."

Persephone insisted on paying for lunch and they

made their way back to her car. Just as they were getting in, her phone beeped with an incoming text.

"They're back," she said as she read the message. "I need to get back to the apartment—" she began as her phone started ringing.

"Hello?" She listened, then nodded. "We're on our way."

She smiled at Jerome. "Well, they're back and they have Cornelius and Dastan with them. They must have come via Canberra and picked them up there. Come on, they're expecting us. Laertius said something about heading to Melbourne."

Cornelius greeted them as they arrived back at the guest quarters. Persephone stayed long enough to say hello, before heading out to see Laertius and the others.

"You're looking well." Cornelius hugged his great grandson to him and smiled. It was good to see him out of the casts and looking better.

"Thanks. How was your trip? How'd you get back so early?"

"It was good. We caught up with the Council in Canberra. Had a few meetings with your grandfather, and other members of the Council in Washington, online. Jacoby sends his best wishes. He was horrified to hear of your accident."

Jerome shrugged. He hadn't met his grandfather, Cornelius's son, yet. He didn't know him. Cornelius and Dastan had become like parents to him. He guessed he'd meet Jacoby at some point.

"Do they know what's happening with Ciccone and Fenton?"

Cornelius sighed. "A little. Still no news on your sister either, I'm afraid."

Jerome hugged Dastan in greeting as the man came through from his and Cornelius's bedroom.

"So, what's going on then, and how did you get back with Laertius?"

"Laertius came to Canberra and met with the coven there. He has been travelling around some of the covens, helping to root out anyone else who has been working with Ciccone and Fenton. Fortunately, the information he sent out to the Coven Masters just after your accident had already warned them what was happening, and many of them had already cleared their houses. None were as deeply involved as some of the vamps here were. It seems that Fenton had sent a few of his more 'with it' Striga to some of the disaffected members of the other covens, and some of them had reported the meetings to their leaders.

"There's a lot more going on than we were

initially aware of. Laertius wants to move on to Melbourne where Ciccone and Fenton were spotted again only a couple of days ago. He flew us back in his private plane, and now he wants to take us all to Melbourne. Seems he has some property by the bay there that he uses when he's in that area. He's having it all fixed up ready for us to arrive there this evening."

"I'd better get packed then," Jerome said as he headed towards his bedroom to grab his luggage.

"Do I need to take everything?" he asked, popping his head out of the door. "Or are we coming back here?"

"I'd bank on taking everything. I'm not sure we'll be back, this trip at least." Cornelius moved over to the dining room table where Jerome's laptop was still set up, after speaking to Roman that morning.

"I'm going to contact Shea and Theo and bring them up to date," he said as Jerome moved back into his bedroom to pack up all his belongings.

Jerome couldn't believe they'd been there nearly three weeks already. He folded his clothes neatly and squared everything away, his army training showing there. His laundry he put into a separate pack and squished it down into any space there was left. His arm was aching by the time he was finished, and his leg was protesting, but he ignored them for the moment. Scooping up his messenger bag, he made his way back into the living room in time to hear Cornelius say goodbye to Shea.

"Give that a minute to cool down and I'll pack it in my messenger bag. I'm not sure but I think it only takes a couple of hours to fly to Melbourne, so we may not need it on the flight."

Cornelius smiled. "You're forgetting we're flying by private plane, totally different experience."

Dastan laughed. "You can say that again."

Just then there was a knock on the door and Dastan opened it to find Rupert grinning at him from the other side. He entered and began helping them ferry things out to the waiting car. Jerome stayed back a bit and grabbed Dastan by the arm.

"What's with the grin? I thought he didn't like you, and vice versa."

"Old history," Dastan replied, following Jerome down the stairs. "We had a long talk on the plane and thrashed a few things out." He smiled at Jerome when they got to the bottom of the stairs.

"What?" Jerome said, bemused by Dastan's amusement.

Dastan laughed. "I caught…" He made finger quotes. "Him, Cassius and Laertius at the airport."

"And?"

"They were making out like teenagers!"

"What? No!" Jerome replied. "Seriously?"

"Seriously," Cornelius replied, coming up behind

them. "Dastan thinks it's hilariously funny. But they're serious. They have to be, given what might be at stake here."

"You're right," Dastan said, kissing Cornelius on the cheek. "As always. I think it's great really. All those years of living in each other's pockets." He grinned. "It's only been a 'thing' for a couple of months now, but they seem happy with each other, and that's what's important."

Jerome shook his head; he didn't care if they were involved. Hell, he was one to talk – he'd always been known as an equal opportunities lover by his army buddies. He hoped it worked out for them.

A few short hours later they landed at Avalon Airport, a small international airport on the outskirts of Geelong, in Victoria. Laertius had explained that they were meeting with the Melbourne coven than night, but in the meantime, they were getting settled in his house in South Werribee, a small settlement on Port Philip Bay.

Jerome shook his head when he heard this. What was it with Laertius and seafront properties?

IX

They hardly had chance to get settled in the new property before Laertius was chivvying them out of the house and into a large black SUV parked out the front. With three rows of seats, it comfortably sat six grown men.

Persephone would meet them at the coven meeting in Melbourne. She was staying with some cousins in South Werribee.

The journey to Melbourne along the Princess Highway took less than an hour. Jerome watched the scenery go by, admiring the blue/grey Eucalyptus trees. They gave off a different hue against the bright blue sky than he was used to in the States. As they neared Melbourne, driving over the Westgate Bridge, Cassius pointed out the Crown Casino. They then passed the Royal Botanic Gardens as they headed for the district of Saint Kilda, where the Melbourne coven was situated.

When they got to the esplanade, they pulled into the underground garage of a large apartment building overlooking the bay. Rupert, who had been driving, pulled them deftly into a parking space next to a small red convertible, which Persephone had just got out of. They all greeted her with hugs. She handed an iPad to Laertius and the two excused themselves to discuss some business.

After a few moments, Laertius returned and led the way through the underground garage to the lifts, which Jerome kept calling elevators to the annoyance of the locals.

When they were all in the lift, Laertius pushed the button for the penthouse. "There are certain rules we have to abide by when we get to the coven meeting. As head of the Sydney coven, I will introduce you first to their leader, Mary. Then she will introduce you to her coven direct. Until that is done, you will not be able to address the coven meeting directly."

"We understand, Laertius. We don't want to do anything to upset them. Especially if they have information for us," Cornelius replied.

Laertius nodded as they arrived at the penthouse. Jerome followed Cornelius and Dastan out of the lift, to where Laertius was greeting a tall Aboriginal looking woman. He bowed over her hand, then kissed her, first on her left, then right cheek.

"Mary, you remember my seconds, Cassius and Rupert?" he said as he drew both men forward to greet the leader of the Melbourne coven.

"I do indeed." She smiled at the two men and greeted them with kisses as well. "It's always good to see you."

Laertius introduced Persephone and Mary asked after her father, Yanni, before turning to the Donati. Her face morphed from a smile for the others, to a frown for them.

"And these are my Donati friends I was telling you about. Signore Cornelius Rossini, his partner Dastan, and his great grandson Jerome Rossini." Laertius bowed again, indicating to the three men to do the same.

Jerome was slightly startled when he heard Laertius use his great grandfather's last name for him as well. He'd only just decided a couple of days ago to revert to his mother's last name and was in the process of changing his name legally to Rossini. But it was typical of Laertius, most likely through Persephone, to be up to date with details.

"Though I am happy to meet you, Signore Rossini, and your companions, I am not happy about the trouble that has landed on our shores." Mary glared at him for a moment, then sighed. "However, I do appreciate that it is not your fault, and that you are as caught up in proceedings as we are."

Mary motioned them into the penthouse proper, where about twenty other vampires were waiting for them.

"My coven." Mary indicated with her hand. "These are the Donati visitors from the United States. We wish them welcome in our home."

Jerome smiled and he, Cornelius and Dastan were greeted and offered drinks and food. Though vampires drank blood to survive, they also ate food. He watched as Cassius, Rupert and Laertius circled the room, greeting old friends and catching up on gossip. Persephone wandered over to Jerome.

"That went better than it could have," she observed. "I got the picture from speaking to Mary's seneschal earlier that she was less than pleased about the circumstances for your visit. Laertius spoke to her this afternoon, and she appears to have accepted that you and your family are in no way to blame."

"I can understand her being upset. Laertius too," Jerome replied. "Though I'd be hard pushed to understand if she blamed Cornelius for the happenings over which he has no control."

"Indeed, young Rossini." A small African man had approached them whilst they had been speaking.

"I'm sorry," Jerome replied. "I meant no insult."

The man smiled and reached out his hand, "My

name is Tochukwu Eneh. You may call me Tock, as many of my friends here do."

Jerome took his hand and introduced himself properly.

"Are you enjoying your visit to Australia?" Tock asked as they followed Mary's signal to gather round her in the main room of the penthouse.

"Very much so," Jerome answered.

Cornelius watched his great grandson carefully, in case he needed to intervene. He was used to Donati politics, and vampire ones were just as convoluted, but Jerome was still learning. He seemed to be doing okay, so he turned his attention once more to Mary.

"Welcome to the Donati, friends of Laertius our fellow coven leader from Sydney. Please, feel at home here." She continued, "It was with a heavy heart that I spoke with Laertius a couple of weeks ago about the treachery within his own coven. I heard with sorrow of the turning of the young man Jack, one of my own people. It's sad that he might not have been able to give being turned more thought. I held my own coven meeting after I heard that Ciccone and Fenton had been seen in Melbourne, talking to both Donati and some known Striga. I had hoped that we had missed the sorrow seen within Laertius's coven, but that was not to be."

She bowed her head then looked up and asked her seconds – Tock, and an androgynous young person with long black hair – to join her. Though they looked young, as vampires they could have been far older.

"Tock and Avon here were able to find that several of our vampires, particularly our younger members, had been approached by both Fenton and Ciccone, to join with them in rebellion against the covens. Two of our members and their human servants were discovered to have been swayed with their arguments. They had made commitments to help in an attack on our coven, similar to that which Laertius's suffered. However, we were able to stop them before this could happen. The two vampires and their human servants have been dealt with."

Cornelius listened, saddened that a second Australian coven had been disturbed by this. He knew that the vampires had more than likely been killed as there was no way a coven such as this would allow them to live. He moved into the centre of the room.

"Thank you for allowing us to attend your coven meeting, Mary," he began. "I spoke with my son Jacoby a short while ago, to warn him of what was happening here in Australia. He told me that he had received reports of covens being infiltrated from as far afield as Amsterdam to Botswana. Donati resources have been set aside to help any coven that comes under attack. Now that we know what is happening, the Donati Council has been contacting as many vampire covens that they know of, to warn them to be on the lookout."

"Thank you, Cornelius. I remember your son from his visit here a few years ago. Now that we know what is happening, we are in a better position to protect our younger vampires who may be tempted by what Ciccone and Fenton are offering. Many of them were swayed with the promise of more control over their local covens, forcing out the old guard. We have cleaned our houses, and put into practice procedures, where discontented younger vampires can explore any issues they have with the establishment. Hopefully we have nipped this in the bud. However, I believe that several vampires from other covens in Australia and further afield have already been recruited by Fenton. To what end we don't as yet completely know."

"I have been giving this much thought." Dastan stepped forward. "Donati as a whole are a peaceful people, we get on well with human and vampire society alike. Our common enemy has always been the Striga. It is my opinion that Fenton allied himself with the Striga to try and increase his meagre gift of persuasion, which he inherited from his mother. By becoming Striga himself he has, it seems, succeeded where many others have failed. In the several years we have known about him, he has not succumbed to the blood lust. We do know that he has been working with Mario Ciccone for over ten years now. Ciccone's work as a defence attorney for some of the less salubrious, but rich, members of society, put him in Fenton's sight. Ten years ago, they kidnapped Ciccone's own son, Jerome here, in a mad scheme to first turn him against his father, then when Ciccone 'rescued' him, to make him their dupe. Fortunately for all of us, our niece Beatrice and her husband Theo managed to extract him from his captivity and thwart their plans."

Dastan stopped and glanced at Jerome, who only smiled at him. Jerome picked up where Dastan left off. "It would probably have worked, at least partially. I always adored my father when I was growing up and his betrayal affected me deeply. I suffered more at Fenton's hands than Ciccone expected, and even if he had succeeded in 'rescuing' me, I would have found a way to get out of his clutches. By leaving when I did and joining the army under an assumed name, I was able to get away from them. When Cornelius and Dastan found me again, I was lucky that Beatrice was with them and able to help me with my memories, whose deterioration were beginning to affect me badly."

Jerome quietened, his face bright red, embarrassed by what he had just shared with the coven. Tock reached over and patted his shoulder lightly in support, and Persephone found his hand and squeezed it in sympathy.

"Thank you, Jerome. Thank you for your frank explanation of your experiences at the hands of the man you called Father, and the Striga, Fenton. I believe it is becoming clearer that Ciccone and Fenton are trying to set off a complete upheaval of the current status quo, with themselves slated to become the leaders of what comes afterwards. A society which would be more conducive to their machinations, than what we now have."

Laertius stepped forward for the first time. "I agree, Mary. Which is why Cassius, Rupert and myself have decided to travel back to New York with Cornelius and his family. We feel that if we are to stop this upheaval in its tracks, then we need to be on the ground in New York."

Cornelius raised his head at that. This was the first time he had heard this, and he was grateful for the support.

"Thank you, Laertius. That news is more than welcome."

Laertius bowed to Cornelius. "Just like old times, eh Corny?"

Dastan laughed. He knew how much his partner hated that old nickname.

"Mary, may I ask a boon of you?" Dastan asked.

"I would like to sit down with Tock and Avon and see if I can read any memories they may have of what your vampires told them about Ciccone and Fenton."

"That would be entirely up to Tock and Avon. I have no objections."

Tock smiled at them and agreed, Avon looked up and pushed their long hair behind one ear, "I have no objections either, Donati."

"Good." Mary smiled. "When will you leave for New York?"

Just then there was a loud banging on the penthouse door. Mary and Tock looked at each other, just as Harley, her seneschal went over to the door. He looked through the peephole.

"It's Danzig!" he cried, opening the door.

Mary shouted at him to stop, but she was too late. A hand pushed its way through the door and Harley was stabbed in the stomach, with the knife it held. Everyone reacted at once, as pandemonium broke out. Danzig it turned out, was one of the younger vampires they had not been able to find. Harley had a soft spot for him and had been worried about his welfare.

Mary had had her suspicions, which she had yet to share with Harley. She sat on the floor holding her seneschal whilst one of her coven – a doctor – worked to stem the bleeding. Danzig himself was being held down by Avon and Tock. As the doctor encouraged

Harley to stand, smiling in reassurance at him, Mary turned to Dastan and motioned to Danzig.

"Do you think you can get anything from his memories?"

Danzig tried to escape from his captors, but they held him too tightly. What he thought he could achieve by coming to the penthouse, Dastan didn't know.

"I can try," he replied.

Mary nodded at him. "Avon and Tock will subdue him for you."

Dastan nodded and left the room following along with Avon and Tock. In the background, he could hear Mary ordering that the apartment building and underground garage be searched. Dastan touched Cornelius lightly on the shoulder as he went by, needing it to ground himself, before he began work on the rebel vampire.

X

Dastan hadn't returned the night before and Cornelius, who had come back to Laertius's beachfront home with Jerome after midnight, hadn't heard from him until about 3am.

He and Jerome had stayed up waiting, but all Dastan could say was that he was staying the night at Mary's.

"Do we have anywhere we need to be tomorrow night, I mean tonight?" Jerome asked him.

"No, nothing. I thought we'd have a quiet dinner – want to come with me to Coles to get some groceries?"

"Exciting!" he replied. "I'll come with you, if only to be doing something normal for a change, but I promised to take Persephone out for dinner tonight before she returns to Sydney in the morning."

Cornelius smiled. "I'm glad you're getting on well with her, it's a pity she's not coming straight back to New York with us."

"She has a family thing this weekend, but Laertius has arranged for her to come out after that. She's a great girl," he ended lamely.

Cornelius reached over and hugged his great grandson. He was really pleased that his true personality was beginning to shine through and delighted in how different he was from that haggard-looking, depressed ex-serviceman he and Dastan had found in the alley in New York.

"Where are you going tonight?" he asked.

"Persephone's cousins here have recommended Shadowfax Winery up the road at Hopper's Crossing." Jerome grinned. "They have some weird name places here!"

"You've obviously never been to the UK. Talk about weird place names, you've not heard many yet – Wetwang, Upper Sodbury, Lower Sodbury... I could go on but won't. I'll let you discover them for yourself when you visit."

Jerome laughed. It felt great to have these times with his Nonno, he really felt as though he had connected with him.

"Come on," Cornelius said. "Dastan won't be back until later today. We might as well get some sleep."

Jerome yawned and agreed.

The two men separated with a hug at Jerome's bedroom door.

The day was quiet. The promised trip to the nearest Coles went off without incident and Cornelius went for a walk, leaving Jerome to have a nap. He still got tired sometimes after the car accident and his continuing physiotherapy.

Cornelius returned in the late afternoon. He was laughing about an old man he'd met down by the bay. Eddie lived in the caravan park near Laertius's house, and was a bit of a talker. He was from London originally and though he'd lived in Australia for over forty-five years, he still had his London accent.

Cornelius had enjoyed reminiscing about the city with Eddie and had promised to call in and meet his wife Patty, before they left for New York.

Jerome smiled. This was typical of his Nonno, he could get on with anyone and was willing to spend time getting to know them, even nosy old men he met by the bay.

Dastan returned just before Jerome was due to leave for his date with Persephone. He looked tired and drained and smiled at Jerome's concern for him, before retiring to his and Cornelius's room, with his partner, to get some much needed sleep. He promised to share what he had learned from Danzig and some of the other vampires when he'd had time to process everything.

Laertius, Cassius and Rupert had gone with Tock to Danzig's apartment to pick up his laptop and search the place for clues.

Jerome said goodbye and got in the Hyundai car he'd hired the previous day, leaving the SUV for Cornelius and Dastan. He input the address of Shadowfax Winery into the GPS and followed the instructions.

He had wanted to pick Persephone up from her cousins, but she'd wanted to travel separately as she was headed to Tullamarine airport straight from their date to stay in an airport hotel, as her flight to Sydney was at 7am the next morning.

When he arrived, Jerome was impressed by the winery grounds. The winding drive up to the restaurant and winery buildings was beautiful. He saw many local birds flying around as he parked and walked over to where Persephone was waiting for him.

He pulled her into a hug, giving her a kiss on the cheek in greeting, when he reached her.

"Hi." She smiled at him shyly. That was new, she'd never been shy with him before.

"All ready for the morning?" he asked as he guided her towards the front door, his hand on the small of her back.

"Yep, not looking forward to getting up 5am to get my flight, but…"

They arrived at the hostess's podium and were quickly shown to their seats with menus for food and wine. Tempted by the house wine, Jerome ordered a bottle for them to share, then he ordered steak and Persephone decided on a crab salad.

Their conversation was wide ranging, sharing their favourite music and books. Persephone laughed when she found that they both shared a fondness for Japanese manga, and they spent some time discussing their favourites.

"I've had a great time," Jerome said as they perused the dessert menu. "I'd love to do this again when you're in New York."

"I'd love that," she replied, with a gleam in her eye. Jerome leaned in closer and took her hand.

"I'd really like to get to know you better," he said, his heart beating faster and butterflies fluttering around in his stomach. He thought she was gorgeous with her high cheekbones, long blonde hair and olive skin. What she saw in him, he didn't know.

"It's not been a great few weeks," she said. "But

one of the best things to come out of it has been meeting you. I really feel we've connected."

Jerome reached across the table to hold her hand in both of his and smiled at her, completely smitten. They were interrupted by their waiter who asked if they wanted dessert. Both of them declined, and Jerome asked for the bill.

"We go back to New York day after tomorrow," Jerome said. "When do you think you'll be free to follow us? I can't wait to introduce you to the rest of my family."

Persephone laughed. "I'm not sure. Laertius is dealing with the details, next week probably. You're close to your family?"

"Not until recently," he replied. "I was estranged from my paternal family for quite some time and have only just begun reconnecting. I think you'll like my step-sister Verity, she's a strong woman. My half-brother Roman is still young. I didn't realise how much he had missed me when I was gone. My cousin Beatrice, Nonno's niece, is my favourite though. She has done so much for me…" His voice broke off and it was Persephone's turn to reach across and offer him comfort.

"I hate to say it, but I should go," she said, smiling across the table at him. "It's already gone eleven and I need to be up early."

Jerome stood up and held her chair out for her.

He led the way out of the restaurant. Persephone's car was parked further away than Jerome's, so he walked her to her car holding her hand, a smile playing about his lips. As they got to the car, he turned round and took her into his arms, leaning down to kiss her softly on her lips. She felt warm and inviting in his arms. He raised his head to smile at her and she lifted her lips back towards his. Taking the invite, he kissed her deeper, nibbling on her lips, before stepping back and taking a deep breath.

"I'll miss you," she said, before opening her car and getting into the driver's seat.

Jerome waved at her, watching her put her seat belt on, before he began walking towards his own car. As he did so he felt a wave of heat and heard a loud bang as Persephone's car exploded in a rain of fire. He was sent flying into the air and landed several feet away, skidding along on his back on the asphalt, his head bouncing off the pavement a few times. Shaking his head, he winced at the pain as he tried to sit up. His ears were ringing and his heart thundering as he looked in disbelief at where the car had been.

Just then, several people came running from the restaurant. Some of them screaming in shock. Jerome sat up slowly, still trying to take in what had happened to him. He looked on with incomprehension as the car Persephone had just got into burned and smoked.

He couldn't believe it, just a few seconds ago he was kissing her…

One of the people who had come out of the restaurant came running up to him. "My name's Tom, I'm a paramedic," he said, already beginning to assess Jerome for injuries. "My wife has phoned the emergency services."

Jerome could only stare at where Persephone's car had been just moments before. The paramedic was checking his eyes and feeling round the back of his head for any contusions.

"My phone." Jerome finally blinked out of his stupor.

Tom helped him sit up further and Jerome fumbled for his phone in his trouser pocket, thankful when he pulled it out that it was still working. Hardly taking his eyes off the burning car, he punched in Cornelius's number.

"Nonno!" he fairly shouted, when Cornelius answered.

"Jerome, what's up?" Cornelius replied instantly.

"I need you. Please…"

Dastan drove the SUV fast through the open countryside, until they reached Shadowfax Winery and Restaurant.

He and Cornelius were worried for Jerome and didn't know what had happened.

As they got closer to the winery, they could see the flashing lights of the local police and fire engines, and more ominously a plume of blackish smoke rising above the car park.

Dastan pulled the car to a screeching halt and they both leapt out, searching the crowd for Jerome.

Cornelius grabbed Dastan's hand as he spotted Jerome sitting on the ground with a paramedic knelt next to him, a blanket around his shoulders.

There was no sign of Persephone.

"Jerome!" Cornelius knelt down next to him. "What happened?"

"Nonno," was all Jerome could manage as he buried himself in his great grandfather's embrace.

Cornelius looked up at the paramedic who had sympathy in his eyes.

"My name's Tom," he introduced himself. "I was here with my wife having dinner when the young lady's car exploded, and Jerome was flung backwards several feet."

Cornelius gasped. "Persephone?"

Tom sighed and shook his head. "Jerome is okay, shock mostly, and a knock on his head. He's lucky he hasn't gotten a concussion. I was just getting my colleagues to check him out, but he didn't want me to leave."

The young man touched Jerome's hand in sympathy as a young woman with a pixie cut and blue eyes came up behind him.

"We have to go, Tom," she said. "The sitter can't stay much longer."

Tom nodded. "Your granddad's here now, mate. You going to be okay?"

Jerome brought his head up from Cornelius's shoulder and nodded. "Yes. Thanks, Tom."

He looked up at the woman at Tom's shoulder. "Thank you for your help."

She nodded as Tom stood up. Holding hands, they moved away to see if their car was okay to drive.

"Can you stand?"

"Yeah, I think so." Jerome took Cornelius's hand and stood up, wincing a little. "I don't suppose there's any chance…"

Dastan put his arm around Jerome's shoulders, he had been chatting with the local police whilst Cornelius took care of Jerome. "I'm sorry, Jerome. She had no chance of surviving that. The police were surprised by the ferocity of the explosion. The detective in charge would like to take your statement, then we can take you back. We'll have to contact Laertius. I don't know how he's going to take this."

"We're about to find out." Cornelius pointed to where Laertius, Cassius and Rupert were just getting out of the SUV.

Laertius's face was grim as he walked over to them. Cassius and Rupert wore similar expressions and were supporting Laertius by holding his hands.

"Jerome," he said when he reached them. "What happened?"

Jerome explained about the explosion, about how he had just put Persephone in her car and was walking away from it when the car exploded. The police detective Dastan had spoken to had said the bomb had been wired to the starter key.

Laertius looked pale, even for a vampire, and his eyes were red where he had obviously been crying. Rupert leaned over and whispered something in his ear and he straightened, turning as the detective in charge reached them.

She held her hand out to Jerome first, then the others. "Detective Chloe Anderson from Hoppers Crossing. Can you tell me what happened?"

Jerome repeated his story. She asked him a few questions then turned to the others. "And you are?"

"Her employer," Laertius answered, he rattled off his name and address in Sydney. "Persephone was my personal assistant, but more importantly than that, she was family."

"Can you think of anyone who would want to hurt her or her family?" she asked, her notebook at the ready.

"No," Laertius lied. There was no point in going

into vampire politics with a police detective. If she'd been Donati he might have shared something, but she wasn't, and he wasn't going to share any info he had.

"Are you sure?" She turned to Jerome next. "Could the bomb have been meant for you?"

Jerome jumped. He hadn't even thought about that. He stared at her in confusion, before Cornelius intervened.

"I'm not sure what you're getting at, Detective," he said. "Persephone and Jerome have only known each other for a few weeks and though they've gotten along, this was their first date. I'm not sure anyone would know of a relationship between them, nor why anyone would want to attack them."

Detective Anderson nodded and sighed.

"Okay, we checked this young man's car out as well, and there's nothing there. We'll follow up with her family, who I understand live in Sydney?"

Laertius nodded. "Yes, I can give you her father's contact details. We will be taking her body back home to be buried, when your medical examiner releases her."

"And you?" She turned to Jerome, Cornelius and Dastan.

"We're due to return to New York in the next couple of days," Cornelius said. "But we will return to Sydney with Laertius for the funeral before we go back to the States."

"I will send you our contact details," Dastan told her.

Reaching for his phone and using the number off the business card she gave him, he sent her their address in Sydney. As an afterthought, he gave her their PO box in New York and Shea's phone number.

"Our steward Shea O'Malley knows where we are at all times and can get in touch with us as and when needed."

Detective Anderson nodded her head at them, then wandered off to talk to the fire brigade and her colleagues.

Laertius drew in a deep breath. "When I find out who's responsible for this, there'll be nothing left of them to bury," he fumed.

"There's nothing we can do here," Rupert said as he put his arm around Laertius and leaned into the older vampire.

"I will go with her to the morgue," Cassius spoke up. "One of us should be with her."

Laertius nodded. "Thank you. I need to let her family know. Rupert and I will be at the town house if you need us."

Cassius nodded then leaned in and gave each of his lovers a kiss. "I'll take the SUV Dastan and Cornelius used. Jerome's car is part of the crime scene yet awhile. I'll leave our SUV for you and the others to use."

Jerome winced as Laertius nodded again. This was the first time he'd seen Laertius this broken up about anything, even the betrayal of some of his coven hadn't affected him this deeply.

He followed them to the large SUV and in a daze got in the back seat with Cornelius and Dastan. Rupert drove with Laertius in the passenger seat. Jerome lost track of where they were and only really came back to himself again when Dastan helped him out of the car and into the town house. It was gone midnight and he allowed himself to be led to the guest room he was using, then got ready for bed.

Once Dastan and Cornelius left him to himself, he laid on his bed looking up at the ceiling, his mind whirling. He wasn't sure he was going to sleep. He mourned Persephone. He mourned the lost opportunity of getting to know the fun-loving young woman even more, maybe falling in love with her. He didn't know if it would have gone that far, but he had been looking forward to finding out.

Sitting up he reached for his phone, which was plugged in by his bedside to recharge, and pushed the contact for Beatrice on FaceTime. She answered almost immediately and he knew Cornelius must have already been in touch with her.

"Oh, Jerome," she answered looking at his blotchy face from where he had been crying. "I'm so sorry."

"Bea…" He sobbed.

"Shh," she replied. "It'll be okay."

He stayed on the phone with her for an hour before he eventually settled down enough to sleep. With promises to see each other soon, he drifted off, thinking of the might've beens and possibilities that he and Persephone had been denied.

PART III

I

Beatrice sat on the sofa in her cousin Jacoby's office. She sipped at the glass of cold white wine he'd procured for her, the flavours bursting over her tongue. She watched her cousin as he sat at his desk checking emails, and reflected on the boy he'd been.

They had grown up together, first in Paris and then in London. It had been the two of them against the world. Until he had taken a job with the Donati Council in London, then moved to Washington DC. He had married an American girl, Emmie, whom Beatrice had loved as a sister. Her peaches and cream complexion was a stark contract to Jacoby's olive, swarthy skin and dark brown eyes. Their daughter, Sherwood, had inherited her mother's complexion and their grandson, Jerome, benefited from it as well.

She sighed, thinking of Jerome. She put her glass

down on the coffee table in front of her. That boy had been through so much in the last few years and now to lose Persephone – a girl Jerome had confessed he was beginning to fall in love with. It was almost too much. But Jacoby seemed indifferent to his grandson's plight. It was as though he wasn't interested in the young man, despite him being all he had left of Emmie.

When Emmie had first disappeared just after Sherwood's birth, Beatrice had grieved for her lost friend while witnessing her cousin's heartbreak. Jacoby had taken a short break from the Council, before returning with a grim smile in place and a determination to help other Donati. Emmie had been suffering from post-natal depression and her disappearance was out of character. Even now, over seventy years later, Beatrice wondered what had happened to her friend. Was she alive, dead, lost her memory? She didn't know, though the memory of Emmie and her loss had kept Jacoby from having a proper relationship with his daughter. It looked like that separation was happening with Jerome, as well.

Jacoby had been horrified about Sherwood's affair with Mario Ciccone, and had not been interested in meeting the child of that relationship. His father, had taken to visiting Sherwood and the young Jerome, until his granddaughter was killed in an accident. Jacoby had shrugged his shoulders when Ciccone had claimed his son to bring up. He'd kept a discrete eye on them to begin with, but he'd shown no concern when the boy went missing. It had been as though time were repeating itself.

Beatrice had somewhat taken Jerome under her wing and today would be the first time that Jacoby, the young boy she'd played with and loved long gone, would be meeting his grandson as an adult. She picked her glass up again and sipped, enjoying the fruitiness of the wine. It would be interesting to see how the meeting would go. It was one of the reasons why she had left the Redoubt early that morning to reach Washington DC and Jacoby's office, before the arrival of the travellers.

She lifted her glass in a toast to her cousin. "Good vintage. Thanks Jax, for thinking of me."

Jacoby's lips twitched in a semblance of a smile at her comment, and the use of his old childhood name.

"I know how much you like a good white," he replied, then stiffened in his seat.

Beatrice leaned forward. "Jacoby?"

"Security just messaged me to say my father and Dastan are here. Jerome is with them. Security are sending them up."

Beatrice nodded and got up from the sofa to stand by Jacoby's desk. She wanted to show solidarity with her cousin but be ready in case Jerome needed her.

There was a ping from the corridor as the elevator

arrived and she could hear the sound of footsteps as they made their way towards them. Cornelius was first through the door and Beatrice stepped forward to hug her uncle and welcome him home. She snagged Dastan as well, placing a kiss on his cheek and giving him a quick hug before turning to Jerome.

He looked... tired. That was the only thing she could think of. His eyes were filled with sadness and he had dark bags under them.

"Oh, Jerome." She pulled him into a full body hug and held on until she felt him relax a bit. "I am so, so, sorry."

Jerome's head was buried in her neck, but he nodded. It seemed he wasn't ready to give up her hug just yet, as though he needed her physical presence to help ground him. A moment later, he looked up at her and offered a small smile.

"It's good to see you, Bea, and to be back."

Beatrice took his hand and led him over to the sofa she had been sitting on earlier. Jacoby was talking to his father and Dastan, who were clustered around his desk. The two older men also looked tired, but they didn't look as worn out as Jerome did. She seated Jerome, then popped her head out of her brother's office looking for his PA, Marcus. Spotting him, she asked if he would bring coffee and refreshments to Jacoby's office. He nodded.

Returning to Jerome, she could see that he was

watching his grandfather. No one had, as yet, introduced them. She smiled at him and turned to the three men at the other end of the office.

"Marcus should be here in a moment with refreshments for you all. Jacoby, don't you want to come meet Jerome? After all, you've not seen him since he was a baby." She smiled at them all, but her eyes were narrowed at her cousin. He was putting this meeting off and making Jerome self-conscious.

"Yes, I'm sorry. Where are my manners?" Jacoby smiled at Beatrice and Jerome, but it didn't reach his eyes. It wasn't really the smile one gave on meeting one's grandson after a nearly thirty year separation.

Jacoby held out his hand for Jerome to shake, but he didn't offer to pull the younger man into a hug as Beatrice had, or as he had with his father and Dastan. Still, she reasoned, he hadn't seen him since he was a child.

Jerome for his part smiled at his grandfather and squeezed his hand in greeting. "You look nothing like I imagined. I thought you'd be more like Nonno, or my mother."

Jacoby grimaced as Jerome used the Italian word for grandfather, for Cornelius. Beatrice knew their relationship was close but obviously Jacoby hadn't picked up on it.

"No, I take after my mother, Elise," he replied

stiffly, just as Marcus entered the room with a tray of coffee and sandwiches on it.

"Please…" Jacoby motioned them all over to the conference table at the other end of his office. Marcus was busy setting up the food, and Jacoby used the distraction to move away from Jerome. Beatrice frowned. She saw from the look on Jerome's face that he had expected more of an emotional connection to Jacoby, like he had with Cornelius. She caught her uncle's eye and he stepped up, putting his arm around Jerome and drawing him to the table.

"Thanks, Jacoby." He indicated the refreshments. "It was a long flight, even in first class. And when you're already bone tired and weary, having that extra luxury still doesn't help with sleep."

"Yes, I'm sorry, Papa," Jacoby replied. "I should have asked how you were. We were all shocked to hear of the explosion."

Cornelius nodded his head, and Jerome busied himself with pouring coffee for himself and Beatrice.

Turning to his grandson for the first time, Jacoby bowed his head. "My condolences. I know what it's like to lose someone you love."

Beatrice was pleased at Jacoby's empathy with his grandson. She drew Jerome closer towards herself as she settled into a chair at the table. They all took a seat and shared in the sandwiches and coffee. Light conversations struck up around the table. Talk of the weather in Sydney, the beaches and the food. Nothing was mentioned about what had taken them to Australia, nor what had happened there, until they had finished their impromptu meal.

Jacoby finally turned to his father. "I was expecting at least Laertius, if not his seconds."

Cornelius smiled wearily at his son. "Laertius, Rupert and Cassius still had some business to clear up in Sydney after the death of Persephone and… well, supporting her father and their family. The funeral was gruelling, a full Greek Orthodox Mass, followed by a burial in the graveyard. Her family were distraught."

"I can imagine, poor Yanni." Beatrice smiled at Jerome in sympathy.

"When can I expect them?" Jacoby continued, almost as if his father hadn't spoken. "There is much we need to discuss."

Cornelius sighed. "They were hoping to catch a flight out day after tomorrow. They should be here by Friday."

Jacoby sighed as though the whole thing was done to annoy him.

Beatrice smiled at her cousin, he reminded her of nothing else but his grumpiness when he was a teenager. Really, he hadn't changed that much.

"It will give us time to prepare for him," she said. "I take it they will be staying with us at the Redoubt?"

"Yes, there is plenty of room there," her uncle replied. "We should head there after this meeting."

The others nodded and Beatrice could see that Jerome was keeping silent, throwing wary glances at Jacoby from time to time.

"We head there next then," she said. "Jacoby, will you be joining us?"

"No," her cousin replied, standing. "I still have work to do here. I'll meet you there when the others arrive."

Beatrice nodded and began organising the other three men to get ready to leave. Cornelius smiled at his niece and kissed her cheek.

"Always looking out for us," he smiled at her. "Jacoby." He extended his hand to his son for one final shake before leaving the office.

II

Jerome sat in the front passenger seat of Beatrice's compact car. Dastan was driving, whilst Beatrice and Cornelius carried out a quiet conversation in the back seat. He was glad to be back in the US, but a bit weirded out about the 'non-event' his meeting with his grandfather, Jacoby, had been. Cornelius had always been warm and welcoming, right from that moment in the alley, but Jacoby... Jerome hadn't really got any sense they were related at all, least of all that he was his mother's father.

He sighed, and Dastan turned towards him.

"Still tired?"

"Some. Dastan, what... Jacoby, I..." he stammered. "It's weird, Mom hardly talked about her dad at all. She said they didn't really get on that well and that she didn't think he was cut out to be a family

257

man. I guess I didn't really get what she meant until today."

"I know. He couldn't be any different from Cornelius if he tried. I… Neely says that he takes after Elise's family. That her parents were more restrained, cold, almost. I wouldn't take it to heart."

"No, it's not that; well, not all of it. It's just that he didn't seem invested in us, in any of us."

"He's been like that since he was a boy," Beatrice replied from the back seat, leaning forward to speak to Jerome. "He was always closed off, more so after Aunt Elise died." She laughed. "I could usually get him to lighten up a bit. He would follow me into my escapades, some of the time."

"You were a little troublemaker." Jerome could hear the smile in Cornelius's voice, but could also tell that his Nonno was almost asleep.

He turned his head back to the passenger window and watched the traffic and the headlights go by. His right hand tightly gripped the seat underneath him; he still had issues getting in a car after the crash in Sydney.

He forced himself to relax. Dastan was a good driver and used to this road between Washington DC and New York. He watched him for a while, marvelling at how well he fitted in with Cornelius, a match that just worked.

It was all quiet in the back seat before Jerome

spoke to Dastan again. "Did you meet her? My grandmother, I mean?"

"Emmie? Or Emmaline as her family called her. Yes, I met her. Neely and I had not been together more than ten years when Jacoby met her in 1920s London, at a party. Emmie was bright and beautiful, and full of life. She was studying at Cambridge but had come to London with one of her fellow students, who had family there. She and Jacoby hit it off straightaway. Her vivacity and his quietness, it shouldn't have worked, but they just seemed to fit somehow."

"She was American? I remember Beatrice mentioning that."

"Yes, from Connecticut. She was born in the town of Hartford, at the turn of the twentieth century. Jacoby was older than her – about fifty years, I think. She'd won a scholarship to attend Cambridge. She was studying chemistry and science, and had been part of a group of women scholars who were taking the academic world by storm. After she met Jacoby, she quietened down a bit. Her parents were pleased by this, they thought she'd never find anyone to marry. You have to remember that even amongst the Donati, at that time, a woman's *raison d'être* was to marry and marry well. Jacoby was considered quite the catch."

Jerome shook his head. He couldn't quite match the man he'd met that afternoon with one who could sweep a bookish, bright, energetic young woman off her feet. His mother had never mentioned her own mother, but then, she'd never met her. Emmie had disappeared when she was a baby.

Dastan smoothly pulled out and overtook a large truck, and Jerome found himself gripping the seat again. Dastan noticed and patted his left leg as he swiftly and competently moved back into the right lane.

"It's okay," he said, smiling at Jerome. "It'll go eventually. I remember once, years ago now, when Neely and I lived in Paris in the 1950s, we got into a terrible accident on the city's streets. Several people died, and we were both lucky to get away with fairly minor injuries. For weeks afterwards though, every time I got in a car, I could hear the screech of metal and smell the stink of oil mixed with blood."

Dastan shuddered. "I still remember it now. There were few seat belts in those days and several people had been flung through their windscreens. We were lucky we were going fairly slowly."

Jerome reached over and patted Dastan's arm. "I... just sometimes, I see that fucking truck coming at us again, knowing we didn't have time to react."

Jerome settled back in his seat again as the traffic quietened down.

"If Jacoby and Emmie met in the 1920s, it must

have been some time before my mother was born? I think I remember her saying she was born in the 50s."

Dastan accepted the change of subject and answered Jerome's question. "Yes, 1952 to be precise. Jacoby and Emmie were very happy. They'd married just before the outbreak of World War Two. They stayed in London throughout, though they could have relocated back to New York. Both worked for the Brits during the war at their code breaking station, Bletchley Park, for a while. Then they moved into intelligence for the rest of the war. Jacoby was even once parachuted into France when it was under Nazi occupation. He had contacts all over the country, not all of them fellow Donati. Emmie was in France for a while as well, in '44 I think, but no-one knew what she was doing. She would never talk about it."

"Wow, I never knew any of that."

"Things changed after the end of the war. Emmie decided that she wanted children and Jacoby wasn't keen. They argued about it endlessly, and some of the light went out of her eyes. She even left him for a while, came to stay with me and Neely when we were living in Carcassonne. She had family there. Eventually though, she went back to him and the next we heard was that she was expecting your mother. They appeared happy for a time." He went on, happy to be able to share what he knew with Jerome. "Emmie doted on Sherwood, and even Jacoby cracked a smile at his daughter's baby antics for a while. Then Emmie disappeared. We didn't know this, but she had been suffering from post-natal depression ever since Sherwood had been born. She was convinced Jacoby meant her ill and was determined to keep him away from the baby. One day we got a frantic phone call from Sherwood's other grandparents asking if we had seen Emmie. They were visiting with Jacoby and Emmie and she had left Sherwood with them whilst she was running errands. She never returned."

"That's awful for Jacoby, and Emmie's parents. What happened? Did she die?"

Dastan turned to look at him, before returning to watching the road. "No-one knows. She never returned, no body was found and gradually life returned to normal. Jacoby employed a nanny to look after Sherwood. Emmie's parents offered to take her, to bring her up, but he refused. They live in rural Connecticut now, and they lost all touch with Sherwood and Jacoby."

"They're still alive?"

"Yes, they're Donati too. Maybe… maybe when this is all over, you'd like to visit them? I'm sure they'd love to meet you."

Jerome shook his head. "I'm not sure. Maybe."

"It's okay, there's no rush."

Jerome must have fallen asleep after his talk with Dastan. The next he knew he was being gently shaken awake by Cornelius, who was kneeling outside his passenger door.

"Hey there, sleepy head."

"Sleepy head yourself," he replied, somewhat grumpily. He hadn't been the only one to fall asleep on the journey.

Cornelius laughed. "Too true," he said.

"Where are we?"

"Nearly at the Redoubt, but we have to get out here and go through one of the other entrances. I don't want anyone possibly finding its location through our laxity."

Jerome slowly got out of the car and stretched. Before they'd left Jacoby's high rise office building, they had gone over the car with a fine tooth comb, checking to see if there were any bugs or tracking devices. They hadn't found any, but they still needed to be wary.

"Catch some sleep?" Beatrice smiled at him. "I know I did. I thought I heard you and Dastan talking about Emmie?"

"A bit." He didn't want to say more than that. There was still a lot to take in of what Dastan had told him. He needed time to digest it.

"If you want to talk, I'm here as well. I was with them for some of that period, so if you have any questions, let me know."

"Thanks Bea. Really, thank you."

Beatrice nodded and went round to the trunk of the car to help Cornelius pull their luggage out. They appeared to be in an underground parking lot of some kind. Dastan was over in one corner pulling a tarpaulin off something.

"Jerome," he called out. "Come here and help me with this."

Jerome did as he was asked and found that Dastan was pulling the tarp from what looked like a golf cart, with a trolley attached. He arched an eyebrow at him as he helped with removing the tarp, before stowing their luggage in the trolley.

"Not quite what you had in mind when I said we had to change modes of transport?" Cornelius laughed, pulling him close.

"You surprise me every time, Nonno," he replied.

Once they were all situated, Cornelius walked in front of them until he came to a metal doorway. He reached into a compartment next to the door and pulled some kind of lever.

Silently, the door slid open and Dastan drove the cart in and waited whilst Cornelius closed the door then joined them.

"Not long now." Beatrice smiled at Jerome.

"About another ten minutes and we can get showers, food and some rest."

Jerome smiled back. He was ready for rest, despite his sleep in the car. His nights had been disturbed recently and the time change coming back to the US from Australia had thrown him for a loop again.

They travelled down a long corridor just wide enough for the golf cart and trolley to fit through, until they came to another door. This one opened automatically and they drove through to find Shea waiting for them.

"Shea," Cornelius greeted him. "Good to see you."

"Welcome back," the other man replied. "Though I'm afraid I've got some bad news."

Jerome's heart sank. More bad news!

"Lilah is missing," Shea said, turning to look at Jerome. "I'm sorry Jerome, your step-mother has been gone since yesterday morning."

III

Jerome's head was spinning. "What? Why didn't you phone us?"

"You were busy with Jacoby, then on your way home." Shea sighed. "It seemed best to wait until you got back. I'm sorry."

Jerome shook his head, it wasn't Shea's fault. "What happened?"

"Lilah went missing yesterday morning and hasn't been seen since," Shea reported. "I've reviewed the security recordings and she slipped out by the east corridor door."

"How?"

"It's my fault," Shea admitted, his cheeks glowing red. "I wanted everyone to know at least one exit, and that one's the easiest to access. Verity and Roman know about it as well. After breakfast yesterday, she retired to the sitting room to read, as she has been doing every morning for the last few weeks. Next thing I knew Roman was in the kitchen, where I was preparing dinner, and asking if I'd seen his mother."

The older man looked distraught. There were stress lines around his eyes as he tried to deal with losing Lilah on his watch.

"It's okay, Shea." Cornelius gripped his shoulder. "You couldn't have known she was going to leave like that. How long after she'd gone was her disappearance found?"

"Several hours, I'm afraid. It was only when Roman went looking for his mother that we realised she was missing. He and Verity are completely stressed out about it."

"Where are they now?" Jerome asked, dropping his messenger bag onto the nearest sofa as they moved into the main lounge area. This was not the homecoming he had anticipated.

"Sedated."

A new voice came from the opening through to the bedroom area. Jerome looked up to see a tall, well-built man, his long brown hair pulled back into a ponytail. He bore a striking resemblance to Shea.

"Who are you?" he asked indignantly as he eyed the larger man.

"Jerome." Dastan put his hand on his arm to hold

him back, as he made to approach the man. "This is Donal, Shea's son. He's here to help out."

Jerome shook Dastan's hand off. He wasn't ready to be placated yet.

"What did you mean when you said they were sedated?" he demanded.

"Jerome…"

"Just that…"

Shea and Donal began speaking at the same time. Donal nodded his head at his father, going to stand by his side.

"Donal was a medic in the US Marines," Shea began. "He has kept his medical training up and is fully qualified to administer–"

"Yeah, yeah, I get that," Jerome interrupted. "I wanna know who gave him permission to sedate my brother and sister."

"They did."

A new voice interjected, and Jerome turned around to find Theo standing in front of him. Bea was tucked under his arm as tight as she could be. She smiled at him in sympathy.

Jerome winced. He knew he was being rude, but it had been a hell of a day… week… He flopped down into the sofa he'd dropped his messenger bag onto moments earlier. Moving it from beneath him with a grunt, he leant forward and put his head into his hands. A moment later he looked up again.

"I'm sorry," he said. "It's been a shitty few weeks and I guess I'm being a shit person."

"No." Cornelius reached out and rubbed his back. "You're just tired, we all are."

Jerome nodded his head slowly and stood up, moving towards Donal. "I'm sorry," he began, holding his hand out. "I'm Jerome Rossini, can we start again?"

Donal laughed, gripping Jerome's hand in a quick pump. "It's okay, I understand."

"I take it Verity and Roman are in bed then?"

"Yes. It was agreed we'd wait for your arrival to see what our next steps will be."

Jerome stretched his neck and then his arms. Dastan and Cornelius had moved away and were talking quietly to Shea in a corner of the large room. Theo and Beatrice announced their intention of going to bed and Jerome could only agree with them. It was gone midnight and he was completely shattered.

"I don't suppose you have any of that sedative left?" he asked Donal with a smirk.

Donal laughed. "A bit. But I have a better suggestion."

He walked over to the wet bar in the corner of the room. Opening the cabinet below, he picked out two highball glasses, pouring two fingers of whiskey into each. Then holding up the ice bucket, he raised his eyebrow. Jerome nodded and Donal added an ice cube into each glass before he walked over and handed one to Jerome.

"Thanks," he said. "I really am sorry."

"Don't worry about it." Donal smiled, sipping his whiskey. Cornelius approached and took a sip from Jerome's glass.

"Hmm, not bad. We're going to bed. Don't stay up too long."

"I don't think I could," Jerome answered. "I'm just going to drink this then go and crash."

Cornelius nodded, turned and followed Dastan to their room. Jerome watched them leave and sat sipping his whiskey.

"Have you known them long?" he asked his companion.

"All my life," Donal replied. "My father was working for Cornelius even before he met Dastan. My mother worked for him for a while as well, but after I was born, she decided she'd rather party than bring up a child." His eyes looked into the distance. "I hardly knew her. She died when I was in my early twenties, during the Second World War in Paris."

"I'm sorry," Jerome answered. "I lost my mother when I was young, but I still remember the pain and sadness."

Donal nodded, then stretched and sighed. "It's been a long day. I'm for bed."

Jerome murmured good night to him, then relaxed back with the whiskey glass balanced on his stomach. He was beginning to fade and knew that if he didn't move soon, he'd end up sleeping on the sofa. Pushing himself up, he wearily grabbed his messenger bag, putting the whiskey glass back on the bar on his way to his room where he flopped down on the bed and groaned. Sleep grabbed him straight away as he idly wondered if Donal had added some sedative to his whiskey after all.

Sleeping in his clothes on top of the bed hadn't been a brilliant decision, Jerome decided the next morning as he stripped off in the bathroom for his shower. He'd been too tired last night to get undressed for bed, and he felt a bit 'off' this morning, but that could just have been the results of the last few weeks.

He turned on the shower and whilst it was warming up, he cleaned his teeth. The shower was the perfect temperature; one thing he could definitely say about living in the Redoubt was that the facilities were top notch. After showering and getting dry, he got dressed in clean clothes. He began feeling more like himself and wandered back into his bedroom, where he found Verity and Roman. They were sitting on the small love seat near the armoire.

Even before he could take a breath to greet his siblings, they rushed him and wrapped their arms around him. He murmured greetings to them and assured them that it would be okay.

"I can't believe she did that," Verity said at last, as she settled on the love seat once more. "It's just so out of character."

"Did she say anything to either of you?" he asked.

"Nothing," Roman answered. "She seemed settled... No, more like, resigned. Resigned that we would have to wait until you and the others got home to see what happened next."

Roman had joined Jerome on the bed and was sitting up against the headboard next to his brother holding his hand, as though he thought he was going to leave him again.

"Shea blames himself," Verity said. "Him and Donal. Kept saying yesterday that he shouldn't have shown her where one of the exits was, that he should have kept a better eye on her. Theo managed to persuade him he wasn't at fault, but you could see it in his eyes that he believed he had let Cornelius and Dastan down."

"It's not his fault," Jerome agreed. "I don't see how he could have anticipated her leaving. She gave no suggestions that she wanted to go?"

Verity shook her head. "She was worried about

273

Lacey of course, we all are. But she was settled. Yes, that's a good word for it."

Roman nodded his head, agreeing with his sister. There was a knock on the door and Donal poked his head round it. "You might want to see this," he said with a grimace. "We've spotted your mom on one of the security cameras."

"What?" Verity was up and out the door before her brothers could join her. Jerome followed at a slower pace. Which security camera? Where?

Donal opened the door to the security room for them. The others were already gathered inside.

"Okay," Cornelius said to Shea, "show everyone what you found."

Shea nodded and after manipulating a few keys he brought up a view of the outside of a large apartment block. "This is where Ciccone is living at the moment," he said. "I've patched into the security camera across the street which keeps an eye on the front door." He pulled up the segment he had been looking for. "This was taken at 5pm yesterday."

They all watched as Lilah stepped out of a cab, paying the driver through the window. Then, appearing to take a deep breath, she turned to the door of the apartment block, entering when the doorman held the door open for her. The view changed to inside the foyer and they watched in horror as one of the elevator doors opened and Mario

Ciccone stepped out. He walked up to his ex-wife and took her hands, pulling her in to kiss her on the cheek. Her white face stood out against the black of his suit as she stiffly returned the kiss on his left cheek. Still holding his hand, she allowed herself to enter the elevator with him.

The security room exploded with loud voices as they all exclaimed over what they'd just seen. Verity was crying, and Bea was holding her, whilst Jerome had Roman.

"I don't understand," Verity sobbed. "Why… why would she go back to that monster?"

"I don't know, Ver," Jerome said as he rubbed circles on Roman's back.

"Any other footage?" Dastan asked Shea.

"No, there are other cameras and security systems in the apartment block, but they are better protected than the one in the foyer, harder to hack."

Jerome sighed. "He must have got to her in some way, played on her fears about Lacey. It's the only reason I can see her going to him."

Cornelius nodded. "We must be ready. She knows where we are. She knows at least one entrance."

"Already on it," Donal spoke up. "I've blocked that entrance. No-one's getting in that way."

"I'll step up the security," Theo said. "Donal, will you join me?"

The two men left the room, talking quietly about access points and air vents.

Jerome watched them go. He looked at the time. "We have to meet Laertius and the others in a few hours."

"Yes." Dastan exchanged a look with Cornelius. "We'll go. Will you stay here, Jerome?"

Jerome nodded. "What can I do?"

"Get everyone ready to leave. If we have to abandon the Redoubt, it will be on a moment's notice. I don't think we will just yet, but Lilah obviously knows where we are."

"I've got it. Come on, Roman. Let's go get some bags packed."

IV

Cornelius stood at the barrier waiting for Laertius, Cassius and Rupert to deplane and get their luggage. A quick text from Rupert, as Dastan was parking their SUV, let them know the trio had landed on time and were taxiing to the terminal.

JFK was a large international airport, and Cornelius knew from experience that it would take at least an hour – even for first class passengers – to go through immigration then customs.

Dastan joined him with a couple of coffees he'd got from a nearby vendor.

He handed Cornelius's large Americano to him and sipped on his own latte. Two bottles of water were also tucked under his left arm.

"Text from Shea whilst I was in the queue," Dastan said.

"Everything's okay at the moment, but he's got Jerome and Donal helping him with checking video feeds from Ciccone's known haunts. No sign of him, or of Fenton."

"He's been a bit conspicuous by his absence recently," Cornelius replied. "Could be Fenton's not in New York at the moment."

"Does Jacoby have any thoughts?"

Cornelius shrugged. "He thinks he might be in California. There were some reports about Striga from the local vampire coven in San Francisco – could be Fenton?"

"Could be." Dastan looked up and nudged Cornelius. "Here they are."

Laertius, Cassius and Rupert strolled through the barrier, and the five friends greeted each other with handshakes and hugs.

"It's good to see you." Laertius grinned.

Cornelius was glad to see that the air of grief that hung round the trio when they left Sydney a few days ago had dissipated. They would grieve for Persephone for a long time, but it wasn't showing in their eyes as much as before.

"Glad you could make it." Dastan smiled.

"Anything new happened since your last message?" Cassius asked, referring to the email Dastan had sent bringing them up to date with the current situation, and Lilah's disappearance.

"Nothing."

"No news is good news?" Rupert asked.

"I hope so." Cornelius sighed. "But I really don't think so. Ciccone's up to something, I'm sure."

The vamps and Donati began walking out of the terminal towards where Dastan had parked their SUV. Rupert and Cassius were on constant watch, checking out the humans and the few other Donati and vampires who were also in the terminal at this time.

None of them blinked an eye at seeing the Australian vamps in their territory. News travelled fast in their circles and everyone knew something big was brewing, even if they didn't know what it was.

Cornelius gestured for the vamps to wait as Dastan got out his security wand and searched the vehicle for bugs and tracking devices. Then he got down on his back and looked underneath, checking for bombs.

Cassius joined him and the two of them gave the SUV a good going over.

"Okay," Dastan finally said, getting up and opening the trunk for the others to put their luggage into. They were taking no chances after the bomb that killed Persephone.

Once they were all settled, Cornelius turned to Laertius in the middle seats. "How are Persephone's family?"

Laertius grimaced. "Doing as well as can be expected. Her father wanted to come with us and take on the mantle of seneschal again, but we've asked him to cover at the apartment in Bondi, and to try and keep the surf shop and the others running. A bit of normality will help."

Cornelius nodded. "The coven?"

Rupert snorted and Cornelius turned to him, raising an eyebrow.

"Left in the capable hands of Agatha," Laertius informed him.

"You met her," Rupert put in, "at the coven meeting. She doesn't always approve of Laertius's methods."

"Hmm, yes, I got that impression." Cornelius laughed.

"She'll keep them on their toes though," Laertius replied.

"I'm sure she will."

Dastan had just pulled on to the Van Wyk Expressway heading for Queens when he noticed that the same black Buick that had been behind them leaving the terminal, was still there.

"I think we've got a tail. Black Buick following us, about three cars back."

Cornelius nodded. "See if we can lose them. Come off at the next exit onto Queens Boulevard and see if they follow."

Dastan nodded and concentrated on the road, not wanting to miss his exit. Entering the off ramp, he could see the Buick as it weaved through traffic behind them to make the exit as well.

"Yeah, they're following us alright," Cornelius said. "Stay on here for a while, then head for Manhattan."

"They're getting closer," Dastan warned as the Buick came up behind them. The dark tinted windows meant they couldn't get a close look at who was driving.

The car behind them sped up and crashed into the back of the SUV, pushing all occupants of the car forward.

"What the fuck!" Rupert shouted.

"Hold on." Dastan grimaced and the SUV shot forward again, away from the Buick chasing them.

"It's coming up on our left," Cassius reported from the back seat.

Dastan tried to move over, but he was impeded by other traffic in the right lane. He hit the accelerator and the SUV surged forward. The Buick, however, had anticipated this and the driver managed to get a sideswipe in, pushing them into the – now thankfully empty – right lane.

Slamming on the brakes, their SUV fell behind the Buick, which roared into the distance, before its brake lights came on when the driver realised what had happened. Dastan swiftly changed lanes and headed for an off-ramp onto some of the smaller streets. The Buick still followed them. Dastan cut across several lanes to take a left turn and just made the lights. There was a shriek of metal and a large bang as the Buick behind them tried to follow them through the junction, getting T-boned as it didn't make it. Dastan slowed down but didn't stop, and they lost the tail.

"Whew! Great way to welcome us to your country!" Cassius grinned.

"Yeah, just what we wanted on day one – a car chase," Laertius replied, but he was also grinning. The adrenaline rush getting to them all.

"Time to swap cars?" Dastan asked Cornelius, who nodded. "Yeah, blue one is closest."

Laertius looked at them. "Blue one?"

"We have a few cars in different places across the city," Cornelius replied. "You never know when you're going to need one."

Everyone laughed at that, the tension broken. Cornelius's phone rang and he saw it was Jerome ringing.

"Nonno?" His voice came over the speaker in the car. "Are you okay? Shea said you were being tailed."

"We're fine, Jerome. It's dealt with. We should be there in about an hour. Would you sort out a meal for us?"

"Of course," he replied. "It's already sorted. Bea and Verity are cooking. Verity was a bit confused that vampires would eat food. She can't understand it."

Cornelius could hear the humour in his great grandson's voice. Many people not used to vampires were confused when they found out they ate food like everyone else. Blood was important to their being, as air was to humans and Donati, but they still needed food for fuel.

"Tell her anything will be appreciated," Laertius spoke up.

"Hi, Lai. I think I've managed to convince her. She's been watching too many films about vampires, so you may get a few questions later."

"We'll be ready." Laertius grinned, then his tone turned serious. "How about you, Jerome. How are you doing?"

They all could hear the sigh as Jerome lowered his voice. "Okay, I guess. I'm trying…"

"That's all any of us can do," Cornelius answered his great grandson as Dastan pulled the SUV into an underground parking lot. "Okay, we're about to change cars so we'll see you soon."

"Okay, Nonno."

Once they reached the Redoubt, with no further issue, Cornelius took great pleasure in showing the vamps around the facility. He showed them to the room they would be using, which had a large king size bed, comfy chairs and an en-suite bathroom.

"Jerome was staying here, but he's bunking in with Roman at the moment. The young man is having a hard time of it, and Jerome wants to keep an eye on him."

"We don't want anyone to give up their room," Cassius said as he pulled his rolling suitcase in behind him.

"It was his idea, so no worries, eh?" Laertius groaned at Cornelius's attempt at an Aussie accent.

"Okay." Rupert came out of the bathroom from where he had been examining the features. "I still can't believe all this is underground in an ex-bunker!"

"Yeah, it takes a bit of getting used to. Beatrice says dinner is ready, so let's go eat and then we can catch everyone up and see what's next."

The fun and friendly dinner that followed, was a welcome break from the strained atmosphere of Lilah's disappearance. Verity and Roman took turns peppering the three vampires with questions, as Jerome warned them they would do.

Could they see their reflections in a mirror? Yes! Cassius laughed and muttered something about how long Rupert took in front of the mirror every day to achieve 'perfection' as he called it.

"How about going out in the sun?" Verity asked, passing Jerome the bread rolls. "You all don't appear to be affected by it."

"It's an age thing," Laertius replied. "The older you are the more you're able to move around during daylight hours and go out in the sun for short periods. This gets longer bit by bit as time goes on. But the sun still affects new vampires, and they have to learn to live in darkness for a time, sleeping during the day."

"That must be hard," Roman said, looking at them.

"It can be, I can't remember," Laertius said. "But Jack, our newest fledgling, is only a couple of months old as a vampire, and he sleeps during the day and hunts on a night."

"Hunts?" Verity picked up.

"Yes, as a new vampire, he needs to ingest human blood every day, preferably from the source."

"He needs to bite someone?" she asked for clarification. "Does he kill them?"

She looked horrified and Cassius hurried to assure her that even new vamps only took what they needed, and they were careful who they approached. Cornelius listened as they discussed vampire traits and habits. Dastan caught his eye and smiled, happy to have their friends and family around them.

"What you have to remember though," Cassius was saying, "is that vampires and Striga are completely different. Striga are driven by blood. They can only ingest fresh blood and they don't eat food. A lot of the popular culture references you're referring to come from the Striga."

"Then why does anyone ever become one?" Roman asked.

"For the blood lust," Cassius replied. "For some, the blood gives them extraordinary strength and extra abilities. Only the strongest survive and can control their need for blood. Fenton is one of those. As a Donati, he had the ability and the strength to remain in charge of his body, and not let the blood lust take over. Not many humans can. Which is why many of them lead short, but very bloody lives…"

He broke off as he noticed that Roman's face had gone white.

"I'm sorry," he said. "That was maybe a bit graphic."

"No," Roman replied, holding his phone out so the others could see it.

"What is it?" Jerome asked, taking his brother's phone in his hand. He read the text that was on the screen, then looked up and read it aloud to the group.

"It's from Mama Lilah," he began. "It says, 'I'm sorry, baby boy.'"

Verity screamed and Beatrice rushed around the

table to her. She too was reading a text from Lilah — hers read 'I'm sorry, baby girl.'

Jerome pulled his phone out of his back pocket when it buzzed and opened it to see the message he'd received. "Mine reads, 'Take care of them.'"

"I don't understand," Roman said, looking at Jerome. "What's going on?"

V

The phone call came early the next morning. No-one had been able to sleep the night before, and everyone was up and around by 6am, staring morosely into their morning coffee.

Jerome took the call and he wasn't surprised when it turned out to be the local hospital. Lilah had been involved in a car accident the day before and had been pronounced dead on arrival. Jerome spoke to the doctor who had been there when she came in, and Shea was chasing up to see if he could find any footage of the accident. Beatrice was following up with the paramedics to see what they knew.

It seemed pretty obvious to them that the accident had been no accident. Ciccone had arranged for his own wife's death, that was the conclusion they came to. But why, was the question.

Verity was sitting with Jerome, her face white and eyes red from crying on and off all night. She'd stayed in his bedroom with him and Roman. The closeness had allowed them to talk about Lilah, and what might be happening.

Shea had confirmed that the phone Lilah had used to send the texts had been the burner phone he'd given her, so she could keep in touch with Jerome whilst he was in Australia. He couldn't find any more information from it; she hadn't used it often.

Jerome arranged with the hospital that he, Roman and Verity would attend the morgue later that afternoon to officially identify their mother. The police wanted to talk to them as well, about the accident and when the last time was that they had seen Lilah. Cornelius was dealing with that as he was friends with the new police commissioner who was married to a Donati. For the first time they were sharing their suspicions about Mario Ciccone with someone who wasn't on the Donati Council, nor a member of their circle.

Cornelius was of the opinion that things were about to get a lot messier for the general public, as well as the vamps of New York and the Donati. He was sure that Lilah's death was a warning – a 'shot across the bows', as he put it.

When the time came to go and identify Lilah, it was agreed that Dastan would drive the siblings and Cornelius to the office of the chief medical examiner. Lilah's body had already been transferred there, as was the practice in New York. Cornelius refused to be left out and wanted to be there to support Jerome and the other two. It was agreed that Dastan would stay in the parking lot and that Cassius, Rupert and Laertius would be on hand as well if they were needed. Donal and Shea would be manning the security cameras at the Redoubt, hacking into any they could, both inside and outside the hospital. Theo and Bea were their backups and in charge of security.

Cornelius was obviously being very cautious, and Jerome appreciated it. He could well believe that Ciccone had arranged the accident that caused Lilah's death and he was wary of what might be waiting for them. But they had to do this. Verity and Roman needed to identify their mother's body and claim her for burial. They needed to see for themselves that she was dead.

They arrived at the Kings County Hospital Centre campus, where they were greeted by a member of staff who asked a few general questions about their identity and relationship to Lilah. Once she was satisfied that they were in fact the next of kin, they were shown a photograph of Lilah for identification.

The photo was of her face only and she looked serene in death, only one bruise on her left cheek marring her face.

Verity nodded. "Yes, that's Mama."

"Thank you," the clerk replied. "I'm sorry for your loss."

All Verity could do was nod as Jerome wrapped her and Roman in his arms.

"Thank you for your help," Jerome said to the clerk. "We will arrange for the funeral director to collect the body shortly."

The clerk nodded, already turning away to deal with her paperwork. Jerome held his brother and sister close and followed Cornelius out of the viewing room.

Dastan picked them up outside the door saying nothing, then they all headed back to the Redoubt.

Jerome's phone rang and Beatrice's name appeared on the screen.

"Hi Bea," he answered. "All sorted?"

"Yeah, the funeral directors will pick her body up in the morning, after the autopsy is completed."

"Thanks. Any chance we can get a copy of the autopsy?"

"You can apply for one as next of kin, though Donal thinks he can get a copy straightaway, rather than waiting."

"Okay, ask him if he would please? We'll apply for

one as well, just in case." He sighed. "Thanks Bea."

"You're welcome. See you soon."

———

The next couple of days passed in a blur, with Jerome doing his best to comfort Verity and Roman and help organise a funeral for Lilah. They had debated whether it was safe for them to attend, or organise anything at all, but had decided that they had to do something. Roman had become hysterical at the thought of not being able to say goodbye to his mother.

Cornelius had met with the funeral directors and agreed that there would be only one visitation on the morning of the funeral itself. He was working hard with the vamps and Theo to ensure the safety of his family, and the mourners. There was a very real possibility that Ciccone could turn up at her funeral, and he wanted to be prepared.

Nothing had come from anyone's efforts to investigate Lilah's accident. The only thing everyone agreed on was that it was suspicious, coming as it did only a day after they had received the texts from her. There were a few suggestions that she had committed suicide, but they weren't taking those too seriously. They were convinced Ciccone had had a hand in it somehow.

Jerome arrived at the crematorium chapel, where the visitation was to take place, followed shortly by the funeral itself. The funeral directors were putting the last touches to the floral tributes that had been received, and he wandered along them checking them out. There was one from her school where she had taught for over twenty years, one from the hospital where she had volunteered as a visitor the previous summer, and various ones from friends and relatives. He stopped when he came to a simple arrangement of begonias, ivy and lobelias, and as he read the card with them, he almost stopped breathing. The arrangement was from Lacey.

Stopping the funeral director as he made his way by, he asked, "When did these arrive?"

"About an hour ago," the woman replied. "Problem?"

"No, thank you."

He looked around but Verity and Roman were talking to some cousins of their mothers. He removed the card from the flowers, not wanting to upset them, but wanting to investigate further. Were they really from Lacey, or was someone playing with them?

The first scream sounded as though it was coming from right beside Jerome's ear. He turned around but didn't at first see anything unusual. Then he saw it. A man he'd not noticed before had Verity, and she was struggling in his arms. As he rushed towards her, he saw Theo ushering mourners out of the chapel, into the grounds.

"Donati," the man – no, Striga – said.

"What do you want?" Jerome asked.

The Striga laughed. "Wouldn't you like to know?" He sniffed Verity's neck and licked a line up over where her artery was. "Hmmm…" He drew out the word. "Good vintage. Almost as good as that one."

Jerome realised the Striga was nodding to where the casket was. He turned, just in time to see a woman, someone he had thought was a cousin of Lilah's, grinning. He rushed over to her but was too late to stop her from lifting the casket lid. Inside, Lilah sat up and smiled at Jerome.

"Hello, Jerome." She smirked. "Surprised?"

Another scream, this time from Roman who was struggling to get closer to his sister, pushing at Theo to let him go.

"No, Rome, stay there," Jerome shouted.

He watched in horror as Lilah was helped from her casket by the other woman. She grabbed her daughter from the Striga who had been holding her.

"Thanks, dear," she said, drawing Verity to her.

Verity screamed, "Mama, no!"

Dastan rushed into the room from where he had

been helping Theo with the other guests. He was too late to stop Lilah from sinking her sharp teeth into Verity's neck.

Verity screamed and shivered, her body going into convulsions, as her mother gulped large mouthfuls of blood from her arteries. The man and woman who were with her kept Jerome and Dastan at bay. Finally, Lilah grinned with bloody teeth as she dropped her daughter's body to the ground.

Jerome took two steps and threw up all over his new shoes. He shook himself and looked up. Verity was dead, she had to be. He didn't see how she could survive that.

He was in a daze as he watched Dastan and Theo fighting with the Striga who had originally had Verity in his grip. The woman who had helped Lilah out of her coffin was dead on the floor with a stake through her heart.

"Jerome," Theo shouted from where he was now fighting with another Striga who had appeared as if from nowhere. "Catch."

Coming out of his daze, Jerome reached out to catch the wooden stake Theo had thrown to him. He turned around to find Lilah just about to grab Roman. He rushed to protect his brother. Gripping the stake tightly in his hand, he plunged it right into Lilah's heart.

Her face went slack and for a moment it was his

Mama Lilah back again, not some crazed Striga. "Take…" she tried to say before collapsing on the ground.

Feeling claws in his legs, then back, he swirled round to find Verity. She was trying to drag herself up from the floor. She looked dishevelled and out of it.

"Blood… must have…"

Jerome shook his head and fought to keep his sister from getting any closer to them.

"Jerome." He recognised Dastan's voice in the hubbub around him. "Jerome… you have to…"

"What?" he screamed.

"You have to stake her." Dastan was trying to keep Roman from reaching his sister. He was crying and calling out her name.

"No!" Roman shouted, slipping out of Dastan's arms and making a beeline for Jerome. "You can't Jer, you can't!"

Jerome had his hands full with Verity, who was now clawing at his arms. He could feel the claws cutting through his flesh. Did that mean he was a Striga now? In horror, he looked at the floor where his step-mother's body lay. He blinked and realised there was only one thing he could do.

"I'm sorry, Ver," he whispered, before bringing the stake up and thrusting it through her heart.

VI

Everything seemed to stop as Jerome found himself staring down at the bodies of his step-mother and step-sister. It took him a moment to realise that Cornelius had arrived with the vamps and had stopped time.

He turned to his great grandfather.

"I...I..." He couldn't get the words out. Cornelius stepped up to him and pulled him into a crushing hug.

"You're okay," he kept repeating. "Ti amo," he said as he kissed Jerome's forehead before letting him go.

There was chaos in the small visitation room. Several dead Striga were laid on the floor. Theo and Dastan had secured one who had survived in the corner. Jerome looked around, still in shock.

Roman lay on the floor where Dastan had lowered him from the mad dive he had been trying to take towards Jerome, in his bid to stop him from staking Verity. Jerome hung his head. How were they going to recover from this?

Theo entered the room from where he had been checking the chapel and offices of the funeral directors. He nodded towards Cornelius. "All clear."

"Good." Cornelius shook his head. "Jerome…" He coughed then started again. "Jerome, I'm so sorry. God, what a disaster."

Jerome just stood where he was. He wasn't even sure he knew how to go on from here. Though they had debated the possibility of Ciccone turning up, not one of them had thought they'd use Lilah against them.

He wondered when they had turned her – before or during the accident?

"I don't understand," he said to Cornelius. "She was dead. The OCME showed us a photo of her dead body – the body that was supposed to be in their morgue."

Dastan came up and put his arm around Jerome. "I suspect, when we investigate, we'll find the clerk was a temp, or a plant by Ciccone. I doubt they'll still be there now."

"You're right, god…. Poor Roman. He's never going to forgive me."

"I can alter his memories slightly, if you think it would help?" Dastan was hesitant in his offer; it would be a break of trust between the brothers.

"I don't know," Jerome replied. "I, it's... shit!"

Jerome wandered away from them, feeling the throbbing in his arms and back from where Verity had scratched her nails down them. He couldn't get over how quickly she had changed once Lilah had bitten her, sending the Striga pathogens into her daughter's blood stream, purely from those in her mouth? Surely there was more to changing into a Striga than that?

Around him, Theo, Cornelius and the others continued to clean up the area before they could even think of beginning time again. Bea and Dastan were with the guests frozen in time. They wanted to work with their memories so that they didn't remember the attack, only a visitation and funeral that ran as smoothly as these things ever did. They couldn't risk humans knowing more about Striga, at this time, than they already did. There wasn't much really – rumours and Facebook groups and conspiracy theories abounded, discussing vampires and Striga as if they were the same creatures. Being part of the Donati hierarchy meant Cornelius and Dastan had to be extra careful in their dealings with humans and Striga.

"I'm sorry about your sister." Laertius had moved

up next to him. Jerome hadn't even been aware that the vampire was there.

He and the others had been to the airport to collect Tock, Mary's second from Melbourne. He could see Tock now in discussion with Theo. It appeared that the two already knew each other.

"Thanks, Laertius. God, what a day." Jerome slumped down onto one of the chairs that had been righted and looked around him. Things were cleared up now, the coffin and bodies had been removed.

Laertius saw where his gaze had gone and rested his hand on Jerome's shoulder. "They've been burned. We couldn't take the risk. Striga are always staked and then burned."

Jerome nodded. "It was just so quick. Verity was normal, then Lilah bit her and she was like some whirling dervish trying to get to me."

"It's not normally that quick. Usually the bite makes people collapse and then if they survive the turning, they will arise within a few hours and hunger after blood. But Verity was Lilah's daughter, the genetic marker was in her blood. It made Verity hunger for blood, even before she'd completely been turned."

"Jerome." Cornelius came up to him and touched his back, right over one of his scratches, and he hissed in pain.

"What's up?" Cornelius asked in concern.

"Verity scratched me, quite deeply in some places." He looked up at his great grandfather. "Will I be like them? Will I become a Striga?"

"Mi amore, no, no, not like that. Scratches can't turn you, only a bite, but they can become infected. Come with me, we must get you seen to before we can do anything else."

"Roman…" Jerome began, then hesitated. "Please wake Roman, he has to know I killed her for a reason."

"Are you sure?"

"Yes."

Cornelius nodded his head and walked over to where Roman had been gently laid on the floor, using someone's rolled up jacket as a pillow. Cornelius touched him. The young man shuddered and then screamed, "Jer, no!" before he realised he wasn't where he had been, and nothing was the same.

"Rome…" Jerome approached his brother, his shirt already half-way off so that Cornelius could examine his scratches.

"No!" Roman screamed. "You killed her, Jerome. You killed our sister."

He was ranting and crying as he got up and began pacing backwards and forwards, his breaths coming in gulps as he tried to rationalise what he had just seen. Before anyone could stop him, he took a step towards Jerome and punched him in the jaw, hard. Jerome just stared in sadness at his younger brother who was shaking his hand out.

"Better?" Dastan asked, taking hold of Roman's shoulders. "Look." He directed Roman's gaze to Jerome's shoulders, arms and back, where the red scratches looked raw and infected.

"What..." Roman began, looking at his brother.

"That's what Verity did after your mother bit her. It wasn't your sister or mother who attacked us, Roman. They were not in their right minds. Jerome was attacked as he tried to protect you."

Roman turned to Jerome. "Oh, god, Jer... I'm..." He couldn't finish his thoughts and Jerome could see how flustered he was getting. He nodded at Dastan who took hold of Roman and led him out of the room. He would make sure Roman was okay, maybe blur things a little, but not let him forget.

Jerome was beginning to feel light-headed as he sat on a chair. Cornelius had found a large first aid kit in the funeral director's office. He worked methodically, cleaning every scratch with antiseptic spray, and putting cream on them. There were one or two that had gone particularly deep, and Jerome hissed as Cornelius cleaned them out.

Tock came over from where he had been talking to Theo. "Jerome, I am so sorry for your loss."

"Thank you, Tock, and thank you for coming." He hissed as Cornelius touched a particularly raw spot on his back, and Tock moved around to see what Cornelius was doing.

"I might be able to help," he spoke to them both. "If you'd let me."

"How?" Jerome asked.

"My saliva closes up bite wounds after I've fed, as it does for all vampires, but I have found that mine is particularly good at sealing wounds." He shrugged, his dark eyes smiling at them. "It's worth a try?"

Jerome nodded, then sat there feeling very silly as Tock spat at a couple of the bad scratches and rubbed his saliva into the fissures. He hissed a couple of times but gradually he could feel their soreness abating and he stopped feeling quite so light-headed.

He grabbed Tock's hand as the big man stepped back from him. "Thank you."

Tock nodded and moved away as he took a call from his coven leader, Mary. Jerome could hear him bringing her up to date.

Jerome flexed his shoulders as Cornelius finished applying band aids and butterfly bandages to his scratches. His skin still felt tight in places, but not as bad as it had been.

"Better?" Dastan asked as he returned to the room.

"Yes. Rome?"

"In my car asleep. Naturally," he added. "He asked me to help, agreed for his memories to be blurred. Said he didn't want to forget, just didn't want to remember it in all its technicolour glory."

Jerome nodded. He felt the same, but knew he had to remember. He needed those memories. Memories of having to kill his step-mother and step-sister, to help him in his quest for justice for all who had suffered at the hands of Ciccone and the Striga.

"The chapel is empty now," Dastan said. "If you wish to go and have a few quiet moments of contemplation before we leave."

"Thanks, Dastan, for everything," Jerome said, before moving over to the chapel where he spent the next few moments remembering Lilah and Verity. He lowered his head in contemplation as he swore to avenge them, and to stop Ciccone's plans before more innocent people could be affected.

Laertius had booked them all suites in the tower at the Lotte New York Palace Hotel on Madison Avenue. Cornelius didn't know how much the Elder Vampire had spent, but he knew it was a lot. Frankly, at the moment he didn't care. His family needed him.

He and Dastan had been booked into one of the penthouse suites, which had two bedrooms. Roman and Jerome were in the room with the queen size beds and he and Dastan in the one with the king. The view from the double height living room over Manhattan was spectacular, as was it from the rooftop terrace too. Cornelius and Dastan had stayed in a number of luxury hotel rooms over the years, but this one topped them all.

Jerome came into the living area from the bedroom he was sharing with Roman. He flopped into one of the comfy wingback chairs. Wincing only slightly when his back touched the chair, he looked out at the city and sighed.

"How are your scratches?" Cornelius asked his great grandson.

"Okay. They still pull a bit, but they're not as red. Those Tock treated look as though they've been healing for days." He paused. "I can't believe he did that."

"Me either." Dastan approached from the wet bar the suite's maître d' had set up when they arrived. He carefully handed round the whiskeys he had poured for each of them and sat down next to Cornelius on the comfy sofa.

"Is Roman still asleep?"

"Yes, out like a light. Not sure I'm going to be able to get much sleep myself though. I keep seeing Mama Lilah and Verity. I'm having a hard time accepting what happened."

Cornelius nodded; Jerome wasn't the only one. He hated that they had underestimated Ciccone and Fenton once more. It was hard being continuously on the receiving end of their combined attacks.

"Have you heard anything more from Shea?" Jerome asked him.

Shea and Donal had been left behind at the Redoubt to monitor the situation through the security cameras outside and inside the funeral directors. This had not worked out as foreseen though, as both of the security cameras had been set on a loop, showing only a peaceful vista. It had taken Donal a while to work out what was going on, but by then it had been too late to warn any of them. The only good news to have come out of the whole fiasco was that the police had not become involved. Though Cornelius had a friendly relationship with the police commissioner for Manhattan, he didn't want to push his luck.

"Nothing new," Cornelius said, as he realised that Jerome was still waiting for an answer. "We've decided it's best to leave the Redoubt for now. I'm pretty sure the whole place has been compromised. Donal and Shea will join us here tomorrow. They are cleaning the place up and removing any computer evidence they can. If Ciccone does manage to gain access, we don't want him finding out anything we don't want him to know."

"Do you think it's likely they will get access?" Jerome frowned.

"I don't know." Cornelius sent a wan smile Jerome's way. "It's a good job we'd already packed some bags, otherwise we'd have nothing to wear."

His attempt at levity fell flat and the three of them subsided into silence.

"We're all tired," Dastan said as he got up and took the now empty glasses from the other two men. "Why don't we try and get some sleep. I've arranged with Laertius and the others to have breakfast served here in the morning. God knows there's plenty of room."

Cornelius smiled as his lover gave him a hand up. "Jerome?"

"I think I'm going to sit here and watch the lights for a while," he answered. "Don't worry though, I'll try and get some sleep."

Cornelius nodded and allowed Dastan to lead them to their suite, where he got undressed and enjoyed a shower in the room's luxurious bathroom. He felt better after the shower and sat in bed with a bottle of water whilst he listened to Dastan take his shower. After a while he emerged wearing sleep shorts and a short-sleeved T-shirt.

Cornelius grinned and pulled Dastan down for a kiss as the other man stopped by the bed to grab a drink of water.

"Ready for bed, love?" He smiled as he grabbed another kiss.

"Hmm, always ready for you, honey."

Cornelius laughed. Trust Dastan to always make him smile.

———

"Okay, thanks Marcus," Cornelius spoke into his phone. "Let him know I'm trying to get hold of him and get him to call me as soon as he can." He listened to the answer on the other end before pressing the off key.

"Still no word from Jacoby?" Dastan asked as he grabbed coffee from the in-suite coffee maker.

"No. Marcus tells me he has been called to San Francisco where there have been a few sightings of Striga by members of the Donati. He has gone to help the Council there as they have had little experience of this."

Cornelius was frustrated that his son was out of contact. Though he understood Jacoby's need to check up on what was happening in San Francisco for himself, if there was a breakout of Striga issues there, it could mean their problem was more far reaching in the States than they had realised.

The doorbell to the suite rang, and Jerome who was closest went to open it. It was the vampire contingent with Donal and Shea, all arriving at once. Cornelius was glad to see everyone safe and sound.

"The maître d' has already been in and set breakfast up in the dining room," Jerome was explaining to the others.

Jerome had been impressed that their suite and the ones that the others were staying in came complete with their own housekeeping and maître d'. Cornelius had smiled at the young man's enthusiasm for the spread that had been set out on the dining table.

The luxury of the suite had temporarily taken Jerome's mind off the deaths of his step-mother and step-sister. Though Cornelius knew the reprise would not last long.

They all grabbed food from the buffet, sitting around the large table or in the more comfortable chairs in the living area.

Roman finally emerged from his and Jerome's room.

"Hey," Jerome greeted his brother. Roman squinted at them all in the room. Beatrice and Theo had just joined them, having been slightly late, and Roman gravitated to Bea who held her arms out for him.

"How are you coping?" she asked the younger man.

"I'm not sure," he replied. "It still doesn't seem real."

Beatrice nodded as she handed him off to Jerome who pulled his younger brother tight into his arms. Leaning down, Jerome whispered something in his ear and Roman nodded before allowing himself to be led to the dining table to get some food.

For a while it was fairly quiet in the suite as everyone ate and drank. Conversation where it broke out was subdued and revolved more around the weather and other lacklustre subjects.

When everyone had finished eating, Cornelius called for the maître d' – a small rotund man called Pierre – to come in and clear the dining room, and to leave fresh coffee and bottled water in its place.

Once he'd gone, Cornelius gestured towards the large boardroom type table in another area of the open plan suite.

Everyone sat around it, and after a few moments of getting comfortable, they all turned to face Cornelius.

"Status report?" Cornelius asked of Donal and Shea.

"Everything of any value has been removed from the Redoubt. We brought any belongings that were left behind here and they're down in our room. We'll sort them out later," Donal replied.

Cornelius nodded. He knew that would include the possessions of Lilah and Verity. He would help Jerome and Roman go through them later.

"Before we left, I transferred all our monitoring over to the mobile control centre. The truck is now parked in the hotel parking lot, and the concierge are keeping a special eye on it for us," Donal went on. "We can access most of its capabilities from here."

"Wow," Jerome spoke up. "We have a mobile control van?"

Shea smiled. "Yep, we'll show you later."

He turned to the table at large. "We made sure there was nothing left on any of the computers in the Redoubt then set small charges to completely destroy the remains."

Cornelius nodded. It was maybe a bit too excessive, but in this case they couldn't be too careful.

"So…" Laertius leaned forward from between Cassius and Rupert. "What's next? What do we have to do to put these bastards down once and for all?"

"That's a good question," Dastan answered him. "We've been on the defensive all this time, waiting for Ciccone to make his move. Well, I think what happened in Australia and the events of yesterday are enough for us to change tactics. I say we go on the offensive."

"I don't disagree," Theo broke in. "But what should our move be? We know where Ciccone is, or at least where he's been these last few weeks, but Fenton has hardly been seen since Australia." He turned to Cornelius. "Have you spoken to Jacoby? Has he heard anything?"

"I tried to speak to him this morning, but could only reach his PA, Marcus, who let me know that Jacoby was on the west coast. The Council leader there, Ratford, I think, had no experience and asked Jacoby for help. Donati in his area have reported the first Striga sightings there in over seventy years."

"Guys, you might want to see this," Donal called, from where he was fiddling with the large screen TV on the wall of the living area.

"What is it?" Cornelius moved over just as the picture on the TV went live. It was showing several views at once, all of which Cornelius recognised.

They were of the Redoubt.

"As we were talking just now," Donal began, "I got a warning on my phone that something was up."

He pointed to the view of the dining/living area in the Redoubt, a view all except Tock were very familiar with. The normal lights had cut off and only the orange emergency lights could be seen. From the outside, they could see that the warehouse where the Redoubt was situated was surrounded by vehicles.

From one truck, which looked as though it had seen service in Afghanistan or somewhere similar, a large projectile was pointed at the warehouse.

"What the fuck!" Jerome said. "They have an RPG on that truck—"

Just as he spoke there was a flash as the Rocket-propelled grenade was fired at the doors of the warehouse.

The Redoubt was under attack.

VIII

"Reports are coming in that a complex in one of New York's warehouse districts has been fired at by an RPG. These are usually used in warzones." The television screen was split, half showing live pictures from their own cameras inside the Redoubt, and the other half a TV report of the Redoubt warehouse, which was still burning several hours after the attack.

"Sources in the police department are claiming this is a result of a particularly malicious gang warfare, which has been raging across the city in recent days..." the reporter's voice continued over the pictures.

Cornelius took the control from Dastan and turned the volume down. The gang warfare aspect had been suggested by him to Clive Browne, the police commissioner he knew, as an explanation for the attack on the warehouse. He left the picture on, which showed the view from the channel's helicopter as it circled the area.

It would be a while yet before they could gain access to the warehouse, to see the damage for themselves, so they would have to rely on their own cameras in the Redoubt in the meantime.

"Nonno," Jerome called as he walked through to the sitting area from the meeting table where he had been ensconced with Theo for most of the morning. He had a phone to his ear and was telling whoever was on the other end to 'calm down'.

He handed the phone to Cornelius mouthing 'Jacoby' to him, so he knew to expect his son's voice on the other end.

"What the hell, Papa! What is going on there?" Jacoby's voice came through loud and clear. "I go away for a few days and the world goes to hell in a handbasket!"

"Jacoby," Cornelius said, "calm down – it's not as though this was unexpected. I'm surprised you actually went to the West Coast and didn't deal with the problem there over video call."

"I needed to be on site," Jacoby's calmer words came back to his father. "Now, what's the situation?"

Cornelius shook his head. It was always the same with Jacoby – he was quick to anger, but quicker to settle to calm again. Cornelius spent the next half hour explaining the current situation to his son, in his guise as Council leader for Washington and New York. In typical Jacoby fashion, he didn't ask how his grandson and the rest were doing, just got down to details about the attack and the cover story. Gang warfare was an understandable event to many people, though New York itself had been pretty quiet for years.

Cornelius asked several times if Jacoby would be returning before his son admitted there was still work for him to do in San Francisco, and that he would be back in a few days. It wasn't the answer Cornelius was after, but he understood the role Jacoby held. After extracting his promise that he would contact them on his return, he hit the end button.

There was a flurry of activity in the suite as several people were coming and going. Shea had set up several laptops in the dining area and spread out across the table were the remains of their lunch. What the maître d' thought of it all was anyone's guess, though they were very discreet, which was one of the reasons Laertius had picked this hotel.

Cornelius joined Shea for an update along with Jerome and Theo. The vampires had left to meet with the local New York coven. They wanted to see if they had any insight into the number of Striga that Fenton and Ciccone could call upon.

Shea fed his screens to the larger TV on the wall

in the main room so everyone could see. They watched not only the RPG attack, but also masked men/Striga entering the Redoubt. It was the entrance that Lilah had used on her exit a few days earlier, which answered the question as to whether she had told them more about their underground retreat. The Striga, all dressed in black, filtered through the Redoubt, and spread through the rooms. There was nothing to be found though as Shea and Donal had cleared as much as they could out.

They watched as the Striga got more and more frustrated at not being able to find anything. After a while, they began destroying the furniture, and tearing pictures off the walls. They piled them up in the middle on the large foyer, before setting fire to them. Cornelius grabbed Dastan's hand as the fire reached the elaborate carved door that Dastan had been so proud of. Dastan squeezed back.

"How many are there?" Jerome spoke up for the first time in a while.

"About twenty in all," Shea answered.

"That many? Are they all Striga, do you think?"

"Hard to tell in this lighting. They're better organised that you would think, but that's probably Ciccone and Fenton's influence."

They were quiet for a few moments until one of the masked figures stepped up to one of the cameras, and slowly pulled his mask off."

Jerome gasped. The figure grinned as though he could see their reaction. Staring straight into the camera was Fenton. So, he was there himself. Unable to take his eyes off the camera, Cornelius watched as Fenton reached into the backpack he was carrying and pulled out a spray can of paint. Just before he sprayed over the camera blocking their view, he mouthed, 'You're next.'

One by one the cameras went out as several of the masked figures applied spray paint to their lenses. The group continued to watch the Striga trashing the place and setting everything on fire through the small amount of cameras they did not appear to know about. They watched as Fenton left via the same door he had entered through, pulling his men out with him. After that the only view was that of burning, both inside and outside the Redoubt.

Laertius and the others returned just after dinner looking weary. Jerome let them into the suite and led them to the comfy sitting area overlooking Manhattan.

"How did it go?" Cornelius asked them as they settled into their places.

"Badly," Laertius answered.

Cornelius arched his eyebrow at Laertius, who sighed.

"We were met by only a handful of vampires from the whole coven. They have been decimated in recent weeks as Fenton and Ciccone have upped their game. Whole scale attacks have been carried out against the coven, and many of them are now afraid to go out, no matter the time of day. Several younger vampires have been converted to Fenton's Striga, some against their wishes."

Laertius looked so downtrodden that Cornelius got up, and with Jerome's help provided drinks all round. Alcoholic for those who wanted it. Both Cassius and Rupert were trying their best to comfort their lover, but Laertius was the most depressed that Cornelius had ever seen him.

"Have you any idea of how many Striga Ciccone and Fenton have managed to recruit?" Theo leaned forward from the wingback chair he had pulled around to face the others.

"At last count the New York vampires believe he has a few hundred here, and several more in other states. Coven leaders have been reporting missing vampires in their areas for several weeks. The word has gone out about the situation, and to warn covens to be extra careful. It has been suggested that they stay together wherever possible, only leaving to feed, and then in groups."

Cornelius nodded. It made sense. They needed to protect the vampires. It appeared that Fenton and Ciccone had moved on from recruitment to forced turnings. This was not good. A Striga army could decimate the human, Donati and vampire population within weeks.

"Any news from San Francisco?" he asked.

"Nothing in particular," Cassius replied. "Why?"

Dastan sat up at that and turned to Cornelius. "Didn't Jacoby say the Donati Council there had called him in because of Striga issues?"

"He most certainly did." Cornelius turned to the trio. "Nothing, you're sure of it."

"None that was mentioned to us," Laertius replied.

Cornelius pulled his hand through his hair. Why would Jacoby lie to him? Dastan already had his phone out and was trying to contact Jacoby.

"Voice mail. I've left a message for him to contact us. I'll contact Marcus as well, perhaps he can get in touch with him."

Cornelius nodded. There had to be an explanation. Likely Jacoby hadn't wanted to let him in on what were probably secret Council affairs. He had been in the same position himself a few times, but none where what was happening had so closely matched what was going on in the wider world.

"There'll be an explanation," Beatrice spoke up

for the first time from where she was sitting on a footstool near Theo. "You know Jacoby can be secretive when he wants."

Cornelius nodded, then turned to the room at large. "We need to stop this from blowing up further than it already has. We have been on the defensive for too long now, and it's time to go on the offensive. Ideas?"

IX

Jerome perched on the windowsill of the suite's living area. He was looking at the lights of Manhattan, and the traffic on Madison Avenue. Watching life go on in the city, even as they plotted inside for the downfall of his own father and his cronies. He laid his head against the windowpane, reflecting on how much and how quickly he had moved on since the night he lay looking up at the rain, in the alley that Cornelius and Dastan had found him in. Despite the events of the last few weeks, he was very happy that they had found him and taken him in. He had come to love the older couple as fathers, replacing the one he had not had since he was seventeen years old. Now, he and they were about to start a war with Ciccone.

They had been planning all day about how and where to take the fight to Mario Ciccone. In the end, they had decided to attack him at his home in the Hamptons. A quick trip by Dastan and Theo had gained the knowledge from the doorman that Ciccone was intending to head to his house in Wainscott for the weekend. Footage from his apartment building showed him leaving there that morning.

He wouldn't be alone. They knew that he would have Striga around him to protect him. They were hopeful they would be able to put a dent in the number of Striga he and Fenton had recruited. And maybe, just maybe, arrange a little payback for Ciccone himself.

"Jerome?" It was his great grandfather's voice. "You should be in bed. Can't you sleep?"

"Nonno." He smiled at the older man. "No, too much going on in my mind, I guess. Worry about Lacey. Roman and Beatrice too."

He grimaced. Earlier that day he had taken Roman, along with Beatrice, to the airport. They had finally had some good news about their little sister. The card with the flowers from Lacey had been traced back to a florist in York, England. A private detective had visited the florist on their behalf and found out that Lacey had ordered the flowers herself. She had been in her school uniform, that of Queen Margaret's school, which they found out was based just outside of the city. She had been accompanied by a lugubrious man, who had not let her out of his sight the whole time she was in the shop. The florist had assumed she was the daughter of someone famous, and that he was her bodyguard.

Beatrice and Roman had both volunteered to travel to England, to visit the school and see what the situation was. They had a copy of Lilah's will, which named Jerome as Lacey's guardian in the event of Lilah's death, and an affidavit from Jerome for them to act in his stead.

He had wanted to go himself, to bring his sister home. But there was too much going on in New York for him to leave. He was determined to stop his father in his tracks, nothing else was as important.

"Any news from Beatrice?" Cornelius asked, resting a hand on Jerome's shoulder and looking out the window with him.

"I heard from them about an hour ago. They landed at Manchester airport and are on their way to York now. They'll spend the night there, then head out to the school tomorrow morning their time."

Cornelius nodded and smiled at Jerome's reflection. "Why don't you try and get some sleep? Tomorrow will be a hard, long day."

Jerome nodded and hugged Cornelius, before heading with him to the bedrooms. He said goodnight outside the door to the master suite, as Cornelius went in to join Dastan, then made his way to the room he had been sharing with Roman. The empty bed near the window looked forlorn, but he was happy Rome had gone for their sister. He needed that. And Jerome needed him far away from Ciccone and his machinations.

The next morning everyone convened in Cornelius's suite for breakfast, before leaving for the Hamptons. Laertius had recruited a few other vampires from the New York coven. Ignatius, Cornelius's brother, and Marcus, Jacoby's PA, had also arrived to help. Jacoby had sent a short message to his father saying that he was on Council business and couldn't talk about it. Cornelius still appeared concerned about what his son was up to.

In all there were twenty of them sitting around the suite eating breakfast and drinking coffee. Theo was in charge of logistics and had divided the group into four smaller groups of five, ready for the attack. Shea and Donal had been trying to hack into any cameras in the area, but there were few outside of the Hamptons villages, and hardly any down Wainscott Stone Highway where Ciccone's house was. They had managed to find some photos of it online from the last time it had sold, which had been less than a year ago, so at least they had some idea of what they were going into.

The house itself was large, just over 19,000 square feet with nine bedrooms and several reception rooms, including an in-house cinema. There would be a lot of territory to cover when they got there, and everyone had been handed schematics of the house and given an ingress point.

"Okay." Cornelius held up his hand. "We'll congregate at the end of the highway leading to Ciccone's house. We don't know what security he has surrounding the house, or how far out it radiates. Be prepared to be attacked anywhere in the area. I will go in the front with Donal, Tock, Laertius and Jenna." He nodded at one of the New York vampires who was sitting next to Laertius.

"My main aim will be to get close enough to the house that I can stop time and allow the rest of you to infiltrate the house. I'm not sure my influence will extend to the whole area, so we may also need to rely on Ignatius finding enough shadows to help him disguise his team, and Jerome using his chameleon talent. We need to take out as many Striga as we can. If we can safely do so, take Ciccone into custody too. If that isn't possible, then we have to kill him."

Jerome met his great grandfather's eyes and nodded at him. This was his father they were talking about, though he hadn't really been his father since the day he had dragged Jerome out of school at seventeen and handed him over to Fenton and his men.

———————

Two hours later they arrived in Wainscott and Jerome pulled the SUV he was driving off the highway. Marcus, Rena, another of the New York vampires, Donal and Theo made up his team. He joined them by the side of the road as they all pulled on undershirt armour and grabbed various weapons. Making sure they all had sufficient weaponry was Theo's job. He checked everyone over, making sure they were as prepared as they could be.

Their reconnaissance had shown that Ciccone had put up new gates and security at the front of the house, though he had not yet had an opportunity to cover all the grounds and woodland surrounding the house. Jerome's group were therefore coming in on foot from the west, through the grounds, and round the tennis courts to the rear.

"Okay," Jerome began nervously, "I've never tried this before in a real situation, so... I've done plenty of exercises—" He broke off, embarrassed. "Anyway, make sure you stick together and keep near me as much as you can, and I should be able to cover you with the chameleon gift."

"How?" That was Rena, the only stranger and vamp amongst them.

Jerome took a breath and bringing his gift to the forefront of his mind he blended into the background. Rena sucked in a breath and reached out to touch his hand. He extended the gift to cover her and she too blended in.

"Holy hell," she exclaimed as she stepped away from his influence, becoming visible once more.

"Exactly," Theo said. "We experimented over the last few days. You don't have to be touching Jerome for him to cover you with the chameleon cloak, but you do have to be fairly close, and he has to deliberately add you in. Six is the most he could cover, so we should be okay with five."

Jerome nodded then turned to the others. "Ready?"

They all nodded.

"Let's go kick some Striga ass," Marcus said, gaining looks of surprise from those around him. "What? Just 'cos I work in an office, you don't think I can fight?"

A nervous laugh rang through their small group at that. Jerome smiled, and taking a deep breath he felt deep within himself for his gift. Slowly, he extended his influence to cover the group. One by one they blended into the background and set off through the five acres of grounds surrounding the property.

X

Something was wrong. His arms felt as though they were being pulled out of their sockets. His hands were numb. Jerome came to slowly, pins and needles charged up and down his arms. He opened his eyes slowly. Squinting against the pale light, he found he was hung from a hook on a beam in a large, cold room.

He groaned, his head flopping backwards. He tried to wriggle his arms, but nothing happened. His head felt thick, and his movements were slow. He couldn't remember what had happened. Swinging his arms, he managed a little movement, but nothing much. Feeling sick, he stopped.

Shaking his head only made it hurt worse. He realised he had been hit in the head at some point, and he could feel a split lip and taste blood on his tongue. Whatever had happened, he had been captured.

His toes barely touched the floor, and it was a hard task to keep himself balanced on them. It was straining his arms even further. His head was clearing a little, and he remembered something – a splash? It didn't make sense.

He drifted in and out of consciousness for several minutes, and slowly things began to come back to him. The raid on Ciccone's house. Casting his chameleon cloak over his team. Moving around the tennis courts to the back of the house. The swimming pool – the splash?

He tried to avoid shaking his head, as that only made the pain worse. He was becoming a bit more clear-headed the longer he hung there. But the longer he hung there, the more pain he was in. He had to try and get free.

Following the rope that was tied around his wrists, he found the hook that the rope was looped around. All he needed to do was loosen the rope enough that he could lift it over the hook. Easy. That was if he wasn't trussed up like a side of meat, with a headache to boot. He looked again, speculating, if he could only…

His thoughts were interrupted by the squealing of a large door being pushed open. A light came on, momentarily blinding him, and he squinted against the pain in his eyes.

"Jerome," a voice he knew came to him, as he tried to see against the light.

Mario Ciccone stood nearby and behind him was a man he had hoped never to see again in his whole life – Fenton. He shuddered. He couldn't help it. It was a visceral reaction to the presence of the man who had caused him so much pain.

"Nothing to say for yourself, I see," Ciccone said with a smug grin on his face.

Jerome managed to find enough phlegm in his mouth to spit at the man who had been his father. Ciccone reacted immediately, backhanding his son before reaching for his handkerchief and wiping the phlegm away.

Jerome swore as the pain in his face bloomed again. He panted slowly, happy to see Ciccone's disgust at his spit landing on his face.

"You think you're clever, don't you?" Fenton growled. Jerome smirked. Couldn't he think of anything more original to say?

"You won't be smirking like that when that old Donati and his faggot husband are swinging next to you!" Ciccone almost hissed at him.

Jerome took a deep breath. They hadn't got Cornelius or Dastan. He had to hope the others were also still free.

He remembered then. The splash. They had been

moving swiftly through the grounds of Ciccone's Hamptons house, heading for the back of the property…

Jerome crossed the lawn and began skirting the pool. He could see several Striga milling around at the back of the house. He counted five. Five against five. He thought the odds were good for them. He turned to whisper to Rena the New York vamp when suddenly, and deliberately, she stepped outside the area of his chameleon cloak.

"What are you doing?" Theo hissed at her.

She ignored him and shouted to the Striga. "Hey, over here!"

"What the fuck!" Jerome had no other time to react. Behind him he heard a splash as Donal grabbed Marcus and pulled them both into the nearby swimming pool. Theo swore and drew several stakes from his body armour. The chameleon cloak was broken and they were all out in the open.

"Jerome," Theo said. "Stop her."

Jerome turned and saw that Rena was launching herself at him. He pulled the stun gun from his vest, and a stake, and managed to catch her with a charge from the gun, before he felt a small puncture in his right hand. Looking down in amazement, he saw a dart embedded in his hand. He began losing consciousness straight away.

"Theo," he gasped as he fell to the ground, vaguely aware of a dripping Marcus and Donal, in hand-to-hand combat with two of the Striga. He fought hard, but consciousness faded.

———

Behind Ciccone and Fenton, Rena entered the room alongside a couple of Striga he didn't know. She was scowling at him.

"I believe you've met Rena?" Fenton grinned. "She agreed to help us capture your sorry ass, in return for the leadership of the New York coven. I think she'll do a good job, don't you?"

Jerome kept silent, watching as the vamp and Striga circled him. Suddenly, he felt the rope above him give way and he came crashing down to the ground, his head bouncing off the concrete as he landed. He groaned as the pain exploded through his skull.

"I owe you one." Rena laughed as she pulled the same stun gun out of her tac vest that Jerome had used on her earlier in the day. Pulling the trigger, she laughed again as he juddered and shuddered through the electric shock being pumped into his body.

"Remember I want him alive," Fenton said, as he

ushered Ciccone from the room. Rena's evil grin was the only response she gave them.

What felt like hours later, Jerome lay on the warehouse floor. His mind and memory flashed back to the time when he had been held prisoner as a seventeen-year-old. But his body was now that of a man in his thirties who had seen combat in the army, and though he was battered and bruised from the several beatings he had taken, and his throat and lungs were sore and wet from the water boarding they had indulged in, he still felt stronger than he had back then.

He wasn't broken, this time. He was older and stronger. They had tried their hardest, and even Rena had looked at him in disgust as she pulled her knife from his belly for the fifth time. He knew he was losing blood badly, but he didn't feel as though he was dying. He hoped it was his Donati heritage coming into play. He also believed part of it was the vampire blood Laertius had given him in Sydney.

He groaned and tried to sit up, the sting of the various cuts and bruises making it hard for him. Eventually he managed it and leant against the wall near where he had been laying.

Using his fingers, he examined the cut on his neck

where they had found Shea's tracking device under his skin. He knew they'd find that one, it was only there as a diversion. The real tracker was implanted in the crook of his elbow. It was tiny and was supposed to be undetectable to current scanners.

He touched his skin around the area where he knew it to be and groaned. His whole body was bruised and tender to the touch. He didn't know if that would have an effect on the tracker. He had no idea of knowing how long he had been here in this hell hole, or even if Shea or the others had survived the attack on Ciccone's house. All he knew was that they had been set up, and he had been captured. He still didn't understand why they wanted him so badly.

Jerome drifted in and out of consciousness for the next few hours. His head hurt worse than any other body part, and he began to worry that he had suffered an irreparable brain injury. He felt woozy all the time and his lungs still felt as though they were soaked in water from the earlier water boarding.

When the door squealed again signalling the entry of another one of Fenton's goons, Jerome could hardly raise his head from the ground where he had laid back down. When gentle hands carded through his hair, he looked up to see a face he thought he might never see again.

"Oh, Jerome," Cornelius said squatting down by him. "What have they done to you?"

"Nonno?" he asked, not quite sure his great grandfather was there with him.

The light came on again and Jerome blinked against the glare once more, but this time Cornelius held his hand over his eyes until he could see better.

Behind Cornelius, Dastan appeared, his blond hair glowing in the overhead light. He was dragging the vamp Rena behind him, and Jerome was never so happy to see his great grandfather's lover than at that moment.

"Okay?" he managed to groan.

Cornelius understood what he was asking. "We lost a couple of the New York vamps. They were as surprised by Rena's defection as we were. Marcus was injured, as was Donal, but neither of them too badly."

Jerome nodded and looked over to where Rena was now being held up by Laertius. He could see where she had taken a beating. He didn't feel like gloating.

She had taken great pleasure in hurting him, and now it was her turn.

"Laertius," he tried to say, but it came out as barely a whisper.

A minute later and the old vamp was by his side, having handed Rena off to Cassius. "Just kill her," he managed to croak out. "No need to drag it out…"

Laertius cupped his cheek and smiled down at him. "I can see a blood transfer in your future, young

Donati," he said, as he leaned down and kissed his forehead.

He stood up, and as Jerome watched he nodded to Cassius who drew his dagger and thrust it into Rena's heart, killing her immediately. Jerome stared in silence for a few moments, then closed his eyes and sighed.

"Jerome?" He could hear his great grandfather's worried voice. He opened his eyes again.

"Fenton, Ciccone?" he asked.

"Ciccone is dead." Dastan answered from where he was kneeling on the other side of Jerome. "Fenton got away. I'm sorry it took us so long to get here, Jerome."

"No," Jerome answered. "You came when you could."

Then it seemed to seep into his brain... his father – no, Ciccone – was dead.

"Dead?" he croaked, wanting to make sure.

"We can show you the body if you want," Cornelius said. "But I'd prefer to get you out of here and to the hospital for a check-up before we take you back to the penthouse."

Jerome groaned out loud as Laertius squatted down and carefully picked him up. He tried not to show how much it hurt, but he felt as though he couldn't stop fighting the pain in his body any longer. He gave in to the darkness as he lost consciousness.

XI

It felt strange being back in the penthouse suite. Jerome had spent only two nights at the hospital, recovering from the torture he had endured.

Laertius had made good on his promise to give him more of his blood, and Jerome could feel the difference.

Cornelius and Dastan joined him in the suite's living area. Coffee and pastries had been delivered by the maître d', and for the moment it was just the three of them.

"Do you feel up to hearing how Ciccone died yet?" Cornelius asked Jerome as he passed him his coffee.

"I need to," Jerome said, taking a pastry from Dastan. "I feel as though he's still out there somewhere, waiting to make his move."

Cornelius shook his head. "He's dead, Jerome. It's up to you if you wish to hear how."

"Go ahead." Jerome sat up in his chair and gave Cornelius his full attention.

Cornelius, along with Donal, Tock, Laertius and Jenna, one of the New York vamps, approached the house on Wainscott Highway from the front. Their task was to infiltrate the house from this side, if they could, and for Cornelius to stop time and prevent too many injuries to their people.

All went to plan until they got inside the house. The house was empty. Cornelius sent Laertius and Jenna to the top floors of the house to double check. The call came back that they were empty.

Sensing a trap, Cornelius called for a retreat to the roadway at the front of the property. Just as they were preparing to leave the house, a soaking wet Marcus came rushing into the house, out of breath.

"They got Jerome," he panted. "Rena, she was in on it. Oh god, Cornelius, I'm so sorry. They got him."

Marcus was out of breath and bleeding from a cut to his forearm. Cornelius grabbed the man's uninjured hand and said, "Slowly, tell me what happened."

Just as Marcus finished updating them, Theo

entered the house. He too was wet. His face was creased in worry as he held up a cell phone.

"I've called everyone else to the house," he said, then he turned to Jenna. "How do we know we can trust you? Rena was a plant."

Jenna held out her hands pleadingly. "I didn't know. Laertius…" She turned to the older vampire. "You have to believe me. No-one knew. But if I get my hands on her…"

Laertius nodded to her. "We'll believe you, but we'll be watching you as well."

Fifteen minutes later, the whole attack force was gathered in the kitchen of the multi-million-dollar home that had obviously been set up as a trap. All so that Ciccone could regain his wayward son.

Dastan came over to Cornelius, offering his silent support as they pieced together what had happened.

"Shea, tell me you have something?" Cornelius pleaded of his steward.

"The tracking device in his neck was abandoned in the woods outside. I'd say they found that one pretty quickly. The one in his arm is still transmitting but it's a weak signal. I've not been able to pin down its location yet."

Cornelius growled. "Then what's the use of it!" he exploded. Dastan reached out and gripped his lover's neck. Cornelius's shoulders slumped.

"I'm sorry, Shea."

"It's okay, we're all worried about him. Let's move this back to the penthouse suite. I have some more equipment there, and Donal and I can work on tracking him down. You work on a rescue plan. We *are* getting him back."

Everyone nodded and Laertius pulled his old friend to him as they exited the house. "He's a survivor, Corny. We'll get him back."

Cornelius sighed at the old nickname but he was thankful for Laertius's help and commitment to finding Jerome.

He couldn't imagine what he was going through. Hadn't the young man suffered enough?

The penthouse suite was just as they had left it that morning, minus the detritus from breakfast.

Marcus, Donal and Theo went off to change out of their sodden clothes and the others scattered around the suite, as well as the two other suites that Laertius had booked.

Cornelius sat at the large table in the dining area with Shea and Donal. He was barely following their conversation as they talked about frequencies and blockages. They were following up with local security cameras as they tried to track where Jerome had been taken.

He felt as if his stomach was being eaten from the inside by acid, and unhappy butterflies danced there. Dastan did his best to distract him, but as the time ticked away and it reached over twenty-four hours since Jerome had been taken, Cornelius found himself beginning to dread the worst.

Dastan persuaded Cornelius to at least lie down and try to get some sleep.

He'd promised to do so, but only if Dastan went with him. He lay in Dastan's arms, looking up at the ceiling in the master suite, seeing only his great grandson. He felt as though he had let the boy down, but knew he'd had to let him get involved. He had lost his step-mother and step-sister in a horrific way, had been brutalised by people hired by his own father, and had still come out the other side.

"I don't think either of us is going to get more sleep," Dastan said after about another hour had passed. "Why don't we shower and go and see where Shea and Donal are at?"

Cornelius nodded and moved away from Dastan, then turned and looked back at him. "Shower with me," he said. "It might help me relax more."

Dastan nodded, knowing his lover needed the comfort in this moment.

It was lunch time before they got the news they had been waiting for.

"Got him," Shea's voice rang out throughout the suite, and Cornelius rushed over to the dining table.

"Where?" He gasped.

"An old warehouse down on the bay in the Bronx area. Looks like it's pretty derelict, which is no doubt why they chose it."

Dastan was on the phone with Laertius, and soon the suite was filled once more with Donati and vamps planning a rescue for Jerome. Cornelius had to believe he was still alive, and that they would find him.

They took four SUVs with them and armed themselves with guns, knives and Laertius's favourite sword. They didn't know what they would be facing when they got there, but they wished to be as prepared as they could be.

Donal handed out military grade ear wigs so that the rescue party could stay in contact with himself and Shea. They were staying behind to co-ordinate things from the suite. They would monitor police bands and the cameras and try to warn the others of any unwanted intrusions.

Cornelius thanked Donal for his ear wig, placing it deep into his ear canal and checking in with Shea. He nodded to the other man when it worked as it was supposed to.

"Listen up," he began. Everyone in the room quietened down and turned to Cornelius. "We get Jerome back by any means necessary. Keep an eye out for Ciccone and Fenton. It would be great if we could capture them, but don't take unnecessary risks."

———————

Half an hour later, the SUVs pulled into position near the warehouse. Cornelius's plan was to freeze time to allow them to get in, check for, and hopefully rescue Jerome. Half of them were going in the front, the other half in the back.

Cornelius was in the party for the front of the warehouse. He pulled Dastan close to him and kissed him. "Take care, bello. Ti amo."

Dastan returned the kiss, then took off with his party for the back of the warehouse. Darkness was just beginning to settle over the city. Cornelius nodded to his brother, Ignatius, who began pulling the dark and shadows to himself. Their group faded into the background, though they did not disappear completely.

Following Ignatius, Cornelius and the rest of their party headed for the front doors of the warehouse. Donal had prepared a small explosive device for them to use to gain access through the locked doors, and Ignatius placed it before signalling for everyone to step back.

The door rattled a bit when the device went off, but it did its job and when Ignatius tested it, the door opened. Smiling at his brother, Cornelius moved past him and into the main area of the warehouse.

Inside, several Striga were waiting for them with wild grins on their faces, hefting knives and daggers. Several were also carrying guns.

Cornelius felt inside himself for his power, sought out his gift and flicked his wrist. Time stopped. Before they could move though, it started again. The Striga were laughing at him.

"What?" He couldn't believe it. His gift always worked. It was as though there was a blockage stopping him from using it for any longer than a few seconds.

Ignatius too was having trouble, but he was too involved in a hand-to-hand fight with one of the Striga to do much about it.

Cornelius tried again and found he could stop time for about thirty seconds. In some cases it was enough for him to move closer to the Striga and take one or two of them out. The others, seeing what was happening, waited for time to stop before attacking, darting in and out of the Striga, dodging bullets as they went.

"Dammit." Marcus pulled himself behind a pallet and grinned at Cornelius. "It's just a flesh wound," he assured the other man, referring to the injury he'd suffered.

Cornelius was beginning to get into the rhythm

that his talent was allowing him. He was covered in sweat as it was taking more out of him than normal.

Just as they were beginning to make progress into the depths of the warehouse, he spotted one figure on the other side trying to escape. He turned and recognised Mario Ciccone across the warehouse floor.

"Ciccone," he shouted at the other man. "Come here and fight me!"

"You won't win, Rossini," Ciccone answered, hiding behind a phalanx of Striga. His voice was gloating, but Cornelius could see that he looked worried.

"You bastard," he shouted. "Where's your son, where's Jerome?"

Ciccone spat on the ground. "He's useless to me! Fenton wants him, he's no son of mine!"

Trying to keep Ciccone occupied, Cornelius moved around until he was facing him. Dastan and Theo were making their way through from the rear of the warehouse.

"Cornelius," Theo shouted. "Laertius has Jerome. End it."

Cornelius nodded and looked to Ciccone. One last time he called his gift to him. Time stopped and stayed stopped. Whatever the interference had been had gone. He killed the remaining Striga around Ciccone, then felt for his gift once more and time started again.

Ciccone looked up, surprised to find himself alone. Hefting the sword Laertius had gifted him with many years ago for saving his life, he looked Ciccone straight in the eyes. The other man quailed, unable to move. Stepping forward, Cornelius swung the sword, taking Ciccone's head off in one easy move. The body collapsed to the warehouse floor, and his head rolled until it stopped at Cornelius's feet.

Dastan appeared in front of him and touched his cheek, bringing Cornelius back from the killing frenzy.

"Neely," he whispered, kissing his cheek. "Jerome needs you."

He nodded and took off at a run to where Tock was indicating that Jerome had been kept.

Jerome was quiet for a while after Cornelius had finished telling him about the attack on the warehouse, and his father's death. He was in awe of his great grandfather.

"Thank you." He reached out and took the older man's hand. "I can't begin to tell you how grateful I am that you killed the bastard. Maybe Lilah and Verity can be at peace now."

He got up and walked over to the large windows overlooking Madison Avenue below him. Wet eyes stared back at him and he wiped tears away from the corners of them both. He turned as Cornelius approached him and walked into the older man's arms.

"It's okay, Jerome. Let it out." Cornelius held him tightly as he cried for the lost boy he had been, who had loved his father only to find out he wasn't what he thought he was. He cried for his siblings and for the loving step-mother Lilah had been. He'd never forget her. And he cried great wracking sobs for the lost opportunities, and what was yet to come.

He felt safe and secure in his Nonno's arms, but he knew it wasn't over. Fenton was still out there, and somewhere was someone or something that affected Donati gifts. There was more still to do, but for now he relaxed and allowed his great grandfather to hold him in his arms.

XII

Laertius had called a meeting for that afternoon saying he had some news to share with the group. He, Cassius and Rupert had been put in charge of interrogating the few Striga they had captured, along with Rena, the New York vamp who had betrayed Jerome. Theo had joined them so that they could make use of his gift of hypnotism and persuasion.

The penthouse suite was once again full of vampires and Donati, joining together to try and stop Fenton's bid to amass more vampires to his side. With the death of Ciccone, he had lost his easy access to funds. Ciccone's estate would have to go through probate and Shea and Donal had managed to hack into many of the accounts that Ciccone had given Fenton access to, and cleared them out.

Jerome was at his favourite spot in the penthouse –

the large windows in the living area overlooking Madison and Fifth Avenues. He was thinking about the phone call he'd had earlier with Beatrice who was in York, England. She and Roman had arrived at the school where Lacey was a boarding pupil, to find that she was fit and well and enjoying her time in the English school. She had had no idea what was happening in the States but had been made aware of her mother's death. Beatrice and Roman had broken the news to her about Verity, but she had taken it okay, Verity had been fifteen years older than her and was an adult with her own life when Lacey was at home with her parents.

Beatrice had suggested leaving Lacey in school until the end of the semester. She was just sitting the English exams which would allow her to choose which university she would like to attend. From what Beatrice and Roman had been able to find out, she was a straight A student, and would likely be able to attend Oxford or Cambridge if she wished.

Jerome was happy for her; whatever she wanted was fine by him. They had both cried when they got to see each other on FaceTime. She kept wanting to touch the screen and assure herself he was there. Even though she had only been a child when Jerome had disappeared, he had been a constant in her life since she was born and was the big brother who looked after her and doted on her. They agreed that she would come to New York, as soon as she was able and it was safe, to stay with Jerome until she went to university. Jerome was already making plans to move closer to her in the UK. He hadn't mentioned it to Cornelius yet as they needed to finish this business with Fenton first.

Jerome turned round to greet Laertius as he crossed the room to join him, a glass of water in his hands.

"Thanks," Jerome took the water and swallowed his pain meds.

"How are you doing?" Laertius asked him as he joined Jerome on one of the sofas in the lounge area.

"A lot better now. Thanks to you."

"I'm glad I was able to help."

They sat in silence for a few moments, watching as everyone who had taken part in the previous clashes with the Striga began to arrive. Amongst them was Marcus. He had brought news from Jacoby for Cornelius, to say that he was deeply involved in a Council matter and would be unable to join them. He'd sent Marcus in his stead. Cornelius had not been happy that his son was absent, but said he understood, having worked for the Council himself for many years. His frown told Jerome that he was worried about Jacoby, though he hadn't shared any details with anyone but Dastan.

Laertius turned to Jerome and squeezed his

shoulder. "I hope this will be all over for you soon, young Jerome, and you can be with your family again."

Standing, Laertius made his way over to the dining table which had become the focus of their activities over the last few days. Jerome stood, glad to feel that the pain pills were beginning to take effect. He needed to be able to move tonight, if anything happened.

"Thank you all for coming." Laertius's loud voice rang through the room. "We have spent the last few weeks on the back foot and lost people – human, Donati and vampire – that we wish we hadn't. But I'm hopeful that the information I'm able to share with you now will help us destroy Fenton and his army of Striga and vamp-Striga hybrids."

He motioned to Cassius, who stepped forward and the large screen in the corner of the room came to life.

"If you could all move so you can see the screen," he said. Everyone complied and watched as Shea connected his computer to the screen so he could share it with the group.

A map of New York appeared, then narrowed in to show an area of the waterfront in the Brooklyn area. The view turned to satellite, and Cassius pointed to an area on the water's edge.

"This is a well-known derelict grain silo on the

Gowanus Bay," he said. "We believe this is where Fenton is holed up."

Murmurs broke out amongst the occupants of the room, and Laertius held his hand up for silence.

"With the help of Theo…" He nodded at the Englishman in acknowledgement. "We were able to interrogate the captured Striga and vamps who Fenton had turned. What we found was quite surprising. Though he has managed to turn a significant number of Striga and enticed many vamps away from their covens, he is not in complete control of them. There are rumblings amongst many of them that they would be better off without Fenton. That he is holding them back from attacking first the Donati then the human population."

Jerome stared at him as he thought of blood hungry Striga on the streets of New York, or any large city. If the blood lust took them, they could decimate a street full of humans in a very short period of time. As they usually stayed on the outskirts of society, feeding off the poor and dying, he was surprised at their ambition.

"That is unusual for Striga," Cornelius voiced his concern.

"Agreed," Laertius answered. "It appears from what we have been able to find out, that Fenton and Ciccone have been promising them a blood frenzy for months now. As they haven't yet delivered, they are looking to take matters into their own hands."

"The interrogation of the Striga we captured tells us that Fenton is not as 'in charge' of them as he at first appeared to be," Theo said. "He has promised much, and not delivered. The Striga we spoke to said they were biding their time, and that if he didn't keep his promises soon, there would be a blood bath in New York – a statement to the human, Donati and vampires in the area. This would be a disaster that has not been seen in any city since the Paris Commune of 1871."

Jerome saw Cornelius lower his head at that. His wife, Jerome's own great grandmother, had been killed by Striga at that time. Dastan, the nearest to Cornelius as always, reached out and pulled his lover into a hug.

"Fenton is also losing some of the vampires who had joined him. They are leaving him, stating that he is unable to deliver what he promised," Cassius said, picking up from Theo. "It appears as though this might be the best time to launch an attack on where he is holed up with the Striga, before they take matters into their own hands."

Shea changed the picture on the screen from that of the map of New York, to photos of the deserted grain silo. "It's a well-known deserted structure in New York, and we are lucky that there are many photos and even some videos of it. I think it tells us that cut off from Ciccone's money, Fenton is running out of options on where he can hide and plot his next move."

"So, if we're going to move, we need to do it quickly," Tock, the vampire from Melbourne, stated.

"Agreed. We can't afford to wait any longer. If we do, the Striga may defy Fenton and cut a swathe through New York. Or he may decide to cut his losses and leave them to their own devices. Either way is not a good outcome for us," Laertius agreed.

Discussions broke out around him, but Jerome could only think of one thing: getting his chance at fighting with Fenton, the man who had plagued his nightmares for years. Before he'd been given his memories back with Beatrice's help, he'd only been a faceless man. Now Jerome knew who he was. He was determined that he wouldn't succeed with his plans.

"When do we attack?" Jerome spoke up over the voices of the others. "Surely it would be best to go as quickly as possible?"

"You're right, Jerome," Laertius answered him, coming to stand by the young Donati. "We must either attack tonight, or not long after."

As they drew up in the car park of the rec ground next to the grain silo, Jerome could feel his heart beating fast. This was it. This was the end. Oh, god, he hoped so. He wanted his life back. He wanted to see Roman and Lacey again, and share in their lives. He also wanted the chance to spend more time with Cornelius and Dastan without the threat of another attack coming at them.

He centred himself then opened the door to the SUV.

Theo was once again in charge of making sure they were armed and protected by bullet and stab proof vests. He checked each of them over in his small party and nodded to Jerome when he checked the straps of his vest. Jerome was armed with several knives and daggers, as well as a few well sharpened stakes.

Jerome was to go in with Cornelius and Dastan. They didn't know if the person/thing that was disrupting Cornelius's gift to control time would be in the grain silo or not. It was Jerome's job to keep with them and see if his chameleon gift would still work. He would use the gift to give them cover. Ignatius was also being used in a similar way, with Laertius and Cassius. His ability to pull the shadows around him and cloak them from view would also be an advantage in the large, dark silo.

As before, Shea handed military grade ear wigs

around, and was checking in to make sure they could hear him.

"Jerome." His voice came through loud and clear. "Report in."

"All okay," he answered, hearing others answering Theo in the darkness around him.

Donal had hacked into the utility company's computers and arranged to have the streetlights around the grain silo switched off. It was only temporary for as soon as it was noticed an engineer would be sent out to deal with it. They had a couple of hours at best. Jerome hoped it would be enough. Night vision goggles had been handed out to the Donati. The vampires didn't need them; their night vision was excellent.

Theo held up his hand to get everyone's attention. "Okay," he said. "Everyone has their assignment. Jerome will go in first with Cornelius and Dastan to see if Cornelius can stop time. Ignatius will follow with Laertius and Cassius, and the rest of us will divide and attack the front and back at the same time. Are there any questions on what we discussed earlier?"

No one said anything or moved. They had spent a fair amount of time discussing tactics back at the penthouse suite, so nothing new should be decided here.

Jerome felt himself grabbed by Cornelius as he

pulled him and Dastan into a hug. He felt the brush of Cornelius's lips on his forehead and squeezed his nonno's arm.

"Stay with me," he whispered. They both nodded.

Reaching deep within himself, he called on his gift. He had been practising more after the debacle out at the Hamptons and now it came to him more naturally. He took a deep breath and allowed the chameleon effect to take over. Shortly, all that the others would be able to see of them was a slight wavering from where he was pulling his power to blend them into the background. Nodding at the other two, he began his trek from the car park to the grain silo.

As they approached, all they could see was the tower where the grain elevator had been. The place was in darkness, and Jerome was more than grateful for the night vision goggles. They entered as silently as they could, aware that Ignatius, Cassius and Laertius were behind them. Inside they went left, as the others went right. Straining his ears, Jerome couldn't be sure if he could hear something or not.

Cornelius raised his hand and time stopped, then about thirty seconds later it started again. Now they knew whatever or whoever was interfering with his ability was somewhere in the grain silo.

Moving slowly through the silo's large, abandoned areas, they saw the spouts that were used to move grain around lying silently. Some were still attached, exposed across the floor. They moved through the area, examining every corner they could.

Then noise of fighting reached their ears. They looked at each other and Cornelius whispered, "That way." He pointed back the way they had come. They turned around and began following the sound of bodies hitting bodies until they found themselves in a wide-open space. They stopped and stared.

There were about thirty Striga and vampires all told, and they were fighting each other. At least some of them were. The others had formed a ring around those who were fighting and were egging them on. As one went down beneath the others, some of those in the 'audience' would dart in and capture them. If they were dead, they would gleefully sink their teeth into them and drink them dry. If they were alive, they'd brush them off and push them back into the fray.

Jerome couldn't believe it. This was not what he expected.

The Striga didn't seem to be aware of them at all, lost in their own world of blood and lust. Cornelius again tried to stop time, and again it worked for about thirty seconds before it started up once more. They knew it wasn't a glitch in his gift as they had worked with him back at the penthouse where it had worked normally. One of the Striga or vampires in front of them was responsible for stopping his gift, perhaps even unknowingly.

Jerome looked around as the Striga continued their bloody fight without appearing to be aware of what else was going on around them. He looked on in incredulity as those in the outside ring bet with others over who would win and who would lose. Something soon would have to give.

There was no sign of Fenton. Jerome was sure he would feel it if the cruel man was anywhere in the large room with the Striga. Perhaps he was elsewhere in the grain silo. He jumped slightly as Ignatius joined them with Cassius and Laertius.

"This is something other," he whispered. Jerome could only agree.

"What's going on?" Shea's voice came through his ear.

"The Striga are fighting and killing each other. Those who lose are being drained of blood by those who win. Talk about blood lust taking over."

There were exclamations from the others who were searching other parts of the silo. "Keep searching," Laertius commanded. "Let us know if you find any other Striga, and particularly if you find Fenton."

The floor around where the Striga were fighting was getting slick with blood. Other fights, apart from those in the middle ring, were now breaking out as the

Striga on the outside caught the blood lust and began attacking their companions. Jerome dreaded to think what this may be like if the ones in the middle were human or Donati. Would the Striga act the same? Was the blood lust so overpowering?

Making sure his chameleon gift was still in place and that Cornelius and Dastan were still covered, he turned to suggest they join the others in searching the rest of the silo, and leave Ignatius to watch over the fighting Striga. Just as he was about to make that suggestion, he caught movement out of the corner of his eye. Turning, he gasped. Fenton. Fenton was in the shadows watching what was happening, almost as though he had orchestrated it.

"Quickly," he hissed to Cornelius. "Fenton's over there."

He pointed in the direction he had spotted his nemesis standing and began moving that way. Cornelius and Dastan followed him.

"Where is he?" Cornelius asked.

"There!" Jerome cried and felt his gift slide off him. He hadn't released it. He saw Fenton through his night vision goggles as he smirked at them. Fenton was blocking their gifts, but how? Cornelius, aware of what was happening with Jerome, lifted his hand and stopped time. Again, it started within a few seconds.

"It's Fenton," Jerome cried. "He's the one stopping us."

367

"How?" Dastan asked. "He couldn't do that before."

Jerome shook his head and started after Fenton once more. He was making his way to the outside of the grain elevator, where some old shipping containers were stacked.

Jerome followed him. They couldn't let him get away. Not now, not when they'd come so far.

Fenton turned round and saluted Jerome. "Another day, Jerome. Another day!"

"No!" Jerome screamed as he saw Fenton take a leap from the edge of the walkway and disappear from view.

Jerome ran over to the water's edge just in time to see Fenton duck into the cabin of a small motorboat, which took off at high speed towards open water.

"Jerome, stop!" Cornelius shouted as Jerome teetered on the edge of the wall for a moment, before falling back into Cornelius's arms.

"He got away," he said, hanging his head.

"I know," Cornelius said, pulling him in tight against his body.

"Come on, let's go help the others clean up in the grain silo. I'd be surprised if any of the Striga are left alive after this. I've never seen anything like it!"

"It had to be Fenton. For some reason he set them against each other."

"Maybe," Cornelius agreed.

"What are we going to do about Fenton?"

"Wait and watch, that's all we can do."

Jerome nodded and followed Cornelius and Dastan into the grain silo. When they got back to where the Striga had been fighting, there weren't many left. Ignatius, Laertius and the others had rounded any stray Striga up and piled the bodies of those who had died in the middle of the silo. A few were still alive, hissing and screeching at the Donati and vamps, and quick dispatch followed for those. Though it sickened Jerome to watch it, he didn't take his eyes away from the bloodshed.

Tock approached them, covered in blood. He had discovered a few vamps from the New York coven hiding in the silo, and also one or two from other covens, including one he appeared to know from Melbourne.

"I've handed the others over to Laertius and the New York coven. I'm taking this one back to Mary in Melbourne," he said. "I think she may have a few questions for him."

"Keep in touch, Tock," Jerome said, shaking the large man's hand.

"I will young Donati, guwayu."

"Until the next time," Jerome answered.

He looked around the large space as the clean-up continued. Shaking his head, he sought out Cornelius and Dastan.

"What now?" he asked.

"For now, we go on with our lives. Fenton might have got away for the moment, but without access to Ciccone's money he will have to start again in some respects. It's the fact that he appears to have gained a new gift that worries me the most. I don't think this is the last we've heard of him. What happened tonight was too neat. He will need to regroup for now."

"We'll alert the Council and Jacoby when he's back," Dastan said. "For now, let's concentrate on us."

XIII

The sun shone down, and Jerome could see it glistening off the water at Cornelius and Dastan's New York estate. He sighed and lounged in the sun like a cat, enjoying the comfortable nest he'd made for himself on the water's edge.

It had been four weeks since the night at the grain silo. All the Striga found there that night had been killed. There had been no further news about Fenton; it was as though he had completely disappeared.

Jerome knew deep down that he would be back.

It had taken them awhile to get the house back to its original state. Fenton and Ciccone had taken their ire out on the structure when they couldn't find Jerome. The Redoubt was unusable, and Cornelius had taken the sad decision to fill it in.

They had rescued Dastan's carved, wooden, steam

punk door. It had suffered in the fire, but it had survived. After some TLC from Dastan, it now formed part of the double doors that led to their bedroom suite.

Jerome picked up a glass of cold water and took a sip. He was content for the moment, though he knew he would have to decide soon what he wanted to do. Lacey was arriving later that day with Roman for a visit. After that, he needed to decide where he was going to live.

Lacey had been accepted into Oxford University to study History and Politics. Roman too had been accepted at Oxford. Jerome hadn't even been aware that his brother had applied to study Physics, but he was very proud of them both. He so much looked forward to where they could take their lives, out of the shadows surrounding their father.

"May I join you?" Laertius's voice came from behind him.

Jerome got up from his nest to greet the vampire with a hug. "I didn't know you were back!" he exclaimed, grinning.

"Just got back about an hour ago. You looked so comfortable out here, I couldn't resist coming to join you."

Jerome laughed and sat down again, suggesting Laertius pull up one of the Adirondack chairs and join him.

"I understand your brother and sister are coming for a visit today," he said.

"Yes, they're both on summer break, before starting at Oxford. I can't believe they both got in!"

"You have a truly lovely family, Jerome," Laertius said, smiling at him.

"I agree. I just… I mean, I know Cornelius and Dastan love me. They've become like fathers to me. But Jacoby, he's still cold to me. He still won't tell Cornelius where he was when we were fighting with Fenton, but Cornelius is hopeful he will trust him one day."

"He's always been a cold man." Laertius helped himself to some grapes that Jerome had idly been eating. "Even after he met your grandmother, Emmie, he was cold to most other people."

"You knew my grandmother?"

"Yes, mostly when she was younger. I know her parents well. Your great grandparents on that side of the family. Have you thought about visiting them?"

"Yes, they extended an invite. I'm going there for Christmas."

Laertius nodded. "I know they miss Emmie so much. They never really had the chance to know their granddaughter, Sherwood. I'm not even sure they met her more than a few times."

Jerome sighed. His family was never

straightforward. He lifted his head to enjoy the sun some more. Laertius was quiet beside him.

"Are Cassius and Rupert here?" he asked, after a few moments.

"Yes, they're at the house with Cornelius and Dastan. You didn't think I'd travel without them, did you?"

"No, not really. How is everyone in Sydney?"

Laertius smiled at him. "Doing okay. Yanni has taken back over as my seneschal for the time being, it gives him some structure to his days now that his wife and Persephone are dead."

Jerome had been sad to hear of the death of Yanni's wife, Lucy, of cancer, only a week after they had buried Persephone. He couldn't imagine losing his wife and his daughter in the same week. Now, when he thought back on the girl he'd known, he felt a mixture of sadness and happiness. Happiness that he'd known her at all, but sadness that it had been for such a short time. He wasn't in any rush to enter into a relationship at the moment. He had his siblings to take care of.

"I'm glad he's found something to fill his days."

Laertius nodded. "Agatha is still in charge of the coven. I'm sure she will keep him busy."

Jerome raised his eyebrow at that. "You're not taking over again?"

"Not yet," he said, squinting in the sun. "I think

there will be a lot to do here in the next few months. Fenton is still out there, and I'm sure he'll be back sooner or later. We all – Cassius, Rupert and I – feel that we are better situated here in the States to help when and as needed. In fact, we've been looking at homes nearby this morning."

Jerome smiled at his friend who was looking down the long driveway, then Laertius turned to Jerome with a smile in his eyes. "I think this might be your visitors…"

Jerome jumped up and nearly toppled into the water. Laertius laughed and caught him, pulling him back onto the floating pontoon.

"Go," he said.

Jerome smiled at him again and rushed towards the house. He got there just as the car turned round in the driveway. He saw that it was Theo driving with Beatrice beside him. He waved at them, and at the other two in the back seat.

As soon as the car came to a stop, Lacey was out the back door and running towards Jerome. He opened his arms to her as she launched herself at him, wrapping her arms around his neck and her legs around his hips.

"Oomph." He grunted as he took her weight. She certainly weighed more than she had as a child.

Jerome swung her round and looked at the glee on her face as she allowed him to manoeuvre her where he wanted her. He pulled her closer and kissed her cheek before putting her back on her feet.

"Jerome," she said gleefully. "I can't believe I'm here! Speaking on Facetime and Zoom isn't the same."

"No," he agreed, turning to greet Theo and Beatrice. Then he turned to Roman who was standing back, apart from the others. He opened his arms to his brother. Roman rushed into them and they rocked together quietly for a few moments. They both remembered the last time they had seen each other, and the horror of Lilah and Verity's deaths.

"I'm so glad you could come," he said into Roman's hair as he hugged his brother to him.

"Me too," Roman said, smiling at Jerome. "Bea has been a godsend to us, she's helped me so much."

"Me too," he replied.

Just then Cornelius and Dastan came out onto the driveway and smiled at the siblings. "Welcome," Cornelius called to them, before greeting his niece and her husband. "Why don't you come in? Shea has a buffet set out near the pool. I'm sure you're ready for lunch."

Jerome nodded and with Roman tucked under one arm and Lacey under the other, he followed his nonno into the house.

ACKNOWLEDGEMENTS

Thank you to my husband Steve, for all your love, help and encouragement.

Thanks also go to my friend Lynne Taylor and the members (past and present) of the Writers@... writing group, I couldn't have done it without you.

ABOUT THE AUTHOR

I have been writing since I was in Junior School, loving English lessons where I got to tell a story. Having grown up reading science fiction and fantasy, my writing has always explored the question of 'what if'.

I live in Yorkshire in the UK with my husband, a fellow author, and our three, sometimes four cats.

I have embraced the independent publishing scene and am looking forward to writing more novels. My work recently has been in the paranormal genre.

BOOKS BY CAROL KERRY-GREEN

The Donati Chronicles:

Of Blood & Shadows

Living in Shadows

Printed in Great Britain
by Amazon